Squirrel Girl

My squirrel-intuition went into overdrive. My tail went fuzzy at the same time mine did. "Back!" I shouted. A bolt of lightning burned through the air above me, right where my friends and I had been standing. The only person in here was a short, wild-haired man clenching a vicious-looking black rifle, aimed at me.

"Squirrel Girl!" he called. "There was a ninety-two-point-seven percent chance it would be you!"

I hated it when people I'd never seen before talked to me like we'd known each other for years. Like the rando above had demonstrated, though, it was part of the public super hero gig.

"This is Squirrel Girl at peak cleverness, peak brilliance, and peak hilarity. And her entire supporting cast is right there with her, including Brain Drain and Mary Mahajan. I love them all. It's a thrilling adventure filled with big ideas explored in fun ways – Tristan Palmgren has truly captured the soul of these characters."

– Ryan North, author of the fictional Unbeatable Squirrel Girl comics, the semi-fictional graphic novel adaptation of Slaughterhouse-Five, and the (so-far-non-fictional) books How To Take Over The World and How To Invent Everything

MORE MARVEL HEROINES

Domino: Strays by Tristan Palmgren
Rogue: Untouched by Alisa Kwitney
Elsa Bloodstone: Bequest by Cath Lauria
Outlaw: Relentless by Tristan Palmgren
Black Cat: Discord by Cath Lauria

MARVEL HEROINES

THE UNBEATABLE Squirrel Girl
UNIVERSE

TRISTAN PALMGREN

ACONYTE

FOR MARVEL PUBLISHING

VP Production & Special Projects: Jeff Youngquist
Associate Editors, Special Projects: Caitlin O'Connell and Sarah Singer
Manager, Licensed Publishing: Jeremy West
VP, Licensed Publishing: Sven Larsen
SVP Print, Sales & Marketing: David Gabriel
Editor in Chief: C B Cebulski

First published by Aconyte Books in 2022

ISBN 978 1 83908 146 0

Ebook ISBN 978 1 83908 147 7

Libary hardcover edition ISBN 978 1 83908 171 2

Cover art by Merilliza Chan

Distributed in North America by Simon & Schuster Inc, New York, USA
Printed in the United States of America
9 8 7 6 5 4 3 2 1

ACONYTE BOOKS

An imprint of Asmodee Entertainment Ltd

Mercury House, Shipstones Business Centre

North Gate, Nottingham NG7 7FN, UK

aconytebooks.com // twitter.com/aconytebooks

For Teresa, a Squirrel Girl's squirrel girl.

No matter what else happens, you gotta believe everything will work out. The worst times in my life have come when I've forgotten that. The best ones come right after I show someone how to see that. It's when everything just... *changes*. When I know that person will be the reason things are going to change for the better.

It's good that I'm *great* at helping other people see it.

My name is Doreen Green[1]. My *other* name is Squirrel Girl. It's pretty easy to explain. Powers of squirrel. Powers of girl. Powers of second-year CompSci undergrad. Powers of eating nuts and kicking butts.

Powers of having *amazing* friends. Powers of having lived so much life in my twenty years that I can't keep it all straight. Powers of surviving a trip across the infinite cosmos with my sanity and sense of self mostly intact.

Mostly being a key word.

Normally I wouldn't share as much as I'm about to write here. As a public super hero most of my life is an open book. There are still a few secrets that decorum and mental health mean that I need to keep. That's why this letter is going into a time capsule. I'm trusting everybody to be cool, uphold Time Capsule Code, and not peek.

If you're peeking, knock it off! Come back in a hundred years. And if you really, really, reaallly have a good reason to peek, then do me a favor and *shhhhh* up about it.

Otherwise...

Glad to meet you, advanced future friends! I hope you're

---

1 Yes, it rhymes, shaddup. – SG

from one of the good futures, but, even if you're not, I'm glad to meet you and hope you're glad to meet me, too. And I hope I'm still hanging around in your day as a cool old lady. Say "hi!"

Secrecy is a hard habit for super hero types to shake. It wasn't all that long ago that I was living the archetypical super-hero double life. Secret identity, rapid costume changes, stretching plausible deniability and all that. I was Doreen Green in the streets, and Squirrel Girl on the beat! While I didn't plan to have my secret identity revealed in *quite* the way it was… I'm kinda glad it's in the open now.

No more covering up. No more double life. It gave me some bad habits. Secrets and lies aren't who I am. More importantly, they're not who I *want* to be.

Ordinarily, when I have something I need to talk about, I'd chat it over with my friends. I can't do that this time. I know a few things that, if I told them, would break their hearts. Yes, even Tippy-Toe the squirrel's furry little spirit would be shaken. I can't do that to them.

It's not just my privacy I'm protecting here. It's the people around me. They have to protect themselves, and I have to help them. It's not my place or my right to blab everything just because there's a story I need to get off my chest.

So I'm taking this seriously. I even hired an editor, someone who owes me a favor and isn't afraid to speak his mind, to look this over. You'll never guess who it is![2]

Sometimes being a squirrel-based super hero means burying things away like acorns in the fall. So you can see why a time capsule is appealing. Just because I can't talk about this particular

---

2 HULK EXCEL AT HIDING HULK'S IDENTITY! – ED

problem, that doesn't mean I can't *write* about it. At some point, when the things I'm holding back can't hurt anybody, I'll be listened to.

So here we are, advanced future person! You and me! I only have one million, twenty-thousand five hundred and fifty-six questions for you – give or take half a question. Is the number of Avengers teams in the triple or quadruple digits? Which of the X-Men are kissing now? Are they calling themselves something more inclusive than X-Men yet? Has humanity finally evolved beyond x86 processor architecture?

If I'm still around in cool old lady form, look me up. I mean, future me (present me to you, I guess) probably knows the answers, but I love meeting new people! It'll be nice to talk over what I'm about to write with someone because… well, you'll see.

And if you are one of my friends? Nancy, Tomas, Ken, Mary, Brian, Tippy-Toe… put this down. I love you all and I'm asking this *because* I love you. Tippy-Toe, I think you even suspect what it is. You said you didn't hear what happened but I don't know if I believe that. There are some things I don't want even you to know, let alone remember me by.

I know saying that is going to be like bait to you. Trust me. *Stop.*

…

All right! Everybody who's still reading this, ready to go? Snap on your safety belts while I point this flashlight under my chin, because it's time to open with a little story I call…

The Unbeatable Squirrel Girl Vs One Thousand and One Character Introductions

It takes a lot to catch me off guard. I've seen so many unbelievable things – dinosaurs on fire off the shore of Liberty Island, alternate-universe reasonably priced New York real estate – but the wonderful thing about the universe is that there's always something new that can stop you in your tracks and really make you say, "Gosh dang!"

One of the few things I was not prepared to see that morning was the neighborhood between Battery Park and Wall Street, piers and streets and cars and everything, phase through the east side of Empire State University's campus.

"Gosh dang!" I said, stopping in my tracks.

"There goes the neighborhood," Nancy muttered. Such a wit, that Nancy.

She and I had been walking together to Algorithms and Ethics and just generally enjoying life. She was my roommate and best (human) friend. It had been hard to find a break to breathe that week. We were coming up on the close of our second year in the CompSci program and spring was breaking everywhere. We were surrounded by huge sycamores with floofy green blossoms, sprouting botanical club flower gardens, the smell of street tacos in the air. And, of course, squirrels cavorting and careening along the campus's trees.

Now the flower gardens had half-transposed with the Bowling Green subway station's boarding platform. The sidewalk ahead was boarding passengers for cruises to the Statue of Liberty. The faces of people standing in line at a falafel cart had only a second to look startled as they ghosted through Nancy and me at interstate speeds.

Then they were all past us. ESU's campus was back to its ridiculously beautiful self. Nancy and I looked at each other. Angry ducks yelled at us in duck, but that was normal.

It hadn't just been sights and sounds that had barreled through us. Reader, I could *smell* the roasting shawarma. A cold breeze had tingled through my skin as the street passed through us. Because we were already going to be late for class, I didn't want to say how hungry that made me.

We started running in the direction the rogue piece of Manhattan had flown. When you spend as much time around squirrels as I do, you learn to pick up on some pretty subtle sounds (and having the proportionate hearing of a squirrel doesn't hurt, either…). The *click-claw* of tiny scampering claws on sidewalk cement is the background noise of my life.

I knew without looking that my best squirrel-friend, Tippy-

Toe, was right behind me. I leaned forward and, after a pause long enough to account for a mighty leap, she landed on my shoulder. Her bushy tail tickled the back of my neck.

"I think one of those Battery Park squirrels phased through my nut cache," she complained. "Now they know where it is! I was even good, and saved some through winter!"

"I feed you," I pointed out.

She didn't have time to answer. I'd been blessed with, among other things, the proportionate speed and jumping ability of a squirrel – which, blown up to human size, is quite a lot. Nancy used to have to get around by more conventional means until I entered her life. I scooped her up, coiled my legs like springs, and leapt to the top of the Gorman Gymnasium.

"*Hup*," I said, because what was I going to do – jump three stories and not say *hup*?

It still felt weird to just jump around in the middle of campus like that. My secret identity hadn't been "secret" for months. I no longer had to hide my big bushy squirrel tail in my pants, or don a costume before leaping around, but I still got moments of self-consciousness. One of these days, I was going to have to get used to Doreen Green and Squirrel Girl sharing the same life. I wasn't there yet. Change is weird. Not as weird as ghost images of New York flying around, but, y'know. Still.

Nancy still complained when I carried her in public. She said it was *undignified*. Dignity is for cats, not squirrels, but Nancy had always been a cat person.

She didn't complain now. If someone was stealing New York landmarks and neighborhoods, we had to figure out where in the world – or possibly in time – they were.

The phantom cityscape had vanished by the time we reached

the gymnasium's higher vantage. The *first* one, anyway. Nancy shielded her eyes from the sun and pointed. The southern tip of Manhattan, just visible against the fringe of the Hudson River, was perpendicular to the horizon.

"Huh," I said, tilting my head.

The concave bowl of Yankee Stadium, flipped upside-down, superimposed over a cloud. The George Washington Bridge crisscrossed through the insurance and bank ads on the left-field scoreboard. A V-formation of panicked geese was too slow to dive out of their way, but nothing struck them.

A moment later, and the images faded. Except for the reeling birds, the sky was clear again.

"Huh," Nancy and Tippy-Toe and I said.

Nancy and I had seen a lot in our lives, even by second-year CompSci student standards. We were immediately in problem-solving mode.

"Hallucination gas?" Nancy suggested.

"Time travel?" I asked.

"No, I just saw that construction on the George Washington Bridge yesterday," Nancy said. "Holographic projection?"

"Total catastrophic space-time inversion?" I asked.

"What the heck does that mean?"

"I have no idea," I said. "But I bet we can find someone who will tell us something that sounds just as alarming."

Nancy braced herself for another jump. Tippy-Toe's tiny claws dug into my shoulder. Once the air between us and our next vantage point was clear of any interleaving parks, subway stations, billboards, and street theaters, I leapt.

New York! It's a heckuva town! Nobody I know is entirely clear on why it's such a magnet for super villainy (not to mention regular villainy). It has a greater concentration of crimebusting super heroes than any other city in the world. I mean, seriously – the Fantastic Four are here, Spider-Man, Tony Stark, Doctor Strange, She-Hulk, He-Hulk, me and my friends…

Kinda makes you think. Do super-empowered heroes attract menaces like mountains attract mountain-climbers? If all of us weren't here, would New York have faced so many terrible threats in so short a time?

You know what? Scratch that. What am I thinking? If it hadn't been for the city's heroes, New York would have been conquered by Doctor Doom, or gobbled up by Galactus, or become the setting for some grim-and-gritty deconstructive reboot about how there's no good people left in the world, only innocents to crush, monsters who call themselves heroes, sad relics of a bygone age, and–

Ahem. Sometimes my thoughts wander. They've been going in stranger directions than they used to.

Anyway, case in point as to the density of New York super heroes: it didn't take me long at all to find my fellow animal-themed crimefighters, Chipmunk Hunk and Koi Boi. (One of the delightful things about super hero callsigns is how much they tell you about the person who chose them. You know a lot about Chipmunk Hunk's personality and interests already.)

It wasn't *too* much of a coincidence that I found them. The three of us, plus Nancy, were all undergraduates at Empire State University. In the same department, even. Chipmunk Hunk leapt along the rooftops, coming from the direction of the Stacy Memorial Dining Hall. Koi Boi skimmed the Harlem River, a white-blue blur of spray and foam.

When I landed atop the Park Avenue Rail Bridge's skeletal

metal counterweight tower, Koi Boi flopped onto the strut right beside mine. Steam from the speed of his passage still wafted from his skin. "You look like you know where you're going," he said.

"Good!" I said. "I kind of do."

"Kind of?"

Chipmunk Hunk slammed atop the tower with an impact that rattled the gridwork. Chipmunk Hunk's other name is Tomas Lara-Perez, but we all have an unspoken agreement to refer to each other by callsign when we're in costume. He was, as you might expect, ludicrously handsome. The wind swept his hair dramatically without mussing it.

Like me, he wasn't traveling alone. His girlfriend, Mary Mahajan, had hitched a ride on his back. Chipmunk Hunk said, "We just saw the Knicks practicing in the Hudson River!"

"And they didn't even drown," Mary remarked. It had not been a good season for the Knicks.

"If we're all seeing the same things, I suppose that rules out hallucination gas," Nancy mused. "Probably. You could all be my figments."

"No, you'd all be *my* figments," Mary said. Her hair was not as windproof as her boyfriend's but that only boosted her mad-scientist image. She was a CompSci student by day, and a superweapon hobbyist at night. And during the day, too, come to think of it. I'd hoped that might have given her some insight into what we were facing, but she just looked somewhere between bemused and irritated, the same as usual.

"Now we figure out if this is happening across the world or localized in New York," Koi Boi said. His short, wavy brown hair was still dripping. His costume consisted of whatever he happened to be wearing (jeans, a shirt, and windbreaker today) plus a pair of fisheye goggles. Even his civilian outfits were all light, quick-drying cotton.

Just in case you were thinking of stereotyping hunks, don't. My man Chipmunk Hunk is razor-sharp. "I haven't seen any clouds near the ground, or buildings too high up," he said. "That suggests a more localized problem. Or at least one that stays low."

"It's okay," Koi Boi said. "Squirrel Girl kind of knows where we're going."

"I'm not ready yet," I said. Seeing my friends in costume had reminded me of my own. I reached back and grabbed a squirrel-ear headband that, until now, had been safely hidden in my tail fuzz. I slipped it over my hair. "Now I'm ready."

Before we launched again, Nancy looked at Mary stretched over Chipmunk Hunk's back. Then back at me. Being held in my arms was, admittedly, not the most dignified position. Too bad! My shoulders were taken. I'd promised Tippy-Toe the seat against my neck the next time we traveled.

I have *tons* of friends around the city. I've only been living here full-time for two years, but it's my friends that make New York feel like home. Some of my friends here, though, I've known for a lot longer than two years.

Like Tony Stark. First among Iron Men.

I made my super hero debut with Iron Man. That was the first time I beat Doctor Doom![3] Since Tony and I go way back, I knew he wouldn't mind me breaking and entering into his offices atop Stark Tower, no matter how many times he'd tried to send me repair bills for that before. Oh, Tony! He knew I was a broke college student. We had a mutual understanding that the

---

[3] To make a short story shorter, Doom's ability to focus on his airship's controls was no match for a scurry of squirrels. – SG

bills are just the motions that, as a titan of capitalism, he was expected to go through.

I think, anyway. We never actually talked about it.

Today though, just getting up there was tricky. A ghost image of the Avengers Mansion drifted across the cityscape, disrupting my sightlines. We were atop skyscrapers now, far enough off the ground that a fall would be bad news even for me, and worse for Nancy. I had to align my next jump through an image of Central Park Zoo. A crowd of people standing vertically across the sky scattered as I barreled through them. A troop of Japanese macaques watched us with jaded eyes.

Our group landed atop Stark Tower's westmost helipad. Alarm klaxons blared instantly. Crackling blue containment fields sprung up around us. The rooftop thudded with the clanging footsteps of security robots. Tony knew the rooftop of his monumental tower was the first place his many enemies would think to attack, and had concentrated his defenses there.

Oh, well. We had to get in, fast. In situations like that, my team preferred to improvise. Things usually worked out – if not the way we intended, then the way things needed to go. I raised my fists, ready for a fight.

The roof suddenly gave way beneath us. The six of us (counting Tippy-Toe, still clinging desperately to my shoulder) tumbled down a surface that had suddenly become a slick metal ramp. We slid down a long, steep drop toward a carpeted floor. That floor was coming up far too quickly. Chipmunk Hunk and I only just managed to position ourselves to cushion Mary and Nancy.

I told you things usually worked out for us. Tony had finally given up and programmed the building AI to let us in and avoid the property damage.

He stood behind a magnificent mahogany desk, surrounded by two dozen half-transparent holographic displays, all flashing urgent red. He looked unsurprised to see us. More tired, really.

"Nancy, Mary," he said. "I would have set some pillows down if I'd known they'd bring you along."

Nancy and Mary have hearts of steel, but their butts were a *teensy* bit more breakable than Koi Boi's, Chipmunk Hunk's, and mine. They're humans with the proportionate speed and strength of a human. Still pretty incredible, but not quite as up to long falls as us.

"Just a little… winded," Nancy gasped. "Pretty normal… day so far."

My butt came with its own fuzzy pillow attached. I refloofed my tail. "So you and the Avengers already know what's happening, right?" I asked Tony, standing up.

"Total catastrophic space-time inversion," Tony said.

"No way!" I said at the same time that Nancy asked "*What?*"

"No, I did make that up," Tony said. "We're still collecting data. It's not holograms, not parallel dimensions, not time warps, not mass suggestion." The latest model of Tony's Iron Man suit stood in the corner. Tony eyed it longingly. But this wasn't the kind of problem repulsor blasts would solve. At least not yet. "The Hulk is already out there, trying to punch things until this stops. Guess how much that's helping."[4]

"What if it's some kind of cosmic reboot?" I asked. "Those have happened before, right?"

"If they had, we wouldn't remember it," Tony answered. "But, no, that's never happened." He scratched underneath his beard.

---

[4] HULK THINK IT USUALLY HELP A LOT ACTUALLY. – ED

"I've got to stay and sort this out. If whatever's happening has a technological or scientific cause, we're the best people to root it out. We'll keep looking."

"So will we," I said.

"Close the roof hatch on the way out, please," Tony said. For the first time, his eyes met mine. "And be careful out there."

See! He cared.

Mary was transfixed by one of the pieces of Iron Man suits on Tony's tables. Specifically, a gloved fist with its repulsor cannon. Chipmunk Hunk and I pulled her away before she could do anything to embarrass us more than our entrance already had.

Back outside, the interior of a Queens penthouse party segued through us – I swear I saw a monocle pop – followed by the guts of a storm sewer. The dingy caverns of New York's Subterranea spilled over the next crosswalk. The Mole Man shook his fist at the outside world in the manner of angry old men everywhere. The city was folding up on itself like a sheet of paper.

No *scientific* explanation meant looking for something wilder. Our next stop was the Sanctum Sanctorum, home of Earth's Sorcerer Supreme and second-leading putting-adjectives-after-nouns practitioner, Doctor Strange.

"Forgive me, for I cannot be distracted," the doctor said, after we'd made a similarly dramatic entrance (knocking on the front door and being let in). Whereas Tony Stark stood in a bubble of rotating holographic displays, Doctor Strange was half-hidden behind a veil of fog and crackling magic power. His cape and goatee were especially dramatic today.

He peered into the æther with eyes aflame. If he hadn't been speaking to us, I wouldn't have thought he'd noticed our arrival.

"I have not located the source of this geospatial madness and need to devote all of my powers to that end. The only thing I can say for certain is that my scryings have uncovered no unnatural swellings of sorcerous might. I do not believe that the cause is within my field of expertise, but I will not give up the search!"

Mary's attention was again lost in the artifacts around her. This time, it was a weathered, chipped, but nonetheless elaborately carved and fearsome-looking axe, vibrating on its stand. Chipmunk Hunk pulled her away even as she stretched her hand toward it.

"You all never let me play with anything fun," she complained once we were back outside. She was the designated chaotic neutral[5] of the group.

"We do fun things all the time," Chipmunk Hunk said. "We just went leaf-watching in Maine last weekend!"

"That wasn't as much fun for me as it was for you."

"And you found that beautiful, wide-open field to test that muon disruptor ray?"

"Oh. Right." She grinned sheepishly. "That was that weekend, wasn't it?"

Our aimlessness was starting to make me itch. My tail twitched back and forth. My friends and I perched on the fire escape of a posh apartment complex overlooking Central Park (when we could see it). People fled from the park entrances, seeking cover, but they were surprisingly orderly about it. Just a little bit of yelling, and no screaming. They were New Yorkers. New Yorkers had been through this kind of crap before.

Sirens caterwauled across the distance. So far, this

---

[5] Every friend group has one. Everyone understands implicitly who it is. – SG

phenomenon was "harmless" , if you could discount all the car accidents and heart attacks it had caused (and I couldn't).

Tippy-Toe yanked at my chin to get my attention, and pointed to my right. I turned just in time to see a red-blue figure swing between skyscrapers, web-slinging toward a tractor-trailer with a smoldering engine. It had crashed into a subway station entrance. The figure took a bad swerve away from one phantom office block, but recovered in time.

The Avengers' Quinjet screamed overhead, slicing through phantom buildings like they weren't there. Its instruments must have seen right through the illusions. But it didn't seem to be going anywhere in particular. It arced across the sky in a slow search pattern.

Nobody knew what was causing this. And everyone else had billions of dollars of sensors or several lifetimes of magical study to deploy. We could have done what Spider-Man was doing: putting out the small fires. Not that that was a bad thing to do, but I flicked my tail irritably.

"Well, nuts! What on earth can we do to stop this?"

I'd meant it as a hopeless rhetorical question. Leave it to my friends to encourage me on the rare occasions when I'm not encouraging myself.

"What do we have that no one else does?" Nancy asked.

Nancy's short hair, sharp cheekbones, and strong chin gave her a hard exterior. It matched her equally hard moral center – though there was plenty of nougaty sweetness if you knew where to look. Like her love of cats or her fandom for all things Asgardian. From her tone, I could tell it *wasn't* a rhetorical question. That little push was just enough to knock me into the answer. I looked at Tippy-Toe.

"The biggest distributed intelligence network on the continent," I said.

Tippy-Toe chittered appreciatively. "Aw, shucks." Flattery gets you everywhere with her.

But of course I didn't just mean her. There were thousands of squirrels in the city. We didn't need billion-dollar Quinjet sensors when we had eyes and ears on every block.

We leapt into Central Park. I set Tippy-Toe loose to spread the word among her fellow squirrels. Chipmunk Hunk crouched to have a chat with his own familiars. Koi Boi briefly left us to visit the Hudson River and speak with its denizens. Just like squirrels, there were more fish in and around New York than most people realized.

It's important to note that none of us have the power to *control* squirrels or chipmunks or koi. That would be mean. They're our friends and fellow citizens of this big ol' planet Earth, and they want to do what's right. Sometimes it can take a little charm and persuasion to get them to *see* what's right and face down doing it, but not this time. The park squirrels were unnerved by reality collapsing, but, like the humans evacuating through the gates, not freaking out. They were New Yorkers too. We'd *all* been through this kind of crap before.

Tippy-Toe was easy to pick out among the knots of squirrels. She wore a pink bow over her neck, both to help me find her in a crowd and because it was super-adorable.

To try and get the space to think, my team and I set up our command center underneath one of the park's many arched bridges. Every once in a while, an office block drifted through us, but the chaos didn't seem so bad from down here.

Our friends' thousands of alert, inconspicuous eyes and ears were spread throughout the city. Very few people take the time to notice squirrels and chipmunks and fish, especially during a crisis. Navigating the labyrinth of illusions was as difficult for them as it was for everybody else, but they were determined little critters, and there were so many of them.

It wasn't long before my squirrels' first reports came in. Ms Jellyfingers said that the phantom images weren't as vivid past Mt Vernon. Whack-a-Tail and Nitpicker said that the squirrels around Greenwich Village could hardly see the physical world through the phantoms.

What was worse was that the images seemed to be taking on more substance. My squirrels didn't think they *were* just images. They reported all kinds of scents mixing together: sewage, salt water, fish, sizzling pizza, burning dust, diesel exhaust. (Yes, I know that was standard New York, but the squirrels said it was worse and I believed them.) Maybe I *hadn't* imagined the smell from the shawarma stand earlier.

The squirrels also said they were hearing sounds through the images. That was new. It meant there was some level of physical interaction, molecules bumping against molecules. If things kept up at this pace, in a few minutes the images would become real, and all of New York would crumple up on itself like a paper ball.

I caught Chipmunk Hunk's cheeks twitching. Koi Boi fidgeted, rubbing his arms. It was increasingly hard to keep my nerves steady. I can handle a lot, but threaten my home, and I won't stop for anything. I didn't know where this was coming from, let alone how to stop it, and that was like an open pit in my stomach.

One of the first rules of data crunching is to pick the right tool for the task. A single, centralized system would never be able to handle the same kinds of jobs as a distributed neural net. The Avengers, Tony Stark, and Doctor Strange were all processing in isolation. Our squirrels and chipmunks and fish were everywhere. With all those eyes and brains working together, we started to see the pattern.

Whenever the phantoms started to get more intense – sounds getting sharper, and smells getting smellier – it happened in one particular part of the city first: around Empire State University.

"Gosh dang it!" I swore. We shouldn't have gone anywhere at all. That's how it is in programming, too. The problem you're looking for is usually right under your nose, but you spend hours figuring out how to see it.

Tippy-Toe scampered back up to my shoulder as St. Patrick's cathedral blotted out the sky. When I peeked out from under the bridge, I saw the East River tilted sideways over one horizon and the Hudson River blanketing the other. I bit the inside of my cheek, trying to develop a plan. Getting back to ESU would be a lot more treacherous than getting out here had been.

"Maybe some of us should try to find the Avengers, or somebody, and tell them," Mary said. A rare reasonable suggestion. But, with everything getting worse, we were going to have trouble finding our way back to a campus the size of several city blocks, never mind specific super heroes.

Nancy said, "I'm not going out there alone."

Mary shrugged. "The responsible thing to do is boring anyway."

Sometimes the best plan is to just dive into the fray. Tippy-Toe's claws dug into my shoulder. I grabbed Nancy. "And a one, and a two, and *hup*."

Chipmunk Hunk, with Mary, and Koi Boi followed close

behind. To navigate, I had to ignore most of what I was seeing, which was a huge problem. Don't get me wrong: I know New York like I know the selection of nuts at my grocery market. But that wasn't enough to jump from rooftop to rooftop by memory alone.

Things kept getting worse. Every time I passed through an image, it felt like passing through a curtain of air. Once, hurtling through an office building, I felt like I was crashing through a thin sheet of glass. Hot pain sliced across my arm. The next time I landed, I looked and saw a thin red stripe running across my elbow. Part of something sharp, the corner of a desk or a window, had become tangible for a moment.

Tippy-Toe and I exchanged a worried look. She burrowed under my shirt collar for her own safety. The next time I leapt, I hunched over Nancy to keep her as sheltered as I could.

Even I had to admit that leaping around the rooftops was foolish now. We descended to the streets and started running.

Nancy pulled out her smartphone. Clever girl. We might not have been able to see where we were going, but the GPS signal was still coming through.

I've said that the thing that makes New York most feel like home is having so many friends here. The tricky part about that, though, is introducing them all. You haven't even met them all yet. But Brian Drayne is pretty hard to forget.

I called him Brian because he was still in disguise. It's his clever alias for his other identity: Brain Drain. Unlike the rest of us, he hadn't given up his secret identity. He was wrapped up in an oversized ESU sweatshirt and a heavy winter cap and scarf to hide the fact that he was actually a disembodied brain and two free-floating eyes in a jar. The jar perched atop a Hulk-sized mechanical body. You'd think most people would have seen through his disguise, but nope. New Yorkers are used to more subtlety from their heroes and villains. Everyone I knew him assumed that any disguise so fake looking had to be real. He was running along... well, I wasn't sure where he was running. An image of Madison Avenue was ghosting along parallel to us, so he could have been there.

"SQUIRREL GIRL," his voice box buzzed, sounding as pleased as he ever did. "CHAOS AND ENTROPY ARE THE FATE OF ALL, AND YET, LIKE KING CANUTE ORDERING THE TIDE TO RETREAT, WE CONTINUE OUR FUTILE STRUGGLE AGAINST THEM."

"Darn straight! If the laws of entropy have anything to do with this, though, I'll eat my tail."

Long backstory on this fella. Decades ago, his dying body was discovered by aliens, who tried to save him but didn't actually know squat about the human body. So they put his brain in a tank to preserve it. Like most of us might in that situation, he went a little bit squirrelly... tried to take over the United Nations, dominate the minds of world leaders, the whole song and dance.

What was happening was that his brain case had been pretty poorly designed. When Nancy and I had found him, we put our programming skills into fixing that. It turned out that, for decades, Brain Drain's id had run his body while the rest of his mind had been helpless but to watch, with nothing to do but regret everything. He'd spiraled around depression, nihilism, and existentialist philosophy.

He's doing great today, though. I'm really proud of him! New York's crimefighting scene wouldn't be the same without him. When I told him we were sure this crisis had originated at ESU, his bobbing eyes rotated to face me. "THE PROBLEMS WE NOTICE IN THE OUTSIDE WORLD ARE OFTEN REFLECTIONS OF THE FLAWS WE DETEST IN OURSELVES."

After a thoughtful moment, he added, "I WILL MEET YOU THERE AND WE WILL PURSUE THESE DEMONS TOGETHER." When I looked over, he was gone. Maybe he'd been on Madison Avenue after all.

When my friends and I got close to ESU, I only knew it because Nancy's GPS said so. We weren't lost for very long, fortunately.

When we stepped onto campus, we rolled out of the dream and into the nightmare.

The Unbeatable Squirrel Girl Vs The Mad Thinker

A terrible clarity burned over the Fields Memorial Physical Sciences Building.

I've erased and rewritten that line five times, but you know what? *Burned* is the right word. It was like turning the contrast all the way up on a monitor, or taking off swimming goggles I'd worn for hours. The clear zone started about fifty feet away from the building. After so long in topsy-turvy freaky nightmare-city, it hurt to be back in normality. Literally hurt – because I still didn't trust anything I saw, I stubbed my toe on a rock I hadn't expected would actually be there.

I hopped around on my other foot for a moment, drawing a rebuking glance from Nancy. After a moment, I realized it was less from the pratfall and more because I hadn't set her down yet.

So I was protective. Sheesh.

The power went out the moment after we reached campus.

Lights in the windows died all at once. With the sun occluded by flying skyscrapers, we were cast under a pall of darkness. Nighttime in the afternoon.

Once my eyes adjusted, I started seeing stars. Little glowing specks, like retinal afterimages, burned into the world. When I turned my head, they stayed rooted against the backdrop, dispelling the idea that they were in my eyes.

The inside of the building was packed. I saw faces in the doors and windows long before we got close to any of them. Students and faculty had flocked to this building for shelter, not realizing that the clarity was more of a bad sign than good.

They were packed so closely together, watching the madness from what they imagined was safety, that I thought we wouldn't be able to get through. The moment the crowd spotted my friends and me, though, they ushered each other back. Sometimes it's good to be the known heroes on campus.

"What the heck are you doing here?" someone yelled. "The problem's out *there*, dummy!"

Of course, being the known heroes on campus can be a nuisance sometimes, too. Like when randos try to explain the heroing business to you.[6] Oh well. New York wouldn't feel like home if it didn't have its nuisances. I pulled Nancy away before she could yell at him.

The interior halls of the building, by contrast with the entrance, were deserted. Everyone had clustered around the

---

[6] At least this time I wasn't trapped in conversation with one, like when they tried to walk with me between classes. "Doreen, I have strong feelings on the Super-human Registration Act. Debate me." "Doreen, I hit a squirrel with my car yesterday and feel really bad, absolve me of my guilt." "Doreen, I like super heroes like the Avengers but don't like mutants like the X-Men, and am going to deal with this cognitive dissonance by trying to justify it to you." – SG

windows. Maybe if they'd come in, they would have noticed the thrum of power behind the walls.

The hallway lights were all on. The Fields Physical Sciences Building was home to the physics department's teaching microfusion reactor. If I had to guess, someone had wired the generator into this building to provide electricity. Someone who either needed a lot of power, or had advance warning that the city's electrical grid would be disrupted today.

Inside, the glowing specks were even easier to see. They were like bright little holes, burning through the universe. They reminded me uncomfortably of a starfield. Like a starfield, the specks were so far away that they didn't seem to have any dimensionality to them at all. It was like this building was starting to phase out of the world... and I was seeing right through the walls, and right through the Earth and sky, to the stars beyond.

"Is anyone else seeing...?" Chipmunk Hunk started to ask.

"Yes," Nancy said tersely.

"If I get radiation poisoning again, I'm going to be very mad," Mary said.

("Again?" Chipmunk Hunk whispered.)

("I had a life before you, you know," Mary said.)

We followed the thrum down a flight of stairs. The corridors there were dingier and less well lit, but that was normal. Physics departments just exude that feeling.

I clamped down on the panic burbling in my stomach. Whatever was happening, we'd found the source. We could beat it.

The thrumming took us towards a set of double doors with foggy glass windows. I didn't hesitate. I kicked them open. Then my squirrel-intuition went into overdrive. Tippy-Toe's tail went fuzzy at the same time mine did.

Prey animals never question their instincts, and neither did I. "Back!" I shouted. I pushed the others to the wall with my tail, an instant before I dived forward.

The moment I slid across the cool tiles, a bolt of lightning burned through the air above me, right where my friends and I had been standing. The crack of an explosion echoed down the corridor, where the bolt met brick wall.

My senses caught up with the rest of me. I'd crashed into some kind of lab, complete with a labyrinth of counters, a bunch of stools, polished tile floors, and laptops and tablets scattered across the table. I scrambled toward one of the counters. A class must have just been in session.

The only person in here now, though, was a short, wild-haired man with shoulders so tense they looked hunched. He clenched a vicious-looking black rifle, aimed at me. And he was dressed in a completely incongruous casual polo shirt and slacks.

"Squirrel Girl!" he called. "There was a ninety-two-point-seven percent chance it would be you!"

I hated it when people I'd never seen before talked to me like we'd known each other for years. Like the rando above had demonstrated, though, it was part of the public super hero gig.

Vivid, fiery red energy splashed across the counter I'd just taken cover behind. Keys from broken laptops skittered across the floor.

At first, I thought my attacker missed. Then I felt the heat spreading across the countertop. He'd set my cover on fire. I couldn't stay there forever. Tippy-Toe dove off my shoulder. Her claws click-click-clacked across tile, and I lost sight of her.

"I think you should know," he said, "that ninety-two percent is exceptionally low for a man of my genius. And now that we've eliminated the variance, I can calculate the *rest* of our destinies!"

He punctuated the sentence with a blast from his rifle.

Somehow, he'd anticipated exactly where I'd hidden behind the counter. The bolt impacted the wood directly between me and him. The cabinet door beside me *whoompfed* open with the pressure of the blast wave, and hit me in the side. It surprised me more than it hurt.

My friends shoved through the double doors an instant after that last shot. Mary led the way. She must have figured out just how long they had between shots. Crouched behind cover, I still had a good view of them. I cringed, expecting our attacker to have planned for that too. But Mary and the others made it to the next-nearest counter, across the aisle from mine. Our assailant didn't seem particularly concerned.

The smoke alarms started shrieking, and water sprayed from the ceiling sprinklers. Of course, "sprinklers" is a misnomer. The torrents that inundated the lab felt like standing underneath a hose... or a waterfall. In seconds, everything was soaked and slippery.

I took the next pause between shots to scramble up to a table that *wasn't* threatening to burn the fur off my tail. Our attacker, whoever he was, had backed away. There was another set of double doors at the far end of the lab. He shouldered through them. The space beyond looked like an industrial nightmare, full of vents and pipes. His wet shoes squeaked on dry cement.

He was grinning ferociously. That was when I realized what he was doing.

That rifle of his didn't just spit fire. The bolts crackled like lightning. He had anticipated my friends charging in here, too, just like he'd anticipated me.

He had just turned this whole room, me, and all of my friends, into conductors.

My breath didn't have the time to catch in my throat.

A brown blur shot underneath his heel.

There is no sound in the world that will raise the hair on your tail quite like a squirrel shrieking. Tippy-Toe squealed as our attacker stepped flat on her back.

He slipped. His shot went wide, into the ceiling. Burning polystyrene tiles rained down on him. And on Tippy-Toe.

Ordinarily, I could have cleared the distance between Tippy-Toe and me in a second. When I started, though, my soles skidded across a sheen of water. I had to grab a counter. Koi Boi had no such problems. He skimmed through the water and vaulted straight toward our attacker, who had just finished batting polystyrene fuzz out of his face. He wheeled his rifle back around, but Koi Boi was faster. Koi Boi grabbed the stock and yanked it out of his grip.

The instant I found my footing, I scrambled toward Tippy-Toe. She lay sprawled amid the smoldering ceiling fuzz. She was moving. Phew. I gingerly checked her over, and detected no broken bones. She was winded, which was the very least any of us would have been if something fifty times our size tripped over us.

"Mostly still here," she said.

"Don't do that again," I said.

"You would have done the same if you could," she said, which, well – fair point.

She probably wasn't going to be much good in a fight for

a while. I tucked her back underneath my shirt collar for safekeeping. Then I caught up with the rest of the world.

Our attacker had gotten away from Koi Boi. Koi Boi, wisely or unwisely, had prioritized snapping that rifle in half over giving chase. And we'd ended up in the science department's microfusion lab.

All of the seats faced a big, heavily insulated metal cylinder. ESU's teaching microfusion reactor sounded a lot scarier than it actually was. We'd entered a warren of vents, exhaust pipes, and gauges, lit by the soft electronic glow of laptop LCDs.

The overhead fluorescents were off. Even when Nancy found the light switch and flipped it, shadows bloomed everywhere. There were annoyingly many places to hide.

Bitter laughter echoed from the walls. "It's always that way, isn't it?" our attacker's voice asked. "Some confounding little variable, something that never should have been there."

"Hang on," I told the others. "This is starting to sound familiar."

Self-styled brainiac villains usually overprepared. I crouched behind a desk, just in case he had another weapon ready. Koi Boi and Chipmunk Hunk immediately flanked my desk, covering me. Hunched on my knees, I pulled out a deck of cards.

Nobody should expect anyone, least of all busy under-graduates living a crimefighting double life, to keep track of every hero and villain who's ever graced or disgraced New York, let alone the world. Hence, collectible trading cards.[7]

---

[7] These ones were custom-made for me by Deadpool. That's a long story, and tangential to the action here. You'll just have to accept it. *Accept it!* – SG

READERS LUCKY. YOU GET EDITORIAL TEXT BOXES REMIND YOU WHO LAST SEEN IN WHAT ISSUE. HULK AND SQUIRREL GIRL HAVE TO FIGURE IT OUT ON FLY. – ED

With a motion honed by years of practice, I thumbed through the tops of the cards until I spotted the face I was looking for:

THE MAD THINKER

The name just comes right out there and says it all, huh? He's not called the Mad Imaginator, I guess. Still disappointing. Like a lot of geeks and nerds, this guy has confused "thinking" for "calculating". The guy's obsessed with probabilities. He thinks that he's fully capable of predicting the outcome of everything in the universe. He's not sharp enough to have figured out that right-brained thinking is thinking too. He has trouble seeing past the little details right in front of him, like a fist in his sinus cavities. –DP

- Once told Spider-Man, "I know who you are, Peter Petruski!"
- Endearingly pathetic. In small doses. Like, two seconds, maybe.
- Has let being verified on Twitter go to his head.
- Once impersonated Reed Richards in an alternate universe while *our* Reed Richards was presumed dead. Apparently? Who even knows anymore?
- Tell him to stop dilly-dallying in STEM, go to art school, and get a real job. See what happens.

I took my turn covering Koi Boi and Chipmunk Hunk while they had a peek.

Someone had left an energy drink by one of the console desks. The next time I saw Mary, she had it open in her hand. Another person might have asked her if she really needed caffeine at a time like this. College students are gonna be college students.

I wished I'd gotten to it first.

Now that I had the chance to look around, I spotted some things that didn't fit. I'd never been here before but, at a place like ESU, you learn the difference between real science and "theatrical" science pretty quick. Real science looks boring: desktops and laptops, CAD software, bad UIs, *Far Side* cartoons, and video game T-shirts.

This was not real science. All around the side of the reactor, someone had set up things that I could only call toys. There was a Jacob's ladder lightning generator, two Tesla coils, a plasma ball, and a silly number of control panels with unlabeled lights blinking in rhythmic patterns. And, against the wall, a table with two long, blinking glass rods atop it – a prop that I would have sworn I'd seen on, like, five different *Star Trek* shows.

If the Mad Thinker hadn't *just* attacked us with a very serious, very deadly superscience weapon, I would have laughed outright. "Come on, my dude," I called. "Do you really think we're going to fall for decoys like these?"

He ignored my question. "To tell you the truth, I've actually started counting on those *confounding little variables* happening to me, because they do every time! *Every* time with you people! And you're looking at the reason why!"

The acoustics in this room were awful. Too much cement and lead shielding. But the place was small enough that he couldn't quite hide where his voice was coming from. I just had to keep him talking.

"Who's 'you people?'" I asked.

"Every time I'm just about to accomplish something, anything, along comes somebody in a costume or a silly mask, and they rip it away from me." As if he'd predicted that I'd been about to find him, he stepped out of a shadow, holding something fist-sized and boxy. It rattled in his shaking hand. "And I think I've discovered how it happens. *Belief*. People see you. Believe in you. And that affects the outcome!"

The object he held was making some kind of soft, high-pitched squeal, like a kettle about to come to boil. "Buddy, I don't even know you. You know nobody talks like that anymore, right?" The man spoke like every other word he said was bolded.

"You don't know me, Doreen Allene Green, but I know you. And Tomas Lara-Perez. And Ken Shiga–" Nancy was making a wrap-it-up motion with her hand. Her expression must have been deadly, because the Mad Thinker cut his dramatic monologue short. "Yes, well. Even before you discarded your secret identities like expired cheese, people were reading about you. People talked about you. People believed in you. That's what shifted the probabilities. I've come realize that belief is a fundamental force of the cosmos. Just as much as gravity or Gamma radiation."

"That's cool," Koi Boi said. "Great. Why don't you send that into a peer-reviewed journal rather than… what are you doing, again?"

"I *have* no peers," the Mad Thinker said, because Koi Boi had, kindly, pitched that one right over home plate. Most people who shout this much at strangers really need somebody to talk to,

and to make what they imagined were witty rejoinders. "I hold the *proof*. And this is going to bring us all someplace where none of it matters anymore."

"All this monologuing and no evil plan yet," I complained. "Come on, make with the exposition!"

"The universe is a vast and wondrous place, Squirrel Girl. There are places beyond our visible light horizon, more lightyears away than there are seconds that have elapsed since the beginning of the universe, where the laws of physics are fantastically different. Where things are more regulated. *Predictable*. And my Quantum Translocator will bring us there. You see, it will 'quantumly entangle' this place with… somewhere else, far out there."

"Pseudoscientific nonsense," Mary said instantly.

"Of course it's not scientific!" the Mad Thinker snapped. "It's quantum!"

Nancy and I looked at each other, and back at him.

"You can stick the word 'quantum' in front of anything you like," the Mad Thinker said, exasperated. "People don't question it. They just accept whatever it does as scientific fact."

Just when I thought I couldn't get any more peeved. "For your information," I said, thrusting an accusing finger at him, "quantum mechanics is a widely misunderstood branch of physics that produces testable, practical results! It's just really difficult to wrap your head around. It's not any more magic than… than… your FACE is magic!" Sometimes it's dang hard to find the words mid-rant, especially when you've got a million other things on your mind.

"No more magic than Newtonian physics," Nancy supplied.

"Thank you," I said, and then, louder, "No more magic than Newtonian physics!"

I'd expected that accusing the Mad Thinker of not thinking this through, or at least insulting his face, would make him mad. He was too enraptured with himself.

"It doesn't matter!" he said, triumphantly. "It's belief! It's what people *believe* about anything with the word 'quantum'!"

No wonder neither Tony nor Doctor Strange could figure out what was causing this. This wasn't mad science *or* magic. It was more like… philosophy. Mad philosophy.

The heck of it was, it seemed to be working. The stars burning behind the walls had only gotten brighter.

Suddenly I realized: the casual slacks, the polo shirt, the carelessly half-buttoned collar. "You're… you teach here?" I asked. "You're a professor?"

For a moment, I couldn't understand why I hadn't seen him before now. But he'd probably calculated his way into avoiding every likely encounter with ESU's public super heroes.

"Adjunct lecturer," he said, in a small voice that told me he was accustomed to correcting students who called him 'professor'. "But that's not important–"

"Adjunct?" Chipmunk Hunk interrupted. "Dang! I'm surprised you had the money to buy the props."

"Or the time to make them," Nancy added. "Shouldn't you be grading?"

"Silence!" he thundered. I could tell they'd struck a nerve. "I've filled my freshmen students' heads with enough of this nonsense that they believe it. And now I have belief behind me, too."

"You can't possibly think the world works like that," Chipmunk Hunk said. "Like – Doctor Doom has people who believe he can do anything, too. Same with a lot of villains."

"Don't you wonder why they never die?" the Mad Thinker asked. "And keep coming back over and over again?"

"Well," Chipmunk Hunk said. He looked at us, and then back at the Mad Thinker. "Kinda."

"Magic is science by other means," the Mad Thinker said. "This is both. Do you see the stars? They're real. It means that we're *already* out there. We're entangled. Soon the effect will encompass the entire city. You costumed vigilantes won't have fate on your side anymore. And those of us with actual ability will be able to *think* our way to the top, like we've always deserved to."

If I was understanding correctly, the device worked in two phases. First, it destabilized space, creating the collapsing and folding cityscape. Then, at the center of the effect, this building was *re*stabilizing... someplace else.

The world was a tub full of water, and the Mad Thinker had just pulled the plug. This building was emptying into the drain. The rest of the city would spiral in after us.

"All right, all right!" I interrupted. "That's enough of this. We're not letting you steal New York and transport it–"

"Entangle!" he said.

"–'Entangle' it some other place in the universe. Sheesh! That is not what quantum entanglement means! That's also a little extreme, don't you think? We've all had those moments where we learn something wild about the universe, and get really shook up about it, you know?" I wasn't going to say his theory was right, but *he* believed it was, and there was definitely some kind of force at work. "So stop trying to origami New York in on itself, and let's talk. Or we'll have to stop you the hard way."

I did not like the grin he wore just now.

"I wouldn't be giving you my villain's exposition if there was the slimmest prospect of you winning—" he started.

I can put on a fairly cool exterior. I like to think of myself as a pretty happy-go-lucky super hero, you know? No angst for me, please. But when someone threatens my home, I get down to business a little sooner than I otherwise might.

While he'd talked, I'd been making some calculations of my own. Though he seemed to have a genuine talent for anticipating my friends and myself in combat, he didn't have the reflexes to match. In the other room, his shots had come close to us, but never quite hit. His plan had hinged on electrocuting us in a water-soaked room... maybe because he knew he didn't have the dexterity to aim any more precisely. Not while he was delivering a line he'd clearly been practicing in a mirror.

I lunged.

A quarter-second before I started moving, he jerked his hand to his side. He'd anticipated me even then, but I was faster. I'd been right to watch for weapons earlier. He *had* rearmed himself.

I swatted the sidearm he drew out of his hand. With chipmunk reflexes and slippery speed, Chipmunk Hunk and Koi Boi were on him, too, restraining his arms.

The other object he was holding – the boxy, metallic, rattling thing – went flying. I caught it.

It was a slender metal box, about the size of my forearm, with sharp corners and home-workshop welding scars. Unlike the rest of the props, it didn't look or feel fake. I turned the device over in my hands. It had a single, monochrome green display mounted in one side, showing a dancing line that looked like an old-fashioned waveform display.

It was moving of its own accord, like something was rattling around inside it. When I'd heard it rattling earlier, I'd thought it was because the Mad Thinker had been trembling. No, it was bouncing around like a squirrel on a sugar high.

Even more alarming, the squealing sound hadn't stopped. If anything, it was louder, and getting higher pitched – like an uncanny power within was begging to get out.

The Mad Thinker could have been lying about everything. But instinct told me otherwise. Like squirrels, I trust my instincts. The pit in my stomach got deeper.

The Mad Thinker didn't seem too concerned about being caught. He didn't struggle against Koi Boi and Chipmunk Hunk.

"You absolutely would have given us a villain's exposition anyway," Chipmunk Hunk accused.

The Mad Thinker vigorously shook his head. "It was too late the moment you noticed that anything was wrong," he said. "The instant the effect started spreading. There's no way to stop the reaction, and it's still growing. Even if you destroy it, it will take us all with it."

The squiggly green line was wiggling around like a jump rope at recess, in an earthquake. And a windstorm. "So the rest of the city isn't quite under this thing's control yet, huh?" I asked. "It's only places where we can see stars that have started to 'entangle.'"

The first thing to know about self-styled brainiac types is that their egos can short-circuit them. A person's perception of their intelligence is more a function of their ego than actual smarts, anyway. Though the Mad Thinker might have been capable of some incredible feats of calculation, he didn't have the emotional intelligence to take full advantage of them.

His voice trailed to nothing as his brain caught up with him.

He realized he'd given away more information than he'd needed. And he calculated what I was going to do next.

"Don't do it," he said abruptly.

"Do you think the fire alarm cleared out most of the people upstairs?" I asked.

"I could go find out," Chipmunk Hunk said.

"No time." The device's keening had built up to a terrific pitch. It just kept going higher and higher. In less than a minute, it would hit its crescendo.

The noise grated on my nerves. I couldn't keep my thoughts straight. But it was probably a good thing I couldn't think too much about this.

"Do you all trust me to do the right thing?" I asked.

Without taking the time to think about it, they all nodded. Chipmunk Hunk opened his mouth to say something – but the Mad Thinker must have calculated a moment of weakness because in Chipmunk Hunk's instant of distraction, he yanked his arm away.

Koi Boi was on the ball, swinging in with a punch aimed at the Mad Thinker's chin. The Mad Thinker must have anticipated that, too, because he had started to duck the instant he tugged loose from Chipmunk Hunk. Koi Boi's swing went wide. He stumbled, balance lost.

The Mad Thinker rushed toward me, snarling. His eyes burned with desperation.

I couldn't afford any more dithering. Not against someone who calculated punches before they were thrown. The Mad Thinker lived halfway into the future, and all I had was *now*.

New York was where I belonged. My people, human and squirrel, all fit here. My life was here. My *future* was here.

Everything I was studying for, and everything I wanted to be, was here.

I didn't just belong *in* New York. I belonged *to* New York. And New York belonged to me.

My friends felt the same way. Maybe they would have chosen differently than I did. But I was the one holding the Mad Thinker's device, and I was the one with the responsibility.

I never shirked responsibility.

I craned my leg up and snapped his device over my knee.

The Unbeatable Squirrel Girl Vs The Cold Equations

The instant I snapped the Mad Thinker's device in half, reality seemed to flex and bow inward. Time held still. Koi Boi's mouth was a perfectly round 'O'. Spittle flew from the Mad Thinker's lips, frozen in midair.

None of which made any sense because, if something had slowed time, my brain was *part* of time and shouldn't have perceived any difference. But I swear it happened anyway.

Then the universe snapped back into itself.

It was like being hit in the nose with a rubber band while you were on an airplane that had lost cabin pressure. My ears popped, painfully. Worse, it felt like pockets of air underneath my eyes had done the same. It was horrible. I do not recommend it.

There was a tremendous *crack* as the laboratory doors whipped open and smacked into the brick walls on either side.

Somewhere, more distantly, glass shattered. A whole ton of glass. Like… a waterfall of glass, cascading onto cement. It sounded like every window in the building had shattered.

A sudden stiff, hard wind yanked me toward the door. It died a split second later. Air had exploded out of all the building's doors and windows at once.

My feet felt strangely lighter underneath me. So did my tail. Tails have a good sense for things like that. I felt like I'd stepped onto an elevator going down.

Next, the floor shook. Unlike the wind, the shaking never diminished. It got worse, and the walls started to buckle. Several ceiling tiles fell loose. Then, with a brittle-sounding *snap*, the metal framework holding the rest broke, and it was raining polystyrene.

"Building's collapsing," I said, ever helpful.

"Thank you," Chipmunk Hunk said. My friends were already backing toward the door.

The Mad Thinker, expression frozen in a mask of horror, vanished under a curtain of ceiling fragments and dust. I doubted he had seen this coming. If he had, though, there wasn't much he could do about it. Not with his limited reflexes and strength.

I was nearest him. I darted forward and found his arm, and pulled him, coughing, from underneath the mound of former ceiling. All of us ran back into the classroom and out into the corridor.

I tugged the Mad Thinker along, hoping that he wouldn't fight back – that he would realize I was looking out for him. No dice. As soon as we reached the first bend in the hall, he used that mighty brain of his to figure the instant when I'd be most distracted, and yanked away from me. I misstepped and didn't have the leverage to pull him back. The strange lightness in my step was playing heck with my balance.

I turned to go after him, but caught sight of an ominously deep crack cleaving its way up through the brickwork. No time.

My friends and I mounted the stairs to ground level just ahead of one of the worst noises I'd ever heard in my life. It was a deep growling, a stone-grinding-on-stone cacophony like the earth was chewing itself apart. Behind us, the basement floor vanished under a torrent of debris. To our left, the ceiling fell inward in a tumble of dust, wiring, and big deadly chunks of stone and metal. The building was collapsing in on itself from the center.

We ran towards the exit. To my relief, the foyer we'd been through earlier was empty. Hopefully the fire alarm *had* cleared everybody out.

In the instant before the lights went out, I hadn't seen any glass on the floor. The windows must have all blown outwards.

Where there had once been windows, there was nothing now… and no daylight outside. No glass, no sunlight, no campus. Just a big, purplish shadow.

The microfusion generator had finally had it. The lights flickered. Half a second later, they died.

The shadows outside weren't completely lightless. By the time we'd crossed the foyer, my squirrel senses had adjusted enough for me to verify that everyone was still with me. For the first time today, even Mary looked panicked.

There was just enough light to see that the university's lawn was still outside. We ran out into the open as the rest of the building collapsed like a sandcastle with water poured on its center.

I dropped to the ground, rolling to protect Nancy and Tippy-Toe as a cloud of choking dust billowed over us.

Half a minute later, when the dust finished settling, Nancy and I and everyone else were still coughing up scads of it.

The university's lawn was comfortingly soft. If I'd been cut by any glass beads, the adrenaline was keeping me from feeling it.

Silence settled over the ruins, thick and awkward as a lecture hall while the TAs were passing exams out.

I pushed myself up on my elbows and saw all the things I'd been too busy to notice a moment ago.

Empire State University's lawn ended abruptly in front of us. It vanished in a clean cut, like someone had taken a paring knife to the soil. Beyond it… orange-purple sand, stretching on to a dim and crumpled horizon.

A warm breeze blew in over us. It was too dry to be like breath, and not acrid enough to be from fire. My spring sweater was suddenly much too warm.

One thing that's hard to communicate about worlds and dimensions far from our own is that none of them smell like you'd expect. There's no place in the Multiverse quite like Earth. Everywhere else, the air and its particulates are different in a way that you never really stop noticing. The mélange of odors that found us now was like nothing I'd ever smelled: gunpowder and gasoline, mixed with something sickly sweet. It was like someone had spiked a gas tank in a war zone. There was something smoky and sulfuric that made me think of volcanism. Not encouraging.

And then there was the *sky*. Violet and magenta swirls washed the horizon. Stars nestled inside their gyri and sulci. None of them were bright enough, or the right color, to account for the diffused light. That seemed to be coming from the colors themselves.

My jaw hung slack. It was hard to look dignified with my mouth hanging open, but that was all right. I didn't have time to think of dignity. I was too busy thinking *holy crap*.

"Well," I said, when I could.

There seemed to be a million things to say, and also nothing at all, so I let that hang.

"I do not accept that just happened," Nancy said. She thought of herself as a pessimist, but she had a talent for directed wishful thinking.

With an amount of effort worthy of a *"hup"* of its own, I rolled to my feet.

Then I nearly fell over on my face. Tippy-Toe squeaked in dismay as she felt my balance waver.

The lightness in my step earlier had not been my imagination. I felt like I was always dropping, like the ground underneath me was falling away. I'd experienced this before, on the moon and other strange new worlds.[8]

If ellipses could make a sound, I would be making it.

"Hah!" Mary said, genuinely delighted. "We're in trouble."

Echoes of the physical sciences building's demise still rolled across the horizon. A particularly sharp crash made us look back just in time to see a monstrously tall figure emerging from the rubble. It clutched a kicking, squirming human silhouette in its grasp, holding it high off the ground.

---

[8] SEE THE UNBEATABLE SQUIRREL GIRL (2015), ISSUE #2. THEN UNBEATABLE SQUIRREL GIRL (2015) #27. IMPORTANT: DESPITE BOTH BEING SAME NAME AND YEAR, THESE COMICS NOT SAME SERIES AS EACH OTHER! IT MAKE HULK MAD TOO! – ED

Under ordinary circumstances, I would've been happy to see him. But I'd hoped a few people I knew had arrived too late to get caught up in all this.

"GOOD NEWS, FRIENDS: I HAVE CAUGHT A VILLAIN," Brain Drain announced, hoisting the Mad Thinker in the air. One of the eyes bobbing in his brain case was facing the sky and the strange new stars. Then the other rotated to join it. "HOWEVER, I DO NOT BELIEVE I AM EMOTIONALLY PREPARED FOR THE BAD NEWS."

"Humph," I said, and rested my chin in my palm.

We were gathered around a pit, having built a fire from the remnants of office furniture. The others shoveled coleslaw into their mouths, as one does in circumstances like these. (The circumstances being finding, underneath the rubble of a collapsed building on an alien planet, an office refrigerator mysteriously stacked with takeout containers of coleslaw.) All of which we had to eat now, before it went bad.

Chipmunk Hunk and I had burrowed the firepit while Koi Boi and Brain Drain collected the fuel. Nancy had found the contents of a paper recycling bin to serve as kindling. Mary had a lighter.[9]

With the warm winds, we didn't need the fire to survive the climate. But the fire gave us something to look at. Otherwise, we would've had to sit in the dark staring at each other and the Mad Thinker, and *that* wouldn't have been survivable for long.

Koi Boi leaned back on his hands. "So," he said. "Now what?"

---

[9] She doesn't smoke or anything. She just carries it around for firestarting reasons. – SG

The Mad Thinker gave him a withering look. "We die miserable and starving, assuming we don't poison ourselves on bad coleslaw first."

For all his complaints about the food, he didn't stop eating.

Digging through the rubble, and piecing together what we knew with what the Mad Thinker was telling us, we'd put together a better picture of what had happened.

The physical sciences building had not collapsed because I'd broken the Mad Thinker's device. It had been suddenly moved to ground unable to support it. The "earth" here was spongier, sandier, and otherwise entirely unlike the world we had been transported from. The building's foundations had been completely unable to withstand the shock.

The microfusion reactor had been smashed to pieces. Nothing usable left. No radiation problems, fortunately. The people of New York had learned long ago not to build things that could cause massive catastrophe just from a little being-battered-apart. Otherwise the city would have been a crater after the Skrull invaded a few summers ago[10]. Or the frost giants after that.

The lawn had once been flat as paper. Now it rippled and rose like a lumpy sleeping bag. The sod had folded, or been shoved together, or stretched out. In some places, it had torn, and mixed with the bruise-colored alien soil underneath.

The "stars" didn't look too much like stars back home. They were too diffused. When I looked closer, I saw that they weren't stars at all, but knots of gas and fog. They looked like lights shining behind a curtain. The Mad Thinker had said his device

---

[10] Again. – SG

was primed to take us into a universe beyond our light horizon[11], to places where physics worked differently...

Under other circumstances, it would have been exciting.

I went into CompSci for a reason. I like math. I like solving tricky puzzles. It made me feel a little better to have puzzled some of this out – even if the equation I'd solved added up into a big ugly zero for our futures.

After a period of resting and hiding underneath my sweater collar, Tippy-Toe was more like herself again.

"Just some bruised ribs," she said. "Tail's fine! My head, too. Probably."

I knew better than most people just how quickly injuries on small, fragile mammals can spiral out of control. So did Chipmunk Hunk, who watched us with undisguised concern.

"Just take it easy," I told Tippy-Toe. "You've done your part."

"Nuh," she said. "I'm tough." She really was. (For those of you who hate seeing squirrels in trouble as much as I do, I'll spare you the suspense right now. Tippy-Toe makes it through this all right.)

I studied computers, not exoplanet astronomy, but this wasn't my first outer space rodeo.[12] I'd learned enough space survival to know what to be wary of... like starting fires in a strange atmosphere. But Brain Drain's filtration system reported that

---

[11] That's over fourteen billion light years, for those of you who don't know the phrase. Farther away than light could have traveled between it and Earth since the beginning of the universe. And – given that the universe is still expanding – it's farther than any light, or anyone stuck traveling below the speed of light, could travel in all the future of time! – SG

[12] IT WAS 1,981,710TH ANNUAL GIANT AMOEBA RODEO AT BARNARD'S STAR. NO COMIC ISSUE BECAUSE NO DRAMATIC EVENTS OR SHOWDOWNS WITH EVIL. SQUIRREL GIRL AND FRIENDS INVITED BY STARJAMMERS AND HAD WONDERFUL TIME. – ED

this air had less oxygen than Earth's, to the point that exercise would make us lightheaded. The gunpowder stink didn't seem to mean there were actual combustibles. A fire wouldn't set the whole sky aflame.

The Mad Thinker could have run away. There wasn't any point, though. There was nowhere to run to. Besides, Brain Drain was seated right behind him – a hard-to-forget reminder that Brain Drain could restrain him at any moment.

There was no point in that, either. Nor in beating him up, or arresting him, or anything else costumed crimefighters traditionally did to villains. The dramatics would have just expended energy that we were realizing we needed to preserve.

Besides, none of us had much to physically fear from him, and he knew it. We were all in the same boat. A great, big, deserted alien world of a boat.

We had nothing better to do than sit around the fire and shoot the breeze.

"You want to tell us a bit more about where we are?" Koi Boi asked the Mad Thinker. "Or sulk about it more first?"

"I never sulk without good reason to sulk." The Mad Thinker nodded to me. "We're doomed because of her meddling. And no – I have no idea where we are, other than impossibly far from Earth."

"Come on!" I said. "We didn't materialize on the surface of an inhabitable world by accident. The odds of that are like the odds of… of finding a squirrel on the moon[13]. You knew exactly where we would end up."

---

[13] Both Tippy-Toe and I have been on the moon a few times, if briefly. So if you picked the right time and place, finding moon-squirrels *was* technically possible, just infinitesimally unlikely. – SG

"I knew *how* we would end up, but not why. I used my Quantum Translocator to scan the infinite universe for suitable worlds, and selected one at random. I have no idea what its physical location is. What would have been the point of finding out? Again, its range is *infinite*. Distance and direction would have no meaning. The odds of us being anywhere near even our galaxy are, oh... well, ask a calculator to divide by zero and you might get the idea."

"So let's say your plan had worked, and you'd brought the whole city here," Nancy said, acidly. "How many New Yorkers would have died?"

"Died? None at all." After a second of letting that hang and a mouthful of coleslaw, he added, "So long as they listened to me."

"I'm extremely impressed by the scope and scale of your issues," I said. "Less so with your ability to make important life choices, but the good news is that now we're in a nice, safe, isolated place where we can work on those issues without endangering anyone else."

"So long as you can do it in ten days," Brain Drain said. "On a related note, I believe I've worked out the survival margins for human beings with our available supplies."

"What about squirrels?" Tippy-Toe asked.

I had a baggie of seeds, dried corn, and nuts with me, naturally. I never travel anywhere without nuts. Good for me and for squirrels. And chipmunks. And ducks[14]. And... just about anything, really.

---

[14] Useful fact time! Ducks will eat all the bread you throw at them, but bread isn't actually all that good for them. It's like junk food. Try feeding ducks with cracked corn, oats, and birdseed instead! – SG

"Given your caloric needs, somewhat longer."

"Ah," Tippy-Toe said. "Darn. Now I'm sad."

The Mad Thinker looked back and forth between us. Unlike me and my friends, he couldn't understand squirrelese, and so this conversation must have been one of those rare things that mystified him. His lip twitched as if agitated by this. He stood.

"Your calculations are off," he told Brain Drain, "by a day."

"Plus or minus?" Brain Drain asked.

The Mad Thinker gave him an awfully rude gesture, like the jerk he was.

"Never mind," Brain Drain said. "We will have the opportunity to learn experientially."

"No, we won't," I said. "I got us into this, and I'm going to find a way out of it."

"Doreen," Chipmunk Hunk said, quietly, "we already told you we don't blame you for this."

But I did. It had all happened very quickly, but when I'd broken that Quantum Whatever He Called It, I'd known what I was risking.

We'd taken a survey of every resource we had left to us. The good news was that the Fields Physical Sciences building had been on a college campus. Food was everywhere. The bad news was *also* that the Fields Physical Sciences building had been on a college campus.

So far, we'd found a crushed vending machine that had spilled some candy bars and cheese crackers, a full vending machine of… coffee and energy drinks. And, of course, enough coleslaw to make us all sick.

The water problem was worse. There was none of it. A search

of the landscape had found no rivers, pools, or hint of moisture in the air. All we had was that one vending machine.

"THERE IS EVERY CHANCE YOU WILL NOT SUFFER LONG," Brain Drain said. "UNLIKE ME. I WILL PERSIST ALONE UNTIL MY POWER CELLS WEAR OUT IN TWO TO THREE DECADES."

"'Every chance?'" the Mad Thinker sputtered. "There's a one hundred percent chance! We are all dead beyond a shadow of a fraction of a doubt!"

For the third time that night, Nancy's patience snapped. "The quakes alone would have killed thousands of people if Doreen hadn't stopped you!"

The Mad Thinker rubbed the back of his wrists anxiously. "The quakes wouldn't have been so bad if I'd been able to transport more of the city," he said, with a glare in my direction. For all his bluster, he couldn't quite meet Nancy's eyes. "If the effect had been as wide as it should have been, the whole of the New York Underground would have come with us. The city would have been mounted in solid rock rather than this unstable regolith!"

To emphasize his contempt for the regolith, he kicked some of the omnipresent purple-orange sand into the fire.

"So you were *just* going to move the entire city out here," Nancy said, bitterer and bitterer. "Off the power grid, away from food infrastructure, with a broken water system and – I don't care what you say – several collapsed skyscrapers, and you expected this to end *well* for you? Or anyone?"

The Mad Thinker waved her off with a flip of his hand. "It wouldn't have been as bad as that. I'd worked through all the outcomes, and it would have been just barely possible to take all of the city's resources and build productive greenhouses, with sunlamps powered by fusion generators, before the city's stockpiles ran out. *If* you knew exactly what you were doing. *If* you put someone who'd weighed every variable in charge."

Chipmunk Hunk snorted. (It is impossible to convey in words how handsome he was even when he snorted.) "You mean if the city put you in charge of everything."

"Of course," the Mad Thinker said, exasperated by the obviousness of it all. A tendril of coleslaw drooped from the Mad Thinker's lip. He slurped it up.

I had to admit that I admired his lack of self-consciousness.

Nancy managed to swallow her comeback long enough to get to the meat of our next problem. "So there's really no way home, huh?"

"There would have been," the Mad Thinker said. "With the city's resources behind me, I could have developed and deployed another travel device, this time without any 'belief' frippery, and brought New York back home. My *new* New York." He kicked more dirt.

"Could you please stop that?" Koi Boi asked. Some of the dirt was hitting him. The Mad Thinker kept kicking.

"*Knock it off!*" Nancy thundered.

He immediately stopped.

In the silence that followed, Mary cracked open another energy drink. Her third that day. Or night. Whatever this was.

This planet, or whatever it was, certainly sounded like it had a mood. A low howl resonated across the horizon. Wind, maybe. Probably. Koi Boi frowned as he listened to it.

Looking at him and the others, I had to resist the impulse to wring my hands.

I hadn't asked any of my friends what they would do before I snapped the Mad Thinker's toy in half. There hadn't been time. It still ate me up inside. While Chipmunk Hunk, Koi Boi, and I sifted the heavier rubble, looking for survivors and anyone else unfortunate enough to be dragged here with us (no one, thankfully), I'd started to try to apologize. Neither of them were having it.

"It's over, it's done, and it's not what matters right now," Chipmunk Hunk said.

"I didn't mean to put Mary in danger," I said, nodding toward the others. They were scavenging for food under the lighter rubble.

"Hey. Mary's one of us. Just like Nancy. She knows this isn't a risk-free life, and she's still here."

Koi Boi still wore his costume's goggles, which, although very cool, also made reading his expression more difficult. "Any one of us would have done the same," he said, as he hoisted a support beam off a fallen vending machine. "Ask Mary and Nancy and Brain Drain, and I'm sure they'd agree."

I liked my friends quite a lot, but I hated it when they gave me the feeling that they were cushioning me. "You two are just trying to make me feel better," I said.

"Yeah," Koi Boi answered. The naked admission of it startled me. "But that doesn't mean we're not telling the truth."

Hmm. Good point.

Not that it allayed my sense of responsibility for all this.

Nancy's voice snapped me back to the present. "Does this planet have a night?" she asked, between mouthfuls of coleslaw. "Is there a day? Do we sleep in shifts, or what?" She did not hide her suspicion when she looked at the Mad Thinker.

The wind moaned over the horizon. It wasn't so loud that we

had to raise our voices, but I wasn't going to be able to sleep with that going on. It raised the fur on Tippy-Toe's tail. Mine too.

"I CANNOT CLOSE MY EYES," Brain Drain volunteered. "EVERY NIGHT, FALLING ASLEEP IS LIKE A NIGHTMARE MY MIND IS CONSTANTLY TRYING TO WAKE ME FROM."

The Mad Thinker stared at him in undisguised horror. "Really? Then how is it that you have not yet toddled off to the front lines of some super heroic battle to try to get yourself killed?"

"A ZEST FOR LIFE," Brain Drain answered.

"We could always eat *him*," the Mad Thinker said, eyeing Brain Drain's brain.

"That's enough of that," I told him.

"No, IT'S TRUE," Brain Drain said. "MY BRAIN MATTER HAS A HIGH CALORIC CONTENT."

"Nobody's going to touch a single neuron of his brain," Nancy said.

"I BELIEVE THE DISPOSAL OF MY REMAINS SHOULD BE MY CHOICE," Brain Drain said. "I HAVE NO DESIRE TO OUTLIVE MY FRIENDS, AND THERE IS A STRONG UTILITARIAN ARGUMENT FOR—"

"We have enough to survive for now," Chipmunk Hunk interrupted, stopping that train of thought before it arrived at the station. "It'll last until we figure out a way home."

"Just what is it you think you're going to do?" the Mad Thinker asked. He looked around at Chipmunk Hunk, Koi Boi, and myself. "Chipmunk-jump back? Commune with space-fish? Collect nuts?" When his gaze fell on Nancy and Mary, he said, "I don't even know *what* it is that you two think you can do, but I don't care to commit even the fraction of the brainpower it would take to explain to you that it's not enough."

He kicked more sand into the fire and then stood and stomped off.

"Yeah!" Koi Boi called at his back. "I think I *will* commune with some space-fish!"

When the Mad Thinker was out of earshot, Koi Boi muttered, "That would show him."

Unless the Mad Thinker went off into the mountains, I could keep track of him, by sound if nothing else. He could not help tripping and cursing wherever he went.

"We'll get out of here," I said, because I needed it to be true. "We just… need time to figure out how."

"I guess I've been on worse camping trips," Nancy said.

"Maybe I can make some kind of caffeine-and-sugar-powered rocket," Mary said.

"I'm surprised you're not one already," Nancy said.

"Give me time," Mary told her, and cracked open another energy drink. "With enough caffeine, anything is possible."

The Unbeatable Squirrel Girl Vs The Solipsism Problem

Chipmunk Hunk nodded in the direction the Mad Thinker had gone. "I hate to say this, but Mr Villainous Exposition out there is probably still our best shot at getting out of here."

Our campfire crackled for an otherwise-silent moment. It was my fault we were here. So all of the messy tasks, like dealing with the Mad Thinker, were my responsibility. I stood.

The firelight gave me a good view of the others. They were doing all right, at least so far. No signs of panic or despair. Mary and Chipmunk Hunk reclined together on a cushion made up of couch stuffing and a fallen curtain. His hand rested idly on the back of Mary's neck. Koi Boi stared at the strange, nebulous sky, hands under his chin. Brain Drain had not returned to the subject of being devoured for food, which, for him, was a stunning display of optimism.

Under other circumstances, this would have looked like a normal campout. Looking at my friends made me feel a little better. Maybe there was something to the Mad Thinker's ideas about belief affecting outcomes. Even if he'd taken us to a part of the cosmos where that was no longer true, I *felt* like I was in a different place than I would have been without them.

They were my responsibility. I could beat this. I was the Unbeatable Squirrel Girl. Together with my team, I was even more… er, unbeatable. Two hundred percent unbeatable. Not even the strange physics of realms beyond the visible universe could stop me.

As I headed toward the Mad Thinker, I heard soft footfalls in the sand behind me. Nancy was following. She knew I was about to tell her to relax with the others while I took care of this, but she preempted me.

"No way am I letting you put up with him alone," she said.

I'd thought the Mad Thinker had just been being clumsy as he stumbled and crashed his way around the rubble. But finding my way through was rough even for me. My reflexes were still catching up with the lighter gravity. More than once, I had to save Nancy from a fall. She struggled mightily to maintain her dignity but that just wasn't in her cards.

We found the Mad Thinker in the middle of the physical science building's remains, not even pretending that he wasn't sulking. At least he was owning his sulking. Good work, guy! Being honest with one's emotions is the first step to addressing them.

He seemed to be trying to scavenge bedding from the torn-up pieces of conference room seat cushions, but it was falling apart in his hands. It was almost pathetic enough to be endearing. *Almost.*

"You're coming to try to wheedle more information out of me," he announced, before we said a word. "While I know more facts and figures than you costumed charlatans could ever manage, it just so happens that none of it is any help out here. Why don't I tell you what's going to happen?" He eyed Nancy, and then told me, "Your rude friend here won't believe that I can't help you, and will try to use the threat of your physical strength to convince me to give up information that, once again, *I don't have*. You'll tell her that you never use force as an interrogation tactic, and this argument will drive a rift between you two that you'll heal hours later, before you even fall asleep."

"Nancy," I said reprovingly. "I would never threaten to beat up someone who's in custody."

Nancy shrugged. "I know it would have been beneath me, but it still would have felt good to say." She glared at the Mad Thinker. "Thanks for robbing me of that."

"You're welcome. And then, after that farcical display... let me see if I can predict what our future holds next..." He held his hand to his temple, and spun it in circles before suddenly snapping his fingers. "Oh, yes! We'll all *starve to death out here*."

"Dehydrate," Nancy corrected. "We'll dehydrate first."

He flapped a dismissive hand at her. "A distinction without a difference."

"C'mon!" I complained. "It's not very true to your persona if you won't be exact about things! It's out of character."

"Forgive me. Forecasting the sufferings of my impending demise is overwhelming my normal capacity for conversational excellence." He paused a moment, then looked at us brightly. "Very well. More parlor tricks to amuse and intimidate you until you go away. You, young lady–" Even when he addressed Nancy, he couldn't quite meet her eyes "–are not as concerned about your fate as you should be, but are worried instead about your cat." Whether he'd somehow deduced the existence of Nancy's cat Mew[15], or just spotted the white cat hair on her coat, it was impressive.

"You don't have any reason to worry," he said. "Someone as adept at fooling themselves into thinking they're prepared to 'hang out' with the likes of Squirrel Girl and her nemeses will have undoubtedly made provisions for your pets."

It was true. Nancy knew that my super heroic life was prone to unexpected absences, but she was determined to be my friend anyway. So she'd made an arrangement with our neighbor. She called him every night. If ever she didn't, he was to come over and feed Mew[16].

"There. Now you can devote what scraps of brainpower you have to dwelling on our own wretched fates instead."

"Are you finished?" Nancy asked.

"My dears," he said, which rankled me more than most of the other things, "I have scarcely begun to make myself intolerable. I can do much worse if you don't leave me alone to wallow."

By sheer perverse coincidence, a lecture hall seat sat mostly untouched among the debris. I sat and crossed my arms. Nancy stood firm behind me.

Something in the Mad Thinker's expression broke. He sat heavily on a slab of cracked wall, and massaged his forehead with his fingers. "Why won't you leave me alone?"

"Buddy," I said. "That didn't sound like a rhetorical question."

"It most certainly was not. It was an expression of despair."

"Don't you already know? Haven't you calculated the answer?"

---

[15] SHORT FOR 'MEWNIR'. SO CUTE IT MAKES HULK SMASH. – ED

[16] And pet Mew. And play with her. And cuddle her. It was *important*. – SG

"I have calculated nearly everything. Based on your past behavior, I knew you wouldn't leave me alone to face death with dignity. There was, in fact, a ninety-eight percent chance you would say those exact words. But that's just behavioral analysis. What I don't understand is *why*." He took his hand from his forehead and made a knocking motion toward mine.

"What is going on *inside* that head? Why would anyone act so obtusely, so muttonheadedly, as you do? Do you genuinely inhabit some different mental dimension than the rest of us? Is it an act? A commitment to the bit so profound as to surpass any definition of comedy?"

"'Behavioral analysis,'" Nancy quoted. "You sure didn't predict her behavior when she destroyed your toy."

"That's the worst thing about it," he said. "I did. Squirrel Girl's past behavior had extremely high indicators for rash and thoughtless action."

My decision to maybe exile us all to save New York had been extremely thoughtful, actually, but I let that one slide.

"I brushed it away because I could not believe your persona was for real," the Mad Thinker continued. "I thought it was an act. I convinced myself that you *did* have a functioning mind underneath your bizarre behaviors, and that you would not, in fact, doom us all. Obviously my mind was poisoned by hope. Of course you're nothing more than the sum of your ridiculous behaviors. I'm beginning to wonder if I'm the only actually conscious being in the universe."

We could still see the campsite from here, but didn't need to in order to hear Brain Drain's lumbering approach. Wood beams crunched like twigs under his feet.

"Solipsism is an interesting thought experiment," he

said as he reached them. "BUT TAKE IT FROM THE BEARER OF PSIONIC POWERS: OTHER MINDS SUFFER EXISTENCE JUST AS KEENLY AS THE REST OF US."

"That sounds exactly like what a figment of my imagination would say," the Mad Thinker said, grumpily. "Anyway, how do you know you didn't imagine that, too?"

"THAT IS A GOOD POINT," Brain Drain said, lidless eyes fixed on the Mad Thinker. "I DON'T. FOR ALL I KNOW, I AM BUT A BRAIN IN A JAR."

The Mad Thinker let out an extremely long breath. He must have anticipated exactly that answer, but it still seemed to cause him physical pain to hear it.

"It must be awful living like you do," I said.

The pained expression did not go away. "How do you mean?" he asked. His voice was flat and incurious, as if he already knew my answer... and I expected that he did.

"Believing that you know everything that's going to happen before it does," I said. "Being trapped in conversations you mapped out before they started." It was like he said: seeing us all as a set of behaviors rather than thinking minds. Like automata. Input stimulus, get response. "If I could do that, I'd had have trouble seeing people *as* people, too."

"I don't just 'believe' that," the Mad Thinker said. "I know it." But he didn't dispute the rest.

Nancy and I have been roommates for long enough that we're adept at picking up each other's thoughts.

She said, "The things that actually surprise you must scare the heck out of you, then."

"'Scare' is not the word I would use," he said. "Irritate. Vex. Provoke–"

"We get it," Nancy said. "You got you a word-a-day calendar every Christmas."

"I've had all evening to foresee this conversation and plan what I wanted to say," the Mad Thinker said, though a little defensively this time.

"And you couldn't choose the right word to start?"

He snapped a glare at her.

Brain Drain reached a metal claw over and patted the Mad Thinker's shoulder. The Mad Thinker must have seen the blow coming, but he still flinched at the friendly pounding.

"I AM ALSO AN APPRECIATOR OF WORDS," he said, "BUT I DO NOT CHOOSE THEM WITH THE AIM OF MAKING MYSELF FEEL BETTER AT THE EXPENSE OF OTHERS. USUALLY THE OPPOSITE ACTUALLY."

"Don't worry," the Mad Thinker said. "Absolutely nothing could make me feel better right now."

"Not even rescue?" I asked. "Going home?" Leaving out the part where he stood trial for his crimes, of course.

"Why would I waste time fantasizing about something that can never happen?"

The poor guy had spent all his life living without hope. What was the point of hoping for anything when you were sure you already knew the outcome? Determinism is a scary philosophy when you get right down to it. What the heck is free will, anyway? Decent people probably shouldn't think about that too much.

"Have we reached the part where you try to get me to reform my villainous ways?" he asked. "Or is that a few seconds off yet? Either way, you can skip it."

"*Never*," I said.

"Come on, Doreen," Nancy said. "Let's leave him to sulk."

The wind's moaning was getting lower, and louder. I wondered if a storm was coming. It sounded more and more familiar the longer I heard it.

A prickling feeling up went my back. I was starting to recognize the noise.

Tippy-Toe tugged on my ear to get my attention, but I already knew what she wanted to show me. I nodded silently. The prickling feeling turned into a cold thrill, and goosebumps.

The Mad Thinker was making a show of ignoring me. He pretended to be gathering bedding again. Time for a different tactic.

"That's fine," I told him. "I'm happy to go on knowing things he doesn't."

"You could not possibly," he said.

"I know we're going to get out of here," I said. "We're going to get back to Earth, and to New York, and Nancy and I aren't going to miss even a day in class."

"I almost believe you've convinced yourself. But, for the slow learners in the class: we have moved to a parcel of the universe where belief has no sway over reality."

"If I'm right, will you admit that there's more to life than treating people like numbers?"

"I will never admit to anything!" the Mad Thinker thundered.

"THERE IS SURPRISINGLY LITTLE REASON TO BELIEVE THAT THERE IS SUCH A THING AS AN OBJECTIVE UNIVERSE," Brain Drain said. "HOWEVER, I HAVE YET TO BE PERSUADED THAT AN OBSERVER'S BELIEFS CHANGE THEIR OBSERVED REALITY QUITE SO STRAIGHTFORWARDLY AS YOU SAY, HERE OR IN ANY CORNER OF THE UNIVERSE. SOME FACTS PERSIST: SUCH AS THE FACT THAT YOU ARE WRONG. WE WILL SURVIVE."

The Mad Thinker gave him a disgusted look. "You've genuinely surprised me. Out of all these buffoons, I thought you had the most sense. Why the sudden turn?"

Brain Drain met the Mad Thinker's glare steadily – or at least as steadily as the tank holding his bobbing eyes allowed. Which was not very.

"I HAVE SPENT A LONG TIME DWELLING IN THE ECHO CHAMBER OF MY OWN THOUGHTS. FOR YEARS, I WAS TRAPPED UNDERNEATH AN AVALANCHE, IN A SENSORY VOID. THE EXPERIENCE INFLICTED UPON ME TRAUMA FROM WHICH I AM STILL RECOVERING. I BELIEVE THAT YOU, WITH YOUR CLOCKWORK VIEW OF THE UNIVERSE AND SUBSEQUENT INABILITY TO PERCEIVE THE PEOPLE WITHIN THAT SYSTEM AS INDEPENDENT BEINGS, ARE EXPERIENCING A SIMILAR TRAUMA.

"INTROSPECTION IS A VALUABLE TOOL, BUT BY ITSELF IT IS JUST ISOLATION. ANY CLOSED SYSTEM OF THOUGHT IS, LIKE THE UNIVERSE ITSELF, DOOMED TO THERMODYNAMIC DECAY AND HEAT DEATH. AND – LIKE THE UNIVERSE ITSELF – WE BECOME HOLLOW ECHOES OF OURSELVES LONG BEFORE WE PERISH, ACCELERATING THE PACE AT WHICH WE TEAR OURSELVES APART AND FLY, SCREAMING, INTO THE VOID." He considered that for a moment, and held up one of his robot claws.

"BUT I DIGRESS. I HAVE MANY FLAWS AND FAILINGS, BUT SINCE EMERGING FROM WITHIN MYSELF I HAVE MADE SIGNIFICANT STRIDES IN ADDRESSING THEM. ONE OF THE MOST SIGNIFICANT OF WHICH IS THAT I AM NO LONGER SO WRAPPED UP IN MYSELF THAT I FAIL TO NOTICE EXTERNAL STIMULI."

The Mad Thinker folded his arms. "I have neither the need nor desire to treat all you zombies as anything but automata."

"Yes, but what about the whale?" Brain Drain asked.

"The... what?"

"The whale," Nancy and I said, together.

The moaning sound resonating over the horizon had seemed disturbingly... alive. It had taken me a while to recognize it. But you're not friends with Koi Boi for long before you've heard all of the sounds of the sea.

Whalesong is distinct, even transmitted through the air rather than the sea.

Koi Boi had stood, and was striding away from the campfire with his hand raised, palm flat, as if in summoning. He was following through on his promise.

An enormous shadow cleaved the horizon. It was much, much larger than any terrestrial whale I'd ever seen, but its silhouette was unmistakable.

Some things were the same the universe over. It's one of the strange and wonderful facts about convergent evolution. The universe was full of aliens with two arms, two legs, a head. We'd encountered many of them. But if there were humanoid aliens all over the place, of course there would be whale analogues, too.

Brain Drain's eyes had not left the Mad Thinker. "Your perspective on the universe is incomplete in ways you have trained yourself not to see." He extended a clawed hand. "Come and improve yourself with us."

The Mad Thinker's jaw hung loose. He'd gone pale in a way I hadn't seen since... well, this afternoon, really. For the second time today, he was genuinely, tremendously surprised. His brain was locked up, trying to recalculate everything.

"I bet you thought Koi Boi was kidding," I told him. So had I. So had he, probably.

"And he'd even told you just what he was going to do," Nancy said, standing and shouldering her coat more tightly.

There was something even stranger than everything else. As the whale approached, I heard a distinctly artificial whine, like a jet engine or rocket thrusters.

Well, unlike my friend here, I was well equipped to cope with surprises.

The Unbeatable Squirrel Girl Vs The Things Dreamt of by Your Philosophy

The space whale was not floating as majestically as all my preconceptions about whales said it should. It seemed to be going one-on-one against gravity and losing. It bobbed, dipped, and weaved. Jets of blue-white flame sprouted from the creature's underside and broad, membranous fins. The whine of engine noises amplified.

Finally, the creature heaved onto the purplish sand with a deep, long sigh. At first, I thought the sigh was some kind of outgassing from those thrusters.

But, no, it really was a vocalization. A long, drawn-out "*Aaahhhhhh.*"

Koi Boi still had his hand raised. Sheepishly, he lowered it. Not the dramatic, inspiring Free-Willy-jumping-over-E.T. moment he'd been hoping for.

"Gravity, my dudes," the creature said, in a booming, syrupy voice.

Koi Boi looked back at me. I shrugged, hands raised. He shrugged back. What was *I* supposed to do? He was the whale expert.

Mary's superpower was that she was impossible to surprise. "Excuse me," Mary called. "What?"

"How do you stand it?" the whale asked. "I mean, stand in it. Heck, you know what I mean. My muscles are turning to jelly, and everything in my head's going higgledy-piggledy."

"Ah," I said. That was a question I could answer, and Mary's attitude had inspired me. "You see, we're terrestrial species that evolved in gravity similar to this, and so our bones and musculature are accustomed to – nay, even required to – exist in a similar environment."

"Dang," the whale said. "I guess that makes sense."

"So far it's the only thing that does," Nancy said.

Koi Boi had gotten more of his wits back about him. "I asked you here to, ah, beseech you." He winced at how he sounded. He cleared his throat. "We need help. We're trapped out here and have no way home."

"How'd you all get out here, anyway?" the whale asked.

"I wouldn't believe our story if I told it to me," Koi Boi said. "So please pretend I said something reasonable."

"Sure," the whale said, and was astonishingly ready to leave it at that.

Its nose was about forty yards from the fire. The ever-present darkness kept us from seeing too much of it, but the firelight showed us a few things: red, leathery skin, broad fins like sails, and at least one solid black eye. Or a spot that reminded me of an eye. It had no iris or pupil, so there was no way to tell if it was looking at us. Somehow, I got the impression that it was.

I looked over the rest of it. Its reddish flesh was crisscrossed with angular black shapes and strange, sharp-cornered shadows. Mechanical protrusions and implants. This whale had had some work done. The metal dug deep into its skin, to the point of looking painful.

Nothing on the creature moved when it spoke. I'd seen no sign of a mouth opening. But its voice had sounded like it was coming from all around us. It spoke in perfect English, too.

The skin on the back of my arm stood up.

"How's its squirrelese?" I whispered to Tippy-Toe.

"Perfect," she said, with no small awe.

Of course. *Telepathy*. Should have realized it when the whale started speaking. First clue.

The voice we were hearing now might have been telepathic, but I was confident the whalesong we'd heard earlier hadn't been. Maybe that was how it *actually* sounded when it spoke, and we were just getting the translated version.

"So where are we?" Koi Boi asked the whale.

I braced myself for the answer. "My guy!" the whale said, with a note of something like boasting, "You are in the best, most private place in all the universe. This is a giant molecular cloud.[17] Like, *massive*. Think hundreds of light years. If your mind can hold that much space. I know mine can't, and I've lived in the open universe for – gosh, has it been all my life? Yeah, it has. All my life."

"That's very *whoa*," Koi Boi said, politely.

"*Very* whoa," the whale agreed. "And this part of it right

---

[17] It's a fancy name for a lot of dust. – SG

here–" The whale raised its tail, and slapped it on the ground for emphasis. It must have forgotten the whole gravity thing.

Once the whale was done wheezing in pain and wiggling around like a human who stubbed their toe, it continued: "This part of the cloud is really special. It's a stellar nursery, my guys. This whole world is just a few hundred million years old. Like, an eyeblink on the cosmological scale. This part of the crust just solidified a few eons ago."

The whale sounded really into this. It was nice to set my worries aside for a while and be amazed along with it. I said, "So all those glowing spots out there–"

"Yes! They're planetary nebulae!" the whale said. Okay, it was a little annoying that it ran over what I'd been about to say, but the whale seemed like it really just needed to talk. "Solar accretion disks mowing down on all the dust out here, spinning planets out of it."

"Have you been out here alone a while?" I asked as diplomatically as I could.

"Yep," the whale answered, and then bulldozed right back to what it wanted to talk about: dust. "And this cloud is so thick that, like, no light from the outer universe penetrates far into it. These stars will drift out eventually, and catch the outside universe by surprise. If you're a star outside, suddenly the cloud's going to peel back and it'll be like you have dozens of new neighbors at once. Think about that!"

"This one is a few fish short of a school," the Mad Thinker muttered. I elbowed him to shut him up.

"I *am* thinking about it," Koi Boi said, in a very good I-support-your-hyperfixations voice. "Do you have a name?"

"Oh. Yeah. I'm Resonant-Hyperbole. But imagine being a

civilization outside the cloud, thinking the cloud is just a void and then one day building, like, a radio telescope and finding all these little pinpoint radio signals in the void. Because the molecular cloud blocks visible light, but not radio, yeah? Then suddenly there's all these new, unclaimed stars and planets that just seem to materialize out of nowhere! Suddenly you've got an intergalactic land rush to get all these fresh new worlds. And it's going to happen here, in just, like a few million years."

"That's very cool, but–" Koi Boi tried.

"So I was figuring on hanging out around here for that long and then watching the fireworks. I'd love to have company until then, though–"

"Look, Resonant-Hyperbole, we have to–"

"Hm? I'm not Resonant-Hyperbole."

A very long pause. There was only so much we could cope with in one day. Beside me, the Mad Thinker let out a drawn-out sigh.

"You're not?" Koi Boi asked.

"Nope. Now I'm Practicing-Gratitude."

"As in… a different identity?"

"Nope. Same me. Only one of me in here, I think. It's just who I am now."

If Practicing-Gratitude planned to be out here for millions of years, it must have had a nigh-infinite lifespan. I realized we had no idea how long it had been out here… in a dust cloud, cut off from the rest of the universe. Alone.

I'd have gone a bit loopy, too. It probably would have taken fewer years than Practicing-Gratitude seemed to have lasted.

Or maybe this species' minds just worked like that, and I was being too human and squirrel-chauvinistic in conceptualizing names. I'm always happy to expand my horizons!

"All right, Practicing-Gratitude," Koi Boi said, "we have a pretty big favor to ask."

"Yeah, I know." It might have been my imagination, but its telepathic voice sounded tired just then.

"Can you get us out of here? Or get us some supplies if you can't?"

"Maybe."

"Well, how did *you* get here so quickly? You couldn't have been waiting in this exact spot."

"Nah, superluminal travel ain't a biggie. When I felt you calling, I came from the next planetary nebula over."

"So, then… can you help?" Koi Boi asked.

"I- I don't know, my dudes. I can get you off this rock, anyway."

"But to where?" I asked.

"Yeah, that's the question, isn't it? I can't stand this gravity for more than another minute or two. Why don't you climb on and we'll talk about it?"

My eyebrows shot up. "What, like on your back?" I asked. This was either going to be impossibly cool, or very deadly, or both at the same time.

"*That's* not very dignified, is it? For me, I mean. You'd look great."

"Also we need oxygen and heat to survive," Koi Boi pointed out.

"Right, right, right! Humanoid species. Forgive me, my guys. It's been a while." The fact that Practicing-Gratitude was communicating with us telepathically but had missed the fact that we were air-breathers told me some interesting things. "Never mind, we can still work it out. I've got space inside."

The Mad Thinker had been caught off guard again. He sputtered. "You don't expect us to crawl inside your mouth?!"

"My mouth? Don't be gross. I don't know where you've been." Practicing-Gratitude shuddered. The vibrations shifted the sand. "No, it's more of a gas-filled sac. Nice and warm and moist. And totally sanitary. For me, I mean."

As we stepped closer to the whale, its biomechanical augments became harder to ignore. Its flabby body[18] was wrapped in a mesh-like gridwork. Standing next to the creature, though, it was apparent that the metal didn't just wrap around its body, but was *part* of it. Some of the gridwork had replaced its flesh. Some of it even went deeper than skin.

Some larger parts of its body – most notably a whole ventral fin – were wholly artificial. The missing fin had been replaced with a dark, rubber-like membrane, outlined in more metal framework and crisscrossed with silver lines. The silver lines traced its muscles. Pieces of other fins had gone missing, too. Similar artificial tissue bridged the big, wedge-shaped gaps in its body.

None of the work seemed to have been done with much care or finesse. There were no signs of swelling or redness or other irritation around the implants, but there were plenty of old white scars. The whale's skin was pitted as if from centuries of micrometeoroid impacts, and the implants' dark coloring was unevenly faded. Everything added into an impression of immense age.

"Been a while since I had company!" the whale said. "Let me

---

[18] No disrespect intended! Whales and space whales are naturally this way, and should love their bodies just as much as anyone! – SG

just do some atmosphere adjustments, some outgassing..."

I braced myself for an incredibly rude noise and a worse smell, but the universe's sense of humor hadn't quite sunk that low yet because all that happened was a muted hissing noise, coming from somewhere on the whale's far side.

"Sweet Prophet-Singer," the whale said. "I swear you never know how much boron you've accumulated until guests come over."

In what I could only describe as "disconcerting" muscular action, a gill-like slit, invisible until now, pulled open in front of us.

Koi Boi shrugged, and stepped inside.

Under other circumstances, I might have hesitated. I trusted Koi Boi to (maybe) (probably) know what he was doing. Or, if he didn't, to make the right decision anyway.

I shrugged too, before I entered. I felt like I had to at least shrug. One by one, everybody shrugged and followed suit. Except the Mad Thinker.

When I looked back outside, the Mad Thinker remained where he'd been. "I'm not going in that monster." He actually sounded frightened.

Practices-Gratitude must have heard that, but, if it took offense, it said nothing. I stepped back outside while the others filed past me.

"Come on, why the heck not?" I asked. "You were the one convinced we were going to starve to death."

"I have no idea what's in there!" he said.

"What, you haven't calculated it out? Figured through the probabilities?"

He glared at me. That was when I realized he wasn't just being difficult for the sake of it. I'd struck a real sore spot.

He and I were alone out here now. I promise you, I had no cruel intentions when I dug in harder. I had a plan. "You just said we had a hundred percent chance of dying here. You wouldn't take a roll of a dice over that?" The glare was no longer quite masking his terror. "What do you think the odds are that we're going to let you stay and die here?"

He must have figured them out. He didn't resist when I reached out, grabbed his wrist, and pulled him inside.

The first thing I noticed when I entered wasn't the smell, which was at least less overpowering than the outdoors. No, it was the squishiness and give of the "floor".[19] I tried very, very hard to keep my footing. I did not want to discover if the surface was as moist as it felt.

The whale didn't just have implants on the outside. All at once, the passage ahead of us lit. The walls were blood-red and worn smooth as the bottom of a river. Lights studded every surface: walls, floor, ceiling. The path branched ahead. Only one of the forks was illuminated.

The lights guided us straight toward a... well, Practiced-Gratitude had called it a "gas-filled sac" , but the word I prefer here is "chamber". It was a broader space than the passage behind it, though still small enough to be uncomfortable for the seven of us.

Just like the lights, someone had grafted metal handholds and railings onto every surface. Big, blocky-looking seats, too. They came cushioned and complete with a restraining harness. Like the handholds, they were all over. I looked up, and saw one of the seats above me, suspended from the ceiling. And, at the far

---

[19] Deck? Bronchi? Arterial lining? The terminology fails, and every suggestion that came to me was somehow worse than the last. – SG

end of the chamber, a circular display monitor glowed, showing us a view of the dim and colorful night outside.

The only one of us who seemed unbothered by this was Koi Boi, who slapped the side of the fleshy walls like he would have a friend's shoulder. "Can you still hear us in here, Practicing-Gratitude?"

"Ouch. And yes. And I'm Many-Waveforms now."

"Um, all right. Sorry."

Koi Boi ran his hand along the back of one of the seats. He gave it an experimental push. It was quite firmly rooted. "Did any of this, um, hurt to install?" Koi Boi asked. He sounded like he already knew the answer.

"Don't worry about it. It's all old stuff. Try not to stomp around in there, though, m'kay? Don't wanna sneeze."

"Hold up," Chipmunk Hunk said. "Sneeze? So are we in your gills, or some kind of sinus cavity–?"

"*Dontthinkaboutit,*" I said quickly. It didn't work. I was thinking about it.

"Whales don't have gills," Koi Boi said. "This is probably more like a blowhole, or nostrils…"

"Stooop," I begged.

Many-Waveforms's voice sounded exactly like it had outside. "All right – so long gravity!"

"Wait," I said, "how are you going to–"

All at once, my stomach dropped out from underneath me, and reality unfurled.

The Unbeatable Squirrel Girl Vs Tossed Cookies

The sky parted in a burst of fog and fire. Then everything went black. The freefall was better than the sudden burst of high-*g* acceleration I'd been afraid of, but not by much. I immediately felt my coleslaw burble up from my stomach. Tippy-Toe squeaked and slipped loose from my shoulder. She fell, scrambling, into the air. I grabbed her, but in doing so pushed my foot into the "floor", which propelled the both of us into the air. The walls whirled.

We were in freefall. I caught another glimpse of the screen as I spun. It was not all black, just *mostly* black. A scattered fringe of light clung to the bottom.

A glowing horizon. Light scattering through a distant atmosphere. A world – probably the world we'd just been on – seen from high above. Its surface was gray-orange, speckled with dark and brackish-looking lakes, and dully glowing volcanic activity. Here and there, a storm revealed itself through a flicker-flash of lightning.

A primordial world. Earth had looked like this once.

"Ooooh, Prophet-Singer, that's better!" Many-Waveforms said. "I'm gonna have rock marks on my belly for days."

"Gosh dang!" Koi Boi swore, when he could speak. "How'd you do that?"

"Oh, I just slammed us through different dimensions until I found one where we were already in orbit, and took that spot."

I swallowed my lunch back where it belonged. "You did not!"

We were already lost in space. The last thing we needed was to get lost in the infinite corridors of the Multiverse.

"Nah, I'm pulling your fin. That's a good way to royally cheese off the alternate-universe counterparts whose spot you stole, and no way am I going through *that* drama again."

"So, then, really... how did you...?" Koi Boi asked.

"Great question!" Many-Waveforms said. "It's complicated."

"You mean you have no idea," the Mad Thinker said. He held himself steady with one of the handholds, piecing some semblance of his wits back together.

"Do *you* know exactly how *your* muscles work, electrochemically speaking?"

"As a matter of fact, I do. I'm a genius."

"Hey, good for you, bud."

Freefall made the space more comfortable in one respect. The extra dimension made it much roomier. I wrapped my tail around one of the handholds that had once been "overhead", swung around, and pushed myself into the nearest seat.

Chipmunk Hunk's cheeks looked puffy, and not in the usual way they did when he hid food in them. My face felt flushed, too. In fact, all of us looked pretty red. Zero gravity, baby! Your blood goes rushing to your head... not all that different than it does when you hang upside-down.

I wasn't actually all that uncomfortable. I was already developing a knack for shoving myself around and coasting to my destination. Squirrels spend a lot of time skittering in all directions, including upside-down. I grabbed a handhold. Chipmunk Hunk and Koi Boi would adapt, too. But Nancy, Mary, the Mad Thinker, and... oh, no, Brain Drain–

"I HATE TO BE A BOTHER." Brain Drain had curled up. The fluid in his brain case sloshed around in globules. His eyes bobbed to opposite sides, tangling in their optical nerves. "THE OPERATIONAL LIMIT OF MY BODY IN FREEFALL IS ZERO SECONDS."

I pushed off my seat. It would have been awkward enough to move him in regular gravity, even with superstrength. Superstrength was no help in freefall, at least not without leverage. I hooked my feet around one of the handholds, and slowly tugged Brain Drain toward them. The problem was his hydraulics. They weren't meant for freefall. At least the power to his brain case and voice box was still going strong. Mary and I each grabbed one of his claws, latched them around a handhold, and manually squeezed them shut. That would at least hold him in place.

"THANK YOU, FRIENDS. PHYSICAL EXISTENCE IS MORE OF A PRISON THAN USUAL." Mary patted his brain case affectionately.

And then she turned green. Nancy made a quiet, subdued *horrf*ing sound as her stomach tried and failed to adjust to freefall.

"Excuse me, Many-Waveforms," I said, addressing the screen

for want of any other direction to look. "You didn't happen to have any, uh, sacs or bladders or other orifices for guests to dispose of unwanted waste, do you?"

I'll spare you the details except to say that some of the consequences of freefall are better described in text than visual media. You don't want to see too much.

After the purging, we returned to the chamber I'd started to think of as the lounge. As I'd thought, there were plenty of other bronchial passages, but this was the only one with seats and other humanoid amenities.

The time I'd spent nursing Nancy through her stomach problems had given me a chance to think more.

"Did you say 'Prophet-Singer?'" I asked Many-Waveforms.

"Gotta say something when you stub a fin."

I'm no stranger to swearing. Compile a list of my most commonly used words, and "dang" and "heck" will be right at the top. Something about that particular phrase triggered a memory, though.

There was so much going on in our big, screwed-up, superpowered universe that anyone would have had trouble keeping track of it all. (Hence, Deadpool's flashcards of heroes and villains.) But I was confident I'd heard that before. Good thing Chipmunk Hunk was just as much of a nerd as I was, and had a sharper memory.

"'Prophet-Singer?'" he asked. "As in the *acanti* Prophet-Singer?"

The Mad Thinker jerked as though given an electric shock.

"Here we go," Many-Waveforms muttered.

Chipmunk Hunk snapped his fingers at – again for want of any other direction – the circular screen. "The acanti are from our galaxy! That means we're not that far away from home! I mean, give or take a few trillion miles and the terrible void of unimaginable space, but–"

"–that is so much closer than I thought we'd be!" I finished.

"I refuse to believe this," the Mad Thinker said. "The creature must have read your mind, found your hopes, and impersonated an acanti–"

Chipmunk Hunk and I were still collaboratively constructing sentences. "I mean," I said, "unless the acanti are spread throughout all the infinite universe–" I started.

"–all we have to do to get home is cross a single galaxy!"

Nancy had been out of things since we'd returned to the lounge, but this brought her back to reality. She looked to the Mad Thinker. "I thought you said you'd sent us out into 'infinity'," she said. "The odds of being in our galaxy–"

"–are infinitesimal," the Mad Thinker said, but he sounded shaken. "Zero. Can't have happened."

Mary had cleaned out her stomach just as thoroughly as Nancy, but she still sounded like herself when she told the Mad Thinker, "One might start to get the idea that you were wrong about everything. How your toy worked, the science that sent us here. Everything."

The Mad Thinker's mouth hung loose as he stared at us and tried to think of something else to say. He couldn't. Without another word, he left the chamber.[20]

I might have followed him, except another pit was opening in

---

[20] At least that's what he was going for. In freefall, he pushed too hard off the wall, spun in midair circles until he came within reach of a handhold, awkwardly shoved himself by hand toward the exit, crashed into its side, and finally hauled himself through and out. But the poor guy was in the process of having his self-image destroyed, so I'll leave him *some* dignity. – SG

my stomach, and this one had nothing to do with freefall. I was remembering what I knew about the acanti.

The acanti used to be more commonplace in the galaxy. People used to be *happy* to see them. They were a spaceborne, spacefaring species of the cosmos. They lived in space, and had a natural ability to travel at superluminal speeds. They'd spent their lives coasting between the stars, philosophizing, and generally being chill.

That was before an alien race called the Brood – hungry and all-consuming alien horde, tried to eat Earth, yada yada yada, you know the type – found them. See, the Brood engineered a virus tailored to acanti nervous systems. It wiped out their higher brain functions. Then the Brood built their homes in acanti bodies. The Brood used the acanti as traveling war machines – their steeds.

At some point, word had reached Earth that the acanti's Prophet-Singer – sort of a spiritual leader – had been freed from the Brood. News after that had been sparse, though.

All of this meant that the seats, the handholds and railings, the lights, the screen, had probably been implanted here by the Brood.

You know, I'm pretty happy-go-lucky for a super hero. Not to mention physically resilient to freefall. For the first time that day, I felt like throwing up. I set my hand on the nearest chair to keep myself steady. And then looked again at what I was holding.

I wasn't the only one of us looking at the furniture and other implants with new eyes. Many-Waveforms seemed to sense this.

"Don't worry about it!" it said. "All that was a while ago. Brain's better now. Furniture's new. I renovated specially for humanoids." In a quieter voice, it said, "When I used to hang out around more humanoids, anyway."

The seemingly casual brushing off was a cue to talk about something, anything, other than old trauma. I took the hint.

"All right," I said, hesitantly. "Look, we're in kind of a pickle here."

"I figured. You know, despite what your 'genius' friend said, I really only used my telepathy to grab your languages and speak with you. Not read your memories. Honest."

"Because you called him a friend, I believe you," Nancy said.

"He could be a friend," I said, which got me a raised eyebrow from her. I was facing her at an angle, so I could pretend not to see that. "Many-Waveforms, will–"

"I'm Slipstream-Eddy now," the whale said.

"Ooo, 'Eddy!' I like that one!" My tail flicked excitedly back and forth. "Anyway, we didn't mean to arrive here and don't have a way home. I know the acanti can travel faster than light, and I also know that, if you've been hanging out in this dust cloud–"

"Molecular cloud."

"–molecular cloud, you must have a good reason. I don't want to pry about what that is. But I am hoping that you could, um, help us get back home."

What followed was a pause just long enough to be meaningful. "I don't know…"

Koi Boi asked, "How long has it been since you left this cloud?"

"Another great question! I don't know."

"You really don't want to leave, do you?" Koi Boi asked.

"I mean… would you?"

Koi Boi shook his head. His affinity for sealife, and apparently for space whales, didn't extend to full mind-reading, but there was plainly a level of communication happening that I couldn't perceive. "We didn't want to leave home either," he said.

"Where are you from, anyway?" Slipstream-Eddy asked.

"We're from Earth," I said.

"Cool name," it said. "But not helpful."

My face fell.[21] "Huh? What do you mean?"

"Like, do you have a location? Coordinates in Sh'iar Imperial? Galactic Council Standard? Distance from the black hole at the galactic center and bearing derived from some mutually known starmark... or... or something?"

My friends and I looked at each other. No one spoke. No surprises up anyone's sleeves this time.

"We're armed with knowledge about Earth's location in different sci-fi universes," I offered.

"Sector Zed-Zed-Nine-Plural-Zed-Alpha," Koi Boi said instantly.

"Alpha Quadrant, Sector 001," Chipmunk Hunk said.

"Sector 8023 of the Third Quadrant," Koi Boi retorted.

"Throneworld Terra, Segmentum Solar."

"I'm so proud of you all," I said, clasping my hands together like a beaming schoolteacher. "And myself for recognizing them." Though Koi Boi's had taken a moment. "But that's probably not helpful, either."

"It could be, if we're actually living in a sci-fi universe," Chipmunk Hunk said. In a quiet, hopeful voice, he added, "Like I've suspected all along."

---

[21] YES, SQUIRREL GIRL USE PHRASES THAT IMPLY UP OR DOWN IN SPACE. ENGLISH LANGUAGE OBTUSE AND UNWIELDY. IT MAKE HULK SMASH. – ED

"I have no idea what any of you said, my dudes," Slipstream-Eddy said. "But I admire the enthusiasm."

"Thanks!" I clapped my hands, ready to approach this like a CompSci major: ask a search engine. "Well… the location thing shouldn't really be a problem. Probably. Maybe. Okay, so it's definitely a problem, but not as big a problem as it might seem. There are lots of folks in the galaxy who've heard of Earth. All we have to do is find a directory, or map, or someone who can point us in the right direction."

"I… suppose I could take you a little way," Slipstream-Eddy said.

I pressed my hands together. "You have no idea how grateful we would be."

"Don't set your hopes too high, my guys," Slipstream-Eddy said. "I can't go very far, or all that fast. Old gray fins ain't what they used to be. Engine implants aren't much better."

"It doesn't matter," Koi Boi said. "We really, really appreciate you going so far out of your way for us. We'll find a way to pay you back."

"Nah. No biggie, dudes." Slipstream-Eddy's voice started to lighten. It was sounding more like it had the first time we met, before we'd had to make things all uncomfortable. "I still need to have somewhere to go, though."

Nancy looked to me. She didn't even need to speak for me to answer the question she hadn't even started. I nodded.

She set her jaw. There was no bravado about not letting me go alone. She wasn't coming with me this time. She could only stand to be so sick at a time.

"There is one person we haven't asked," I said.

• • •

"No, I have no idea how to find Earth from here," the Mad Thinker said, before I even finished pulling myself into his chamber.

He'd found some kind of small, fleshy sac to rest and hide in. I'd only found him because of the cloud of despair hanging around outside. That, and the angry muttering.

He'd already disposed of my excuse for being here. "Sounds like you've got that calculator brain back into gear again," I said.

"I can't turn it off." He snorted. "Unfortunately."

"That's rough, buddy," I said, folding my arms.

"I don't understand how I could have been so wrong," he said. "It doesn't make sense. *Nothing* makes sense."

"Everybody's wrong about something," I said.

"But I *wasn't* wrong! We're here because I wasn't wrong!" He raised his fist as if to strike the wall. If the mechanics of freefall wouldn't have sent him flying, I expected he would have. I reflexively pulled myself back to the entryway.

Evidently, I wasn't the only one alarmed by his outburst. He looked appalled, too. His shaking fist unfolded. The next time he spoke, he sounded considerably calmer. "My device worked," he said. "Radical reconceptualization of the metaphysics of the universe and all. It sent us across the cosmos. It brought us to a world of *my* specifications. It would have brought the whole city here, and I would have become its leader before we returned, if I hadn't allowed you to disrupt it." He rubbed his forehead with his knuckles. "But it should not have brought us anywhere near our own galaxy. It worked, and it didn't. That is what I do not understand."

"You were right about some things," I said, planting my hand on the entrance because I'd started to drift too far. It turned out to be hard to maintain the dignity of a good, stern arms-folding in freefall. "And you were wrong about others. What's so hard to figure out about that?"

"Because I'm too good to be wrong," the Mad Thinker said. "Not like the rest of you squirrels or dolphins or whatever else you all cosplay as."

"*Most* people are right about some things and wrong about others."

"I am not like most people."

"Really?" I asked. "What are the odds of that?"

"Very good," he said grumpily. "One hundred percent."

"Even in light of all this new data you've received?"

He shifted uncomfortably and hugged his arms to his side. "There must be... hidden variables. I only need to... un-hide them."

I hoped what Brain Drain told him had had a chance to reach him. "Like the fact that other people aren't probabilistic automatons?" I asked.

"You all very much are. I only... need the discipline–"

The stammering meant he was losing track of the conversation he'd mapped out in his head. His lips opened and closed several times. He looked ill, and not just in the flabby, clumsy way that freefall made everyone look sick. I mean, there was *that*, too, but this was atop it.

My tail lashed back and forth, like it always did when I was upset.

"Excuse me," he said abruptly. "I need to be alone."

He turned toward the far wall. After that, he made no attempt to acknowledge my presence. Letting him stew was probably the best thing I could do for him at the moment. I left him.

I returned to the passenger lounge humming. I grabbed a

handhold with my tail and swung into one of the cushioned seats.

Tippy-Toe was having a blast in freefall. She and Chipmunk Hunk had already started horsing around. Mary had lost her grip on her energy drink the moment we'd gone into freefall. It had not been long before Tippy-Toe and Chipmunk Hunk were bouncing off the walls, slurping up fizzy green globules, and getting wiggy on caffeine and sugar.

Nancy looked a little more like herself. A puffier, greener version of herself. "You look too happy for what you must have just gone through," she said.

I tried to catch Tippy-Toe and place her on my shoulder, but she bounced off my palm instead. Off she went, careening toward the back of the lounge.

"You're a terrible influence," I told Chipmunk Hunk.

"I'm a *delightful* influence," he said.

As Tippy-Toe zipped past me in a blur of pink bow and brown fur, she flicked her tail in and out to adjust her spin. (Squirrels have an innate sense for conservation of angular momentum. You know how, when you're spinning in a chair and stick your legs out, it slows your spin down? And when you pull your legs back in, you speed up again? Same thing applies to squirrels in midair.) She raced around like Mew at four o'clock in the morning.

"Still no idea where we're going," I reported.

"Not a problem," Chipmunk Hunk said, despite the overwhelming evidence to the contrary. "Earth's pretty big in the galactic community. We've turned away Galactus and fought off the Skrulls, like, ten times. Not to mention saved the universe more than once, I'm pretty sure. We just have to find someplace where lots of folks from the Milky Way are gathering. We'll find someone who knows where Earth is, and doesn't mind helping some aliens out."

"Well…" Slipstream-Eddy said, "I do know a place. Not all that far away, relatively speaking. A big old space station. And I don't mean *big ol'* space station, I mean *big* and *old*. Lots of humanoids hang out there. Or did when I knew it."

"I could kiss you," Koi Boi blurted. "I mean, if you *do* kissing."

The lounge had no central seat. With the way the chairs ringed the cabin, and without any sense of up or down, *any* seat could have been the center one. Mine *felt* more central, though. And I'd always wanted to do this. I raised my hand, finger extended – as much as anything could be 'raised' in freefall, anyway.

"*Make it so,*" I commanded.

"Nerd," Nancy said softly.

"Trapped in space with nerds," Mary agreed. "Terrible."

The Unbeatable Squirrel Girl Vs The Fault in Her Stars

We were still arguing over what a "nerd" was when we reached our destination three days later.

"We're all CompSci students!" I insisted. "The definition of 'nerd' includes all of us, by default!"

"I AM A STUDENT OF PHILOSOPHY," Brain Drain said.

Fair point. "Even nerdier!" I said.

"The left hand of dorkness," Mary agreed. "And for CompSci – there's a difference between being smart and being a nerd."

"You were geeking out about all of Tony's war toys!" I said. We were rationing the food scavenged from the Fields Memorial Physical Sciences Building, and so we were all getting a little nippy. "At Doctor Strange's house, you looked like an unsupervised toddler in the checkout aisle. You would have taken things if we hadn't stopped you!" I turned to Nancy. "And you're just as bad! You write fanfiction!"

"I never would have shared it with you if you're going to weaponize it all the time," Nancy muttered.

I stuck my tongue out at her[22]. On my shoulder, Tippy-Toe did the same. Adorable.

"I write fiction about Asgard," Nancy said. "Asgard is real."

"And Cat-Thor, the cat version of Thor? Cat-Thor is real?"

"He's real to me. And Loki *loves* Cat-Thor![23]"

"I have learned, like, so much over the past three days," our whale friend said. They were going by Hyperlogic-Bubble right now.

They had also never professed to having a gender, and my friends and I had settled on referring to them as, well, "them". When we'd asked, Hyperlogic-Bubble had only seemed confused. Maybe gender was one of those things that didn't bridge our cultural divide, telepathy or not. They seemed perfectly happy with that pronoun regardless.

"Very little of what you learned about us is useful," Mary said.

"Useful is overrated," Hyperlogic-Bubble said. "Hey, just to let you guys know, we're coming up on that place. The station."

"All right!" I said. As fun as it was to argue about the many and exquisite ways we were all nerds, that had been the fifth time today. We'd had to do *something* to distract ourselves from the fact that we had no changes of clothes and no shower.

We hadn't brought much stuff with us but, like college students everywhere, we'd somehow spread what little we had

---

[22] DO NOT ATTEMPT IN ZERO GRAVITY. TONGUE MAY GET BITTEN. THIS HULK SAFETY MESSAGE BROUGHT TO YOU BY HULK HARD LIFE EXPERIENCE. – ED

[23] HULK NOT SCARE EASY. LOKI'S CAT-THOR COSPLAY IN Unbeatable Squirrel Girl #8 SCARE HULK. – ED

in more mess than seemed possible. The crumbs from the nuts I'd brought with me had gotten everywhere. I brushed some out of our airspace. One of the many ways that space travel is less glamorous than it seems. I somersaulted through the air, caught my free-floating squirrel-ears headband, and then my left sneaker. Tippy-Toe, helpful as ever, vaulted off me to go retrieve my right one. I landed upright in one of the cushioned seats.

"Space lanes are pretty empty," Hyperlogic-Bubble remarked. This was about the third time today. It seemed to be making them edgy, or as edgy as they seemed to be able to get. "This used to be a pretty happening place."

"How long ago was that?" Nancy asked.

"Oh. You know. A few... thousand years..."

"And you don't think things could have changed since then?"

"I'm not old, if you're calling me old," Hyperlogic-Bubble said, defensively. Neither Nancy nor I spoke. There wasn't a safe answer. "Anyway, this is one of those places that, the more it changes, the more it stays the same, you know?"

Before I could ask about that, Chipmunk Hunk pushed his way into the lounge, looking exhausted and frustrated. He and Mary had spent long hours trying to get Hyperlogic-Bubble's subspace radio working.

There had turned out to be a handful of other chambers inside Hyperlogic-Bubble made for humanoids. One of them had a whole bunch of old radio and subspace communications equipment, made for whoever had been in here last. Hyperlogic-Bubble said they never used it. They preferred telepathy.

"We picked up a few sounds like voices here and there," Chipmunk Hunk had said, the first time he and Mary had gotten it working. "Nothing we could understand. Most of the frequencies are filled up with something that sounds like a siren."

"Right," I said. I would've bet a lot that he and Mary had been getting up to more than being subspace HAM hobbyists in there. Maybe I was wrong. Mary had given up on the subspace radio hours ago, and Chipmunk Hunk hadn't seemed to have gotten anywhere. With a sigh, he pushed himself into one of the chairs.

The image on our screen had been pretty same-y the past couple days: a single bright blue dot, centered directly ahead of us. Everything else was solid black. No stars, no nothing. Really pretty fascinating if you knew what you were looking at[24], but not much in the way of scenery to admire.

Hyperlogic-Bubble had told us how they traveled faster than light… in three different and mutually exclusive ways. Yesterday, they'd said that the acanti had gotten an exemption from special relativity from the One-Above-All when they created the Multiverse. The day before that, they'd insisted

---

[24] Okay, so light moves like a wave – kinda, as it can act like particles, too (it's complicated), but for the purposes of our discussion it's a wave. The waves can be close together or spread out. The different spacing between waves is what gives light its properties, like color. Blue is a short wavelength, with lots of waves bunched tightly together. Other colors, like red, are lower energy, with lots of space between waves. If you travel toward light, they seem to bunch up because you're plowing through them that much faster. So everything becomes slightly bluer. And if you're traveling really fast, like we were, everything becomes much, *much* bluer.

Here's another effect: according to special relativity, the mass of an object traveling close to the speed of light will, to the outside universe, seem to get bigger and bigger. And we were breaking all kinds of physical laws to travel at Silly Speed, so the rest of the universe perceived us as having a very big mass indeed. A mass large enough for its gravity to bend light. All the light reaching us had bent light into a single, high-energy point right in front of us. Never let anyone tell you Squirrel Girl isn't educational! – SG

that they, personally, had renegotiated the laws of the universe with C, the anthropomorphic personification of light speed[25]. Today, Hyperlogic-Bubble told us that they didn't move at all, but picked up the whole of space-time and juggled it until they ended up where they wanted to go.

We took this as an admission that Hyperlogic-Bubble had no idea how they traveled faster than light. The only thing we knew for sure was that, for the most part, traveling inside Hyperlogic-Bubble didn't feel like moving at all. No feeling of acceleration. However Hyperlogic-Bubble traveled, they had enough control of inertia to keep us (and themselves) from compressing into pancakes as we moved.

On the screen ahead, the blue star was starting to blur. Other colors were smearing in.

Hyperlogic-Bubble said, "All right, we should be in–"

Then silence.

On the screen, the colors hazed, and blossomed into a full starfield. I pursed my lips, waiting.

"Hyperlogic?" Koi Boi asked. "You all right–?"

"Whoa there!" Hyperlogic-Bubble said abruptly. "I *am* slowing. See how good I'm slowing?"

They didn't seem to be talking to any of us. I had no idea what was going on, but it was easy to get the idea that things were about to get rough. They may not have been able to tell us how they traveled faster than light, but they had warned us that their

---

[25] Just about every idea or concept you can imagine has an anthropomorphic personification in this big, messed up universe of ours. It's true! I met the anthropomorphic personification of anthropomorphic personifications once. – SG

SQUIRREL GIRL NOT MAKING THAT UP. HIS NAME IS ANTHROPOMORPHO. THAT MAKE HULK SMASH. – ED

control got a lot less certain when they had to start and stop abruptly. *That* seemed worth believing.

Each seat was equipped with safety belts. I slipped mine on. All over the lounge, my friends, no fools, did the same. Tippy-Toe wriggled under the collar of my sweater.

"All right, all right, I'm heaving to!" Hyperlogic-Bubble said. "Sheesh!" However their telepathy worked, they couldn't seem to help broadcasting their voice to us whenever they spoke with whoever was out there.

I jerked forward, hard, into my safety harness. It was sharp enough to knock the breath out of me. Across the lounge, Nancy wheezed. As if someone had taken offense to Hyperlogic-Bubble taking offense, a white-blue crackle of weapons fire blazed across the screen. We got knocked into our seats a second time, even harder.

"Hyperlogic?!" Koi Boi asked, when he had the breath.

"Hmm?" Hyperlogic-Bubble asked, as though they had just remembered us. "No big deal. Just pirates, is all."

"That deal sounds very big!" Nancy said.

"Also, I wasn't *going* to worry until you said not to," I added.

"Have some faith, my guys! It's just a warning–"

Another bolt of fire, another shove.

"–I mean, *two* warning shots. More aggressive than I remember."

"Are they going to board us?" Chipmunk Hunk asked. "Are we going to have to fight them off with our dashing moves and unflappable attitudes?"

"Nah," Hyperlogic-Bubble said. "Warning shots are just how the locals communicate around here."

Nancy and I looked at each other.

"Hyperlogic," Nancy said, "what kind of station did you say this was?"

"I told you. Built into an asteroid."

"Yes, but run by *who*?" Nancy asked.

"No idea. This is the kind of space where things change hands pretty quickly, you know? Lots of nebulae and molecular clouds for ships to hide in around here, which has always made it a pretty lawless part of space."

Nancy closed her eyes and massaged her forehead.

Hyperlogic-Bubble said, "Those pirates are directing us to a landing on the asteroid. Thought you'd like to know."

"So they *weren't* attacking us?" I asked.

"Nah. They're more like... over-aggressive parking monitors."

"But you say they're still pirates."

"Oh yeah. They've got ships built out of blasted chunks of other stolen ships, transponders broadcasting crosshatched bones, the works. And they *are* kind of forcing me to land."

So long as Hyperlogic-Bubble sounded calm, I wasn't going to panic. I was, however, *concerned*. At least there was no more weapons fire. That we could see.

The starfield began to roll. A pause – signifying what, I had no idea.

A great big void slid onto the center of the screen and stayed there. It took me too long to realize it wasn't empty space, but an object. Something was occluding the stars behind it. Without knowing how fast we were traveling relative to it, it was impossible to judge distance, but my gut said "big".

When Hyperlogic-Bubble spoke again, their telepathic voice came across as quieter. "A lot more ships than there used to be."

As we cruised on, some of the stars shifted. They weren't stars at all. They *were* ships. As we drew closer, their lights became more recognizable: running lights, the glows of active engines, and probably some honest-to-gosh windows, too.

Hyperlogic-Bubble made a telepathic noise suspiciously like a low whistle. "Wow!" they said, delighted. "This is seriously bad news."

"Why are you making it sound awesome?" Nancy demanded.

"I forgot how exhilarating it is to be out in the thick of things," they said. "You know – really doomed by galactic turmoil. Takes me back! Don't worry, my mood's gonna crash soon."

My squirrel-senses spotted a few more lights dappled along the object's surface. The lights were dim, difficult to spot even against starlight, but there were so many different colors among them I figured they had to be artificial. Violets and blues and pinks.

"It's awfully dark out there," Chipmunk Hunk said.

"Well, yeah, it's space," Hyperlogic-Bubble said. "We're not near a star or anything."

"Look, I'm trying to ask if you can, uh, enhance that view?" Chipmunk Hunk asked.

"Sure," Hyperlogic-Bubble said. The screen blinked to a deeper, darker shadow.

"Not helpful," Chipmunk Hunk said.

"Whataya want from me? Be specific."

"I want to see what that is!"

"Oh. Nah, you don't want to know that."

A long silence followed.

"Hyperlogic-Bubble–" Nancy started to say.

"Light-Horizon now," the whale said.

"Light-Horizon," Nancy said, slowly, "why wouldn't we want to know that?"

"I mean, it would just alarm you."

"Not helpful!" Chipmunk Hunk said again.

"IGNORANCE HAS ITS VIRTUES," Brain Drain said.

"All right, fine," Light-Horizon said. "You all didn't seem to take kindly to those pirates earlier. I didn't think you'd want to know there are thirty more of them out here."

My eyes may have bulged. I tightened my grip on my safety harness, but no more turbulence followed. Nancy sputtered so hard that she coughed.

"ALAS, THAT IGNORANCE, ONCE LOST, CANNOT BE FOUND AGAIN," Brain Drain said. "TAKE COMFORT IN THE FACT THAT THERE ARE MANY OTHER UNPLUMBED WELLS OF KNOWLEDGE, CONTAINING HORRIBLE TRUTHS THAT WE WILL LIKELY NEVER UNCOVER."

"The pirates aren't alone," Light-Horizon said. "There are, like, thirty kinds of warships… some freighters – probably smugglers – pleasure yachts, cruisers, clipper ships, licensed privateers, unlicensed privateers, light sails, stolen police cruisers–"

"AS THE WALLS OF IGNORANCE COME CRASHING DOWN, I LEARN TO FEAR THINGS I COULD NOT HAVE CONCEIVED OF JUST MOMENTS AGO."

"Yeah, okay," Light-Horizon said. "I'm a little antsy, too. It isn't usually like this. There are more ships out there than the station has docking berths to hold. Like… three times as many. Something's up."

Koi Boi chewed on his thumbnail. "So… in theory, with so many aliens here, we ought to have an easier time finding someone who's heard of Earth, right?"

"In theory," Light-Horizon said.

I wished I shared Koi Boi's optimism. Anxiety gnawed its toothy little teeth on my gut. I didn't know exactly what waited for us here, but it was easy to get the idea that getting home was going to be a lot more trouble than I'd thought.

Just getting to the asteroid was a hassle. Other ships headed in and out in a higgledy-piggledy hodge-podge of trajectories. After one arrow-shaped craft whooshed past our screen, leaving a searing exhaust trail etched in our retinas, Koi Boi asked, "Is this safe?"

"Nope," Light-Horizon answered. Their voice showed no sign of concern. Thinking about what Brain Drain had said, I refrained from asking for more.

Mary hummed as we weaved through meteorite-speed traffic. Khachaturian's "Sabre Dance."

Nerd.

The darkness was so complete that I didn't know we were almost at the asteroid until Light-Horizon told us they were about to set down. "I don't *think* my organs should squish around too much, But, you know, I could've misjudged our relative speeds. Just to warn you."

"What are we supposed to do if your organs 'squish?'" Nancy asked.

Light-Horizon didn't answer. We never had to find out. Light-Horizon settled their body onto bare rock. They set down so lightly we didn't even feel it. We all shifted, subtly but unmistakably, toward what had again become the floor.

"Ahh," they said. "Microgravity. I guess I can tolerate that. The station's a couple miles over the horizon from here. There's no open docking berths, so I can't get you any closer."

So. To get to the station, we were going to have to walk.

Light-Horizon had several spacesuits lodged in various cavities inside them. The helmets and rebreathers smelled about as nice as you would expect for having been stuck inside a space whale's mucus membranes for years. At least they were resizable, apparently having been made from the same space-age stretchy fabric as Bruce Banner's pants[26]. The only exception was that it didn't have space for my tail but, as someone who'd had a secret identity most of her life, I was well accustomed to shoving my tail down a pant leg. I've dealt with kinks in my tail before.

The Mad Thinker joined us. He didn't say a word, not even to ask us where we were going. He just suited up along with the rest of us.

I stared at him. He didn't acknowledge me. We'd seen him several times over the past few days, but, to my friends' not-so-quiet relief, he spent no time with us. He probably would have called it "brooding". I called it "sulking".

Brain Drain's body wasn't any more cooperative in microgravity than freefall. At least he was still easy to lug around. He had insisted on being left behind – "I HAVE BECOME AS UNWIELDY IN FORM AS IN SPIRIT" – but we weren't leaving him alone to marinate in that attitude. Mary and Chipmunk Hunk tugged him along between them.

He was the only one of us who didn't need a spacesuit to survive. Downside was that he had no built-in radio. The only way to communicate with him was to plant our helmet visors against his brain dome. Sound transmitted through the glass.

---

[26] PUNY BANNER ALTER-EGO VALUE MODESTY. – ED

"I BOTH RESENT AND APPRECIATE YOUR DESIRE TO INCLUDE ME."

"That's friendship for introverts!" I told him. "You're welcome, and I'm sorry."

Muscle walls in Light-Horizon's innards closed behind us, mimicking the function of an airlock chamber seal. In a burst of dissipating sound and freezing gasses, its blowhole opened into darkness.

The outside world was the deepest night I'd ever seen. There was no nearby sun to illuminate the asteroid, and the starlight wasn't bright enough to reveal much, even to squirrel-senses.

The suits must have been made by someone with visual acuity similar to humans' and squirrels', because they had good flashlights built into their wrists. Our dancing wrist-lights fell across ancient, craggy, and crater-pitted rock. Everything looked sharp enough to trip on – sharp enough to cut into a spacesuit. No erosion out here in space to smooth those edges.

"This isn't goodbye, right?" Koi Boi asked. His radio voice crackled in my ears. "You're gonna stick around in case we need a quick ride out of here?"

"Don't worry, dude. I don't ditch friends." Light-Horizon's voice sounded as clear as ever. Even via telepathy, I heard what sounded like a frown in their voice. "I'm not sure I *could* leave, anyway."

"Am I going to regret asking you to explain?" I asked.

"Probably," Light-Horizon said, but went on anyway. "It's just that I haven't seen any ships leaving. Plenty taking off, sure, but only going to a parking orbit. And those pirates are keeping an awfully tight watch on everyone. They might not, uh, want anyone here to leave."

I glanced up. With everything around us so dark, I had a clean view of the sky and the starfield. Nothing had changed, but the sky seemed a lot less open than half a minute ago.

"Wonderful," Nancy said.

"Isn't it?" said Light-Horizon, whose mood had not crashed. "It's exciting!"

The Unbeatable Squirrel Girl Vs The Water Rising Above Her Head

Our spacesuits came with compressed gas thrusters. Good thing, too, because in the asteroid's microgravity, one wrong step might have propelled us off the surface and into the void. Charming to think about. "Walking" wasn't so much walking as shuffling: pushing off the rock with as little vertical force as we could manage. It was like we were trying to keep our footing on ice.

Ever been on an airless world before? I've been on the moon more than once, and I still never got used to it. It's not just the gravity, or the incredible danger, or your breath fogging your helmet's faceplate (seriously underrated annoyance). It's the whole look of the place. It's got a different eye-feel.

There's an incredibly sharp distinction between light and shadow. So sharp that it feels like you could chop veggies with it.

There's no light scattering from an atmosphere. Which, well – of course there wouldn't be. But it's one thing to recognize that intellectually and another to realize what that actually looks like. You can see this same phenomenon on pictures taken from the moon, where there are really sharp distinctions between shadow and sun-lit or Earth-lit areas.

When we waved our wrist-lights around, it was like we'd taken a hole-puncher to the fabric of the universe. Like nothing existed except where we shone our lights. When I looked *really* closely, I could see some areas illuminated by the light bouncing off the asteroid itself, but the rock wasn't highly reflective, and so there wasn't much of that.

The second really strange thing about how the asteroid looked was the closeness of the horizon. There wasn't anything you'd think of as a "horizon" like back home. The asteroid was tiny by comparison to a planet and so, even from the ground, its spherical shape was much more noticeable. The "land" just seemed to go forward for a few hundred feet, and then… disappeared. There was suddenly no more of it. Just open space, like a cliff falling away. But we kept walking and never reached any cliff.

I understood why that was, but that didn't stop it from being disconcerting. I'd noticed the same thing each time I'd been on the moon, but that hadn't been so pronounced as this. And, on the moon, I'd had the comfort of seeing Earth and knowing that I'd be going back home soon. I didn't have either of those things this time.

Nothing quite underscores just how small Earth is like going out into the broader universe. Special, but small. There was an unimaginably broad range of experiences in the universe beyond us. It made me dizzy.

In retrospect, I should have seen that as a warning sign about how I would feel later. But, at the time, the vertigo seemed like just one more thing to get through.

The close horizon and lack of light scattering meant that, when we reached the station, we came up on it suddenly. There was no light pollution, no spotlights, no sign of any light at all. It seemed like we took a few steps forward and a big, black octopod-like structure suddenly rose into the sky.

It was massive enough that we couldn't even see all of it before it fell over the "horizon" and vanished beyond the curve of the asteroid. It had no windows. Not that spaceships or space stations needed windows (cosmic radiation shielding is expensive, especially for transparent materials!), but it gave every impression of a place that did not want to be seen, or noticed, ever. At the very least, the hull did not have to be as black as it was. Our flashlights didn't so much shine on it as fall into it.

For lack of other options, we walked along the side of the station, flashlights slicing across the hull, until we came across a door-sized airlock hatch – just as it was opening.

Six figures in spacesuits stepped through it. They were unmistakably alien. Their suits had four arms and long, spindly, spiderlike legs. Each of their four hands had wicked, bayonet-like blades sticking out from the wrists.

My friends dropped into defensive crouches. I held up my fists in classic put-up-your-dukes boxing stance. But the aliens strolled right past us. Most of them didn't even look at us. The one that did just paused and shook their faceplate as if in pity, and moved on.

We hustled into the airlock door before it closed. Air began hissing into the chamber, heralding the return of sound.

"I CANNOT SAY WHICH I PREFER," Brain Drain said. "THE FEAR OF GOING IGNORED OR THE TERROR OF BEING NOTICED."

"I'll take being ignored," Nancy said.

"Always make the opposition underestimate you," Mary said.

That was all anyone *could* say, because at that moment gravity reasserted its hold and we all crashed to the floor. It was like someone had flipped a switch, or there were magnets in the floor, or something. Not only did I fall over, but I also felt like an anvil was laying atop me.

The gravity was not so strong that I couldn't stand again. But standing again was a mistake. All the blood that had gotten comfortable in my head for the past couple days went rushing back to my feet. Even with the powers of squirrel *and* girl, it was a little much. The world turned dim and spotty. I had to lean against the wall for a moment.

There had not even been a warning before the artificial gravity turned on. Nancy had toppled over on her stomach. I helped her up as she muttered something about an interstellar OSHA.

Brain Drain's body made a bunch of unsettling cracking and gurgling noises as his hydraulics readjusted and the fluids in his brain case resettled. He stood and offered each of the others a claw up in turn.

"MANY THEORIES OF THE MORE CYNICAL PHILOSOPHIES OF MORALITY HOLD THAT KIND ACTS, SUCH AS YOU HELPING ME, ARE COMMITTED WITH AN EXPECTATION OF REPAYMENT," he said. "COUNTERPOINT: I AM NOW HELPING YOU AND YET I DO NOT FEEL MY DEBT FULFILLED."

"Someone sure owes me something," Nancy said.

"I'll buy you a week of coffee when we get back," I said. Heroism lesson: projecting confidence is important for keeping spirits up!

"You may find it useful to know that the air here is a breathable oxygen-nitrogen-argon mix," Brain Drain said. "With a barely tolerable level of exotic toxins."

I slipped up my visor and immediately regretted it. If I'd thought the planet we'd landed on had smelled "weird", this was "troubling". This was a mix of nail polish and vinegar and chlorine.

"I would not recommend breathing too long," Brain Drain advised.

"Way ahead of you," Koi Boi said, covering his nose and mouth with his shirt collar, yanked up through the neck of his spacesuit.

Then the inner airlock doors opened, and we forgot all about that.

Dancing colors filled the space beyond. A burble and babble of alien voices, a subdued susurrus so thick that they blended together into a rushing like a waterfall. Sounds like no human throat could ever produce. A purring, squealing, squelching nonsense. Heavy thumps as proboscises and tentacles smacked against the deck.

I instinctively raised my arm to block a flicker-flash of violet light playing over my visor. To my dark-adjusted eyes, it was like a sun had been unveiled in front of me, only… more purplish[27]. It vanished as soon as it appeared. The space on the other side of the airlock was dim, but at the same time it was full of changing

---

[27] Generally a bad sign for suns. Remember I mentioned blue being a short-wavelength, high-energy color? The whiter and bluer a sun, the more it's also blasting you with even higher-energy rays – like deadly, deadly radiation. Stay away from blue stars! In fact, don't get too close to any suns! Safety tips you can use in everyday life! – SG

colors, flashing and weaving in and out, like stepping into a nightclub. A nightclub run by a headache.

When I blinked away the afterimages, they resolved into shapes: a bottle, a ray-gun, something that looked like sushi, sunglasses but for someone with three eyes... the images weren't the objects themselves, but floating, fluorescent shapes.

Advertisements. Even off Earth, you can never escape them.

The space we entered was enormous, like a market bazaar. There were too many aliens about to see to the other side of the place, but, even if there hadn't been, ramshackle structures and stalls formed walls and alleyways that would have blocked sight anyway.

They had been constructed haphazardly, out of debris. Dented bulkhead plates and metal girders stacked against each other like card castles. It was easy enough to spot the signs of poverty and misery, even here. If there was any such thing as "urban decay" in space, this station had it. Space stations weren't cheap to build or maintain, but these people had been left to their own resources.

The crowds underneath the floating images didn't have as many lights focused on them, but they were no less eye-catching. Humanoids – even using a loose definition of humanoid that fit the four-armed aliens we'd passed – were a bare plurality of beings here. I'd never seen so many different entities all together in one place, not even the other times I'd been to space.

This place was infinitely smaller than the void we'd just come from, but I'd never felt tinier. I took a few steps ahead, not bothering to hide my starry-eyed awe. Silver spheres with three eyes and three nostrils bounced past us. Their bodies spun even as their faces remained level. Blueberry-colored amorphous masses exuded limbs from their gelatinous central bodies when needed, crawling across the ground on undulating centipede-legs. Vaporous smog-creatures billowed between passersby. Gray-and-black-skinned spider-form aliens avoided the crowds by skittering across the ceiling. My friends and I clustered closer together to avoid being swept away by the tide.

No one paid attention to us. I was starting to understand what Brain Drain had meant about the fear of going ignored. A "hello" would have been nice. We were not significant enough to warrant attention. And it soon became clear that most of the beings here were being treated the same way.

The smells were getting worse. Every time I moved, or every time the air shifted, there was something new and off-putting. Next up was lemons. Then burning coal. Then a whole cooked turkey that had just been left out on the kitchen table all the way from Canadian Thanksgiving to American Thanksgiving.

(Thinking about the smog-creatures I'd seen, I sure hoped I wasn't inhaling any of the residents.)

From the way the smells shifted, it was plain that most of them were coming from the aliens themselves. Which was fair – humans probably smelled like old tires or something to them, at least those with olfactory faculties. But it was still a shock to the senses.

Just because there was no order, though, that didn't mean there were no cops. Motion just behind us made me spin. Two pearl-white humanoid robots had stood astride the airlock hatch. Once we were far enough past them, they stepped in front of the hatch, blocking us from returning to it.

So – getting in was the easy part.

"This is a trap," the Mad Thinker said mildly. He stood a pace away from my friends and me, just far enough to maintain his dignity while not being pushed away by the traffic. I was surprised, and a little pleased, that he hadn't tried to slip into the crowd. Whatever his reasons, good or bad, he was sticking with us. For now.

I nodded at the crowds. "It doesn't seem like it's for us."

"Not *just* for us."

"Light-Horizon?" Koi Boi asked, quietly. "Were you in on this?"

Light-Horizon's telepathic voice sounded like it was coming from right next to me. "Nope. They're doing it to me too. Lots of sensor pulses. They're *very* ticklish. Nothing's come at me yet, but I'm being watched, and it doesn't look like any ship out there is being allowed to leave."

"I'll figure it out," I said.

I swiveled on my heel and turned back to the airlock. Nancy hissed at me to stop. Too late. I marched towards the nearest of the robots.

"Hiya," I said, and then spread my arms. "What the heck?"

Neither of them moved, but I got the impression that their featureless faceplates were looking down at me.

"Don't tell me a space station with this many different aliens in it doesn't have some kind of universal translator," I said.

"A space station with this many different aliens in it doesn't have some kind of universal translator," the nearest robot answered.

I was *almost* amused. "That's very cute," I said.

The robot answered in a strange language that trailed into a polite, uncomprehending question mark.

I walked back to the others. "Definitely messing with you," Chipmunk Hunk said.

"Oooh, yeah," I said. I looked back over my shoulder at them and narrowed my eyes. "Let's experiment."

When Chipmunk Hunk and I moved back toward the airlock as a group, the robots shifted to block our path. The one that had spoken spoke in that same alien language again. Its voice was pleasantly polite, edging toward friendly – not that that meant much. The Mad Thinker folded his arms, frowning, as he studied the aliens. His lips moved like he was calculating under his breath.

We could have fought them. From the way that Chipmunk Hunk was tensing up beside me, I could tell he was getting ready to. That wouldn't have gotten us any closer to finding a way back to Earth, though. Or to figuring out just what was going on here, and why. Or who in the crowd might help us, or work against us. I set my hand on Chipmunk Hunk's shoulder and led him away.

He looked at me questioningly. "I may be here to eat nuts and kick butts, but I've still got some nuts left," I told him.

"That reminds me, I'm hungry," Tippy-Toe said.

"Those nuts might not hold out for long," I said.

"How'd the aliens that we passed on the way in get through?" Nancy asked.

"They could have been part of whatever's going on," I said. Somehow, though, that explanation didn't sit well with me. Something in their stance, the way that one had shaken its head at us, didn't give me any impression of hostility. Just resignation.

"Maybe they gave the guards something they wanted," Nancy suggested.

"A bribe?" Koi Boi asked.

"A toll," Mary said.

The Mad Thinker sighed. He probably thought he was twenty

steps ahead of us, and knew all the answers already. Maybe he was, but I wasn't ready to trust his judgment just yet.

The flow of the crowd pushed us on, through strange new frontiers of smells, and nearly pushed us into (through?) a transparent, amoeba-like blob.[28] Without Brain Drain there to be a wedge in front of us, I'm not sure we could have stayed together.

The flux of passersby pushed us into an eddy where at last we could catch our breath. While I did a headcount to make sure none of us had separated, Nancy's attention fixed on a market stall. She walked toward it. Once I verified none of us had been engulfed by any amoebas, I joined her.

The stall looked for all the world like a newsstand. If you replaced the newspapers and magazines with holographic projectors, metal-and-crystal rods, floating images, and alien lettering. A furry white hominid lounged behind the counter.

I did not need long to find what had caught Nancy's attention. A great big holographic image of warships, bristling with pointy cannons and missile tubes, hovered in front of the screen. *Several* warships, in fact, once I looked closer. The weaponry looked dangerous to the point of ridiculousness. The ships were like giant thistles. The holography was so sharp that I could have cut myself on that thing.

That hologram was only the most prominent image in a field of images. The others showed legions of battleships, alien troops lined up in regimented ranks, and, most concerning of all, a map of stars crisscrossed with bright lines. Past space travel experience told me this was a map of travel lanes between

---

[28] The blob was, and I swear this was true, busking. With a half-engulfed electronic keyboard. – SG

star systems. All of them, every single star and connection, was blinking red.

"War, huh?" Mary asked.

"WHAT IS IT GOOD FOR?" Brain Drain asked.

"Good gosh, y'all," I said as I waved all the others over. "Take a look at this."

My poor stomach had been through a lot these past couple days. Now it felt like it dropped through the floor. I would never get used to the feeling.[29]

There was one little silver lining. These were recordings of warships and soldiers, but *not* battles. The ships weren't firing any weapons at each other. The soldiers were lined up in parade formation, none of them looked injured. These images were of people getting ready to fight. Not actually fighting. Yet.

The Mad Thinker was still with us. He could have escaped at any time... if he wanted. He trailed, arms folded. He was the only one of us who'd kept his spacesuit helmet's visor up. I couldn't see his face underneath the reflected holograms on the glass.

"Ah," he said. "This explains a few things."

My friends' open-mouthed gawking finally got the proprietor's attention. It pulled its furry feet back from the seat it had propped them up on, and raised a rectangular device to point at us.

Traveling out in the universe, dealing with alien technology, gives you no choice but to trust your gut to figure out what things are. Without having seen any of the particular kinds of cannons on those warships, for instance, I was sure that they *were* weapons. I didn't have any way to prove this, but the rectangle

---

[29] HULK'S STOMACH POWERFUL. EAT SADNESS, DIGEST INTO RAGE. – ED.

pointed at us didn't feel like a weapon. A shimmering blue-white light washed over us. Then all of the floating holographic text blinked into English.

"WAR WAR WAR" read one headline. The next read the same in a larger font. The next, a larger font still. The first hologram, as if angry at the others for out-competing it, grew larger as we watched.

"Hey, careful," the furry creature said. "You collapse those photons' wavefunctions by observing them, you bought them."

I *knew* this place had universal translator tech. I ignored what the creature had said, and went right into Chipper Mode. "Hi there!"

"Are you here to loiter or buy something?"

"I'm here to learn," I said. It was the truth.

The creature showed us some astonishingly sharp teeth in what I chose to interpret as a warm and welcoming smile. "You've come to the right booth," it said. "You can learn anything you want, if you can pay."

My friends and I looked at each other. Nancy asked, "What kind of payment?"

"I've got ten dollars and some gum," Chipmunk Hunk offered. ("You've got gum and haven't shared?" Mary hissed.)

The newsstand-monster's eyelids opened and closed horizontally. "Well, I don't know yet. A stanza? A rhyme?"

These past few days, I'd had to do an awful lot of standing and staring while I made sure that I had just heard what I'd thought I'd heard. This was going to all make sense eventually, but, at the moment, I just had to roll with it. One rhyme was rarely far from my mind.

I said, "I'm here to eat nuts and kick butts!"

The creature looked at me for a long moment, as if waiting for more. Finally, with a sound that could only be a sigh, it returned its feet to their prop. "It's not as though I've got much else to sustain me. Ask your questions."

"We're looking for a planet called Earth," Koi Boi said. "We're hoping to get in touch with someone who can point us toward it, and take us there."

("It's a perfectly good rhyme," I muttered.)

("Great, even!" Chipmunk Hunk said.)

The creature answered with a wheezing noise. Laughter, maybe. With aliens, it could equally well have been sobbing, or just breathing. "And I'd like to go home and never see this place again, but here we all are."

"We need to find a way to Earth," Koi Boi reiterated. "We're *going* to find a way to Earth."

I could not read this alien's facial expressions. But its pause before it spoke said enough. "Even if you *could* leave this place, you don't want to. How'd you get here?"

"Space whale," I said, and just because everybody had been intentionally obtuse so far, I left it at that. "I'm pretty sure we want to leave."

"We've got finals coming up in a few weeks," Nancy added, as though it would add weight to our request. She took finals *very* seriously.

The alien said, "I mean, if you find a way to travel without getting incinerated by what's about to happen out there…"

"What *is* about to happen out there?" Koi Boi asked.

"The Itrayans? The Eradu? The war?" The alien blinked black, beady eyes at us. We stared blankly back. "It's like you stepped through a portal from a cosmic backwater."

"Let's pretend for a moment that we did," I said. Earth had made contact with plenty of alien species, from Aakon to Zn'rx. I'd never heard those names. But the galaxy was a big place[30]. Plenty of space for names no one from Earth had heard of.

"Then you should know that there's a great big system of political alliances and defense pacts about to come crashing down on this quadrant because of the Itrayans and the Eradu. It's going to be impossible to travel anywhere without getting blown to bits or conscripted. There's not a single ship that'll risk traveling while that's happening. There's not a single ship that *could* breach all the blockades." The alien's gaze flicked to passersby behind us. "And that's all you *need* to know because none of us are getting out of here anyway. Not until the shooting stops. And not even then."

"Who's stopping us from leaving?" Koi Boi demanded.

The alien looked again at the beings behind us. Had the passersby been human, they would have just been inside eavesdropping distance.

"The poetnappers," the alien said, in a much softer voice.

"Excuse me?" I asked.

"*Poets,*" it hissed, and waved us away with a flourish of its clawed hands.

Sure. Made just as much sense as anything else today.

I tried to get more answers out of the newsstand alien, but it didn't want to talk – or at least be seen talking – anymore. Not to us, and not about the poetnappers. It looked deliberately away. When I kept being my charmingly persistent self and stepping in front of it, it resorted to projecting one of the news holograms in the space between us.

---

[30] UNDERSTATEMENTS MAKE HULK SMASH. – ED

While the rest of us had been talking, Mary had studied the market. She nodded in a direction with slightly fewer holograms.

"This is giving me a migraine," she said.

"Same," Nancy and Koi Boi and Tippy-Toe said in unison.

"Light-Horizon, you there?" I asked the air.

"'Course," they answered telepathically.

"Can you sense anything about the aliens running this station?"

"Sorry, friend. Need more to go on than that. It's a mess of minds out there."

There was nowhere here free of bustle, but there were a few places with a little less hustle. The marketplace eventually ended in towering walls that curved up and into the dome overhead. From the walls, corridors snaked away into obscurity. This station was probably bigger than any of us could map out. Its tentacles both clung into and dug underneath the asteroid. The only places that seemed more threatening than this market were places that had absolutely no one at all. We stayed away from the corridors.

The quietest-but-still-occupied space was a little nook in one of the bulkheads, where tables and chairs to fit all forms and sizes were arranged in no particular order. The smells over here took on a decidedly less chemical, more organic flavor. A long counter stood close to the far wall, tended by three orange-skinned humanoid aliens. Lumps and blocks of food-like material sizzled on counters.

It was some kind of restaurant, or soup kitchen, or the like. Not that my stomach was ready to eat. Or would be ever again. None of the aliens paid us much mind when we claimed a table for ourselves.

Chipmunk Hunk laid his hands on Mary's shoulders and started rubbing[31]. She shook her head and held out her hand instead. He sighed, reached into his pockets, and fished out a package of gum.

"Why do I get the feeling that we're farther away from home now than when we were stranded on a deserted planet?" Chipmunk Hunk asked.

"If it makes you feel better," the Mad Thinker said, "these obstacles were always here. This is just the first time you've perceived them."

"That doesn't make me feel better at all," Chipmunk Hunk lamented.

The Mad Thinker smiled, thinly.

---

[31] GOOD MIGRAINE TRICK. HULK THREATEN TO USE ON FRIENDS AND THEY SAY THEY FEEL BETTER. – ED

The Unbeatable Squirrel Girl Vs The Non-Interference Principle

After the third time the Mad Thinker recounted our odds of finding a way out of this, Nancy slammed her elbows on our table. She turned to the Mad Thinker. "Are you going to use that incredible brain of yours to calculate a way back home, or what?"

"I could," the Mad Thinker said. "There's no point."

Brain Drain's eyes rotated to face the Mad Thinker. "You ARE TAKING MY PLACE IN THIS GROUP'S DYNAMIC."

Nancy ignored Brain Drain. "Why the *heck* not?" she asked.

The Mad Thinker looked toward me. "What's the point in opening a door for someone if they're not going to walk through it?"

I blinked. "You think I wouldn't use a way home if I found one?"

"You wouldn't believe my answer if I told you," he said, and stood. "Excuse me. I need to gather more data." He strode back toward the busier parts of the market without looking back.

"Should we stop him?" Nancy asked.

"He'll be back," I said. I was having to trust my gut a lot out here, and my gut said that didn't feel like an escape attempt. A fight wouldn't have been a good idea in so crowded a place, anyway.

"I WILL KEEP MY EYES ON HIM," Brain Drain said, tapping his brain case. He waded into the crowd that the Mad Thinker had disappeared into.

"The Mad Thinker has the right idea," I said. "We need to find out a lot more about what's going on."

After some discussion, we decided the best way to start on that was to split into pairs, stay close, ask around, and meet back here in a few minutes. Chipmunk Hunk and Mary stayed at the table while Mary mainlined sugar to help her headache. Nancy and Koi Boi approached the aliens at the counter. Tippy-Toe and I surveyed the aliens sitting/slouching/undulating over the tables.

Most of the aliens were in groups of two or more. One sat alone: a green-skinned, green-haired humanoid with crossed legs and a pleasant-looking smile. For whatever value I could trust "pleasant-looking" with aliens, anyway. She was at a table that had been shoved against a wall, holding a tablet in one hand. Every once in a while, she glanced past it at the others. It was a good place for her to keep an eye on all the tables as other beings came and went.

I walked up to her, trying to think of a way to start the conversation, but I didn't need to bother.

"I have a wonderful memory for faces," she said, in a

refreshingly pleasant voice, "and I haven't seen you before." She looked to Tippy-Toe next. "And I certainly would have remembered you."

"Thanks, probably!" Tippy-Toe said.

Whatever universal translator was in effect here was picking up squirrelese, too, because the alien nodded. "Which means you're either the shapeshifters from the Andromedan cruise ship, or you're unlucky enough to be new here."

"No way!" I said. "You've memorized everyone in this station? How?"

The alien tapped her head slyly. Weird alien memory. Got it.

"We *are* new here," I said, "and extremely confused."

She shrugged. She glanced again at her tablet before returning her attention to us. Greeting newcomers seemed to be rote for her, like she'd said all this a hundred times before. She sighed.

"I suppose you'll want to know the whole story."

I hushed my voice. "Who are 'the poetnappers?'"

Her already-wrinkled nose crinkled more. "Gangsters, the lot of them. War-profiteers."

"Okay! So far, this is making less sense than before, but I'm still with you."

"Well, there's no poetry like poetry that comes out of war. You know, the 'sweet and honorable to die for one's country' stuff. Sweet, sad, ironic stuff written by soldiers in trenches. War poems will still be read for eons after a war ends."

I nodded. "Still wobbly on the making-sense scale."

"Well, there's a war coming. No better time to harvest poets to grind into war. All kinds of aliens, local to the region and otherwise, are looking for shelter from the storm. Some of them look here, especially the ones who don't have anywhere better to go. Isn't that why you're here?"

"No, we're just a bunch of humans, looking to get home."

"Humans?" the alien spat, rearing up. Suddenly she seemed a whole lot less sweet. "From *Earth*?"

I was so caught off guard by the change in tone that I was more curious than surprised. "Um... yes..."

The map of wrinkles on her forehead shifted. New detours ran along the suddenly bulging veins in her neck and forehead. Her chest puffed out like a bullfrog's. She drew one of her arms back. I stepped away, but not fast enough.

Rather than hit me, though, she just poked me in the sternum. Hard.

"We don't need any meddling humans meddling things up out here! The galaxy's had enough of humans. Always thinking you're at the center of things. What brings you out here this time? Siccing Galactus on worlds you've never heard of, because, *hey, at least they're not Earth?* Stealing the Black Vortex because everybody absolutely *loves it* when you unleash an all-powerful MacGuffin on the universe? Throwing gamma-irradiated angry green giants into the cosmos like yesterday's trash, dusting your hands off, pretending it's down, and only caring when it gets back home?[32] Hurling the Phoenix Force off your planet and only bothering to think about it again *after* it devours a star?"

Yellow spittle flew from her lips. The creature leaned over me, panting with just as much rage as she had shouted. It was like

---

[32] HULK VERY ANGRY AT THE TIME, BUT MAY HAVE MADE MISTAKES AND HAS REGRETS HULK ONLY CAPABLE OF EXPRESSING AS PUNY BANNER ALTER-EGO OR IN EDITORIAL FOOTNOTES. – ED

standing under the mister in the grocery store produce section, only much warmer.

So it turned out that talking to someone with weird alien memory may have had some downsides.

I didn't need to look to sense the other aliens at the tables staring at me. The sounds of their voices and the swishing of their appendages had gone silent. The creature seemed to be waiting for some kind of response.

"It's okay," Tippy-Toe said, from my shoulder. "She's with me."

The panting hitched. The creature's breath became slightly less intense as she turned to Tippy-Toe.

"I'm teaching her to be better!" Tippy-Toe said, and tugged at my headband. "See? Squirrel ears! And she's got a tail somewhere under that suit!"

The panting abated. I cracked an eye open. The creature's height was rapidly deflating.

When she spoke again, her voice was all sweetness. "It's very good of you to take an interest in the meddling-impaired," she told Tippy-Toe. "See that you keep a close eye on her."

"Always do," Tippy-Toe said cheerfully.

When I felt safe enough to step away from the creature, I wiped the spittle off my face and slunk off. At least that alien had heard of Earth. But if I'd asked her for directions – assuming she even knew where to look – she'd probably steer us into a sun.

When my friends and I reconvened, they had a few more scraps of information.

"No one has seen the 'poetnappers' that run the place," Nancy said. "They have those robots we saw earlier running everything for them. The pirate ships keeping everyone penned in here are probably some kind of mercenaries."

"There's some kind of underground poetry exchange going on," Koi Boi said. "People keep asking each other for stanzas. There's a whole bunch of aliens on the other side of the market scribbling on scraps of paper. One of them was playing the drums."

"I hope those were drums," Nancy said.

"Could've been skulls," Koi Boi admitted. "Didn't look too closely."

Brain Drain rejoined us. "THE MAD THINKER FOUND AN EMPTY BOOTH, SAT IN IT, AND IS STARING AT THE WALL," he reported. "I UNDERSTAND HIM MORE NOW."

I watched two aliens furtively exchange slips of scrap paper.

"There's some kind of poetry-based black market here," I said. "And, unless the translators are mangling words, it seems like whoever's managing those robots is kidnapping anybody who might be a poet." And, though this was more of a hunch than a certainty, shipping them off to war to produce poetry.

Nancy had seen the same exchange I had. "No wonder these aliens are passing everything around on the down-low," she remarked.

"And we are farther from home than ever," I said. "We need to escape this place. Get through space traffic lanes shut down by war. And find out where we're going. And that's if we can get the means to travel, too."

"You feeling all right?" Nancy asked. Her polite way of saying she was picking up some very un-Squirrel-Girl-like pessimism.[33]

"Discombobulated," I said. "Like I've spent most of my life in a

---

[33] It was true, it *wasn't* very much like me. This should have been another warning sign. – SG

world full of pictures and art and now I'm living in plain old text."

"Plain text can be art," Nancy said, defensively. She had once gotten into an acrimonious debate with an English major about whether programming qualified as art.[34]

I gave her a look I hoped wasn't too jaundiced. "Thoughts?" I asked the others.

Brain Drain considered. He held up a metal claw. "THOSE WHO SAY THE JOURNEY IS WORTH MORE THAN THE DESTINATION HAVE PLAINLY NEVER EMBARKED UPON THE LONG ROAD OF WRESTLING WITH DESPAIR."

"That is so true," I said. "But I meant about our current situation."

"SO DID I."

Mary said, abruptly, "I want to get my hands on some alien technology." Migraine or not, she stood.

"No weaponry," Chipmunk Hunk said.

"Yes, weaponry," Mary said, heading into the crowd.

"It's not that I'm hungry now," Nancy said, "but someone should investigate the food and shelter situation. We're going to need to collapse eventually." She stood too.

Gradually, everyone split apart on their own missions again. I was at least focused enough to make sure that everyone traveled in groups of two or three, but, eventually, Tippy-Toe and I were left alone.

"Humph," I said, still grumpy about being yelled at on behalf of humanity. My tail squirmed in my spacesuit's leg, anxious to

---

[34] It's true! Like art, code can bury meaning and have multiple valid readings. Look no farther than the Annual Obfuscated Code Contest, whose goal is to abuse C in the most elaborate, creative ways possible. Like a Tic-Tac-Toe game consisting of a single print statement in a while loop and that's also ASCII art. Or a program that calculates pi by measuring its own area. Look it up! – SG

get out and twitch around. I didn't have anywhere safe to leave the suit, though, so I kept it on.

"What's wrong with meddling, anyway?" I muttered.

"Well…" Tippy-Toe said.

I raised an eyebrow. "Don't tell me you agree with that alien."

"Humans do have a way of pushing themselves into the center of things," Tippy-Toe said.

"We do not–" After giving that a quarter-second's thought, I cut myself off and said, "Okay, maybe."

"Even on Earth, humans act like they're the only species on the planet."

"*I* don't," I said.

Tippy-Toe patted my cheek. "That's why we squirrels love you."

"And I feed you."

"That too! But you're also one of the reasons why we keep giving humans a chance to grow out of it."

I rested my chin in my hand. "Humph," I reiterated. I hoped Tippy-Toe got the message that I didn't want to talk about it. I had enough to mope about just now.

The worst part was that Tippy-Toe and that alien were right. I *was* thinking about meddling. Fantasizing about it, even! There was only so much misery and chaos a squirrel-girl could see before she leaped into the fray, no matter how unwise it was. I've done interstellar diplomacy before.

Maybe Tippy-Toe was right. Maybe I *was* shoving myself into problems I didn't understand. Letting my own sense of self-importance get to me.

The two aliens who'd furtively exchanged scraps of paper lingered a moment at the edge of the cluster of tables. One of them had soft, azure skin. The other was mostly hidden underneath a heavy cloak, but I caught a glimpse of chitinous gray skin. And then a scorpion-like stinger tail, slipping out from the back of the cloak, and curling around the other alien's legs.

Lightning-fast, the stinger plunged into the blue alien's backside. The blue alien jerked and, silently, started to fall. Its assailant quickly caught it before it made too much noise. Moving just as quickly as its tail, it started rooting through the blue alien's pockets, collecting more scraps of paper and stuffing them under its cloak.

Involuntarily, I bunched my hands into fists. I stood.

Maybe I wasn't letting my self-importance get to me *enough*.

The insect-alien's compound eyes caught me starting to move toward it. It let its victim slump to the ground, and dashed down an alley between ramshackle stalls.

Things suddenly seemed a whole lot simpler. Here was a crime. And I was a crimefighting dang *super hero*.

Heck, this whole *place* was a crime. Getting home wasn't as important as unraveling it. If anything, focusing on getting home was a distraction.

Without hardly thinking about it, I was giving chase. In that instant, everything crystalized.

Time for some meddling.

The Unbeatable Squirrel Girl Vs The Ultimate English Major

I felt a lot more like myself after I left the scorpion alien dangling from an overhead girder, tied there with its own stinger-tail.

Back on Earth, I would've dragged it to the nearest police station, all the while telling it what awful choices it was making with its life, but a) the stinger would have made that impractical, and b) the robots that amounted to local authorities here seemed worse than this creature was.

So the suspending-from-the-ceiling bit was a compromise. This way, I could keep an eye on it from anywhere in the market. Large as the market was, it had very few tall structures to obstruct my view. And if any alien here tried to take revenge on the insect alien with any cruel and unusual measures, I could see that, too, and put a stop to it. Hopefully, the insect alien's species felt something like humiliation. I didn't have many other tools to persuade it to change its ways.

The blue-skinned alien was, so far as I could tell, all right. It moaned on the ground, pale and sweaty, until it saw me and the scraps of paper I'd recovered from the insect. The alien snatched the papers and wobbled to its feet. Without saying a word to me, or even seeming to register my presence, it retreated into the crowds.

"You should maybe see a doctor!" I called to its back.

It continued to ignore me. I assumed that was a "thank you".

The little green alien who'd yelled at me was gone when I returned to the cluster of tables. Good. *Meddling*, my butt. This place was full of injustice, everybody was miserable, and the only way that was going to change was if somebody rolled up their fuzzy sweater sleeves and got to work.

I checked up on the Mad Thinker, but he was right where Brain Drain said: sulking in an empty market stall. It seemed cruel to force him out when I didn't know what to do with him, and frankly didn't want him around. I let him be, for now.

This was a good a time as any to poke and prod and test our captors. The robots had no sidearms or other separate weapons. They didn't need them. Each of their wrists had a protruding, deadly-looking weapon barrel.

I circled them. "Doesn't that get in the way of your mobility?" I asked them. "Are you able to move your wrists freely with those?"

They didn't answer.

"Do androids dream of electric squirrels?" I whispered. "*Tell me.*"

The robots stood guard silently, hour after hour, never

moving from their posts. Light-Horizon said they didn't detect any telepathic signatures in them. By which they meant to say, no living minds of any kind. Not even the kind of mind they might have detected from a sentient android.

I had no other clues as to where to start looking for who was responsible for this. This whole thing reminded me of when New York started warping around itself. Heroes like the Avengers and Spider-Man had put out every fire they could reach, but they hadn't been able to find the cause.

This time I didn't have a worldwide network of squirrels, chipmunks, and fish to help. The count was one squirrel and one whale. So far. But I still had my friends, which put me miles ahead of the enemy.

Nancy had watched some alien travelers present the robots with tablets and notebooks. She'd been too far away to read any of them, even if they had been written in a language she understood, but it was easy enough to guess what was on them. *Poems*.

The robots turned most of the aliens away from the airlock. Others, they'd let through – after an appropriate literary bribe. One alien, traveling alone, had been less fortunate. Nancy and Koi Boi had been out on their own when they'd seen their first poetnapping. The robots had taken a long look through the alien's notebook, and then hauled it off, dragging it away by its flailing tentacles. It had taken all of Nancy's energy to keep Koi Boi from charging after them.

If I'd been there, she wouldn't have been able to stop me.

"We tackle this as a group," Nancy said, after recounting the story. She gave me a pointed look.

I *was* a little prone to charging ahead sometimes. I pretended not to hear.

"ADVANCED INTERSTELLAR CIVILIZATIONS LIKELY HAVE ECONOMIES BEYOND THE SCOPE OF OUR IMAGINATIONS," Brain Drain pointed out. "BASED MORE UPON INTELLECTUAL AND CREATIVE WORK THAN MATERIAL GOODS. THEY MAY BE HARVESTING POETS LIKE ORES FROM A MINE."

"Or committing a really violent form of literary criticism," Mary said.

"I've never trusted poets," Nancy said.

"Yeah, they know their way around words too well," I said. "You just know they're gonna roast you one day."

"And it's gonna sting," Nancy said. "Everything gets more personal in meter."

"POETRY IS CAPABLE OF RIPPING MY HEART OUT AND DISSECTING IT IN FRONT OF ME," Brain Drain said. When we looked at him, he added, "METAPHORICALLY SPEAKING."

"Right," Chipmunk Hunk said, "I don't know about anyone else, but I'm hungry."

"How can you stand the thought of food in air smelling like this?" Nancy asked, but Chipmunk Hunk was already out of his seat and heading toward the counter.

"It's either think about food or think about everything else," Chipmunk Hunk said.

"That's fair," Nancy said.

We still had food with us, but we couldn't survive on it indefinitely, and we might need more of it for the trip home – assuming we ever got a chance to make it. Might as well check out the local resources.

The variety of aliens at the counters was an encouraging sign. If they were all eating food from the same source, there probably weren't all that many biochemical barriers between us and nutrition.[35] A line filtered toward the counter. It was long, but moving fast. Immediately, a bronze-skinned humanoid alien stepped into it behind us.

There were three aliens behind it, tending equipment that looked halfway between a kitchen stove and a laboratory. Another alien waiting for food tried to pay with scraps of poetry, but the cooks waved it off. *Someone* around here was doing something good without expectation of debt or payment.

That didn't last. The alien who'd tried to pay held out its tentacle. Quick and casual, one of the cooks picked up a knife and sliced off a segment of flesh. The first alien quivered. I almost leapt to its defense, but the cook set the knife back down. The cook took the bit of flesh, stuck it into a piece of laboratory equipment that looked like a microwave with a whole bunch of computer displays, and flipped a switch.

The machine glowed, and its displays showed rotating DNA-like molecules. More machines on the countertop whirred into action, slowly exuding a pale, yellow-white spongy substance like scrambled egg.

So *that* was how these aliens were getting around biochemical

---

[35] Fun science facts! When you look into it, it actually should be impossibly difficult for human beings or any life from Earth to derive nutrition from life that evolved elsewhere! Life on Earth uses the same basic biochemistry. Varieties of alien life very similar to us could use nutrients that the human body would have no idea what to do with. For example: there are even ways to structure amino acids – called "left-handed" and "right-handed" – that mean they'd function identically but be incompatible with each other. All life on Earth uses left-handed amino acids only. There's no reason that life elsewhere couldn't have used the right-handed amino acids. Alien life using them could even evolve to be identical to us, but still be completely incompatible as far as nutrition goes! All of which is to say: I should have known better. (Foreshadowing!) – SG

FORESHADOWING NOT CLEVER WHEN YOU POINT IT OUT, SQUIRREL GIRL – ED.

barriers. Taking chunks out of each other, analyzing them, and growing food from the sample.[36]

The cook folded the eggy substance over itself like an omelet and, as an afterthought, returned the piece of tentacle it had sliced off. The alien inclined its head in appreciation, and slid off.

The cook turned toward us next. As a single movement, all of us stepped back.

Surviving off our own food it was, then, at least until we had no other choice. I didn't think I'd be able to eat scrambled eggs again in my life.

"I scoffed at what you said about ignorance," Mary told Brain Drain, "but now I understand."

"EXPERIENCE IS A CRUEL TEACHER," Brain Drain said. "AND I HAVE LEARNED A LOT."

We were so preoccupied with these thoughts that it took us a moment to realize someone had approached us. I looked up.

The bronze-skinned humanoid alien who'd been in line at the counter stood over us. His hair was a deep, dark purple-black – slick and well-kempt and tucked into a bun behind his head. He had an equally well-cared-for pencil-thin beard, like a goatee but without the mustache. Aside from the strange coloration and uncomfortably sharp cheekbones, he would have looked closer to human than most of the aliens here… except his eyes were solid black.

The next line is going to read a little odd, but you're going to have to trust me in that he said it exactly as quoted here. Read it twice if you have to.

---

[36] HULK HAVE STRONG STOMACH BUT GIVE HULK A BREAK, SHEESH. – ED

"'Who are you?' the hero demanded. 'You who walk away from omelets?'"

I was getting better and better at reacting to things like this with equanimity. "Hi!" I said. "I'm Squirrel Girl."

"The arrogance of the stranger was almost as striking as her brashness," he said. "It was plain, at least, that he had found their leader, though whether the others followed her from lack of will or lack of character was yet to be apparent."

I blinked. The equanimity was getting harder to come by again.

"Hey now," Nancy said, though more confused than offended.

I pretended this was all expected. "Squirrel Girl is the name I usually go by, anyway. I'm also called Doreen Green. What's your name?" I asked the stranger.

"He dispensed with the introductions as quickly as possible, telling Doreen Green naught more than his own name." Without invitation, he took a chair from a neighboring table and scraped it closer to ours. "He told them that they must be more careful about flaunting their wealth. The fools didn't seem to realize how it had looked to turn down free, biocompatible food as they had just done."

"Look, now, Hadrian, we–" I started, and stopped.

The alien's name was Hadrian. I had no idea how I knew this. The name had popped into my head fully formed.

"More telepaths," Mary said. "No wonder I have a migraine."

"He allowed them to vent their misplaced anger," Hadrian said. "Not for the first time that minute, he wondered if this would be worth the trouble, but the thought of the treasure this misbegotten group was surely sitting on steadied his nerves."

Nancy seemed about ready to tackle the alien, or run, or first one and then the other. I set my hand on her arm.

I leaned forward. Realization prickled my brow. "You're a *poet*," I said. And the uniform maybe meant that he was not just a poet, but one of the poetnappers.

"He was many things, but not a poet. Still, he allowed his interlocutor to keep her misimpression. It could be useful, something to exploit."

I don't know how to explain what went through my head at the moment. I had heard him speak, knew he had denied being one of the poetnappers running the place, but I couldn't get the idea out of my mind regardless. It was like my conscious and subconscious had taken off running in two different directions. Or like my reaction wasn't entirely under my control.

The alien wore an outfit that resembled a uniform with a skirt or kilt, and thick golden buttons down the front and two overlapping ovals as a chest insignia. The fabric was nearly the same color as his skin, which made it difficult to register at first. His skirt only went to his knees, and his uniform sleeves ended at his elbows. His forearms were intriguingly tattooed. One arm had a stylized sun. The other, an inverse starfield. With the alien's solid black eyes, it had taken me a while to realize that he wasn't looking at us when he spoke. He didn't seem to be looking at anything at all. At least not anything present.

"Look, if you're part of the group that's keeping all these people prisoner here, you and I need to have some words, buddy," I told him.

"He was not Doreen Green's buddy, and anyway was growing impatient with their questions," Hadrian said. "He had urgent matters of his own to discuss. He explained how the group had been drawing more attention to themselves, and how their behavior thus far had signaled enormous wealth to the station's desperate inhabitants. Hadrian nodded to the thief hanging by its tail."

Hadrian did not in fact nod at anything, just kept staring over my shoulder.

Now that I thought about it, I could see what he'd meant. The arguments he'd never made, but only described himself making, formed in my head. They seemed reasonable. I'd returned the stolen property and not taken a reward or a ransom. Our group had never shown any interest in poetry, or seemed to consider paying for anything. We'd approached one of the few charitable operations in the place, a food kitchen, but refused to eat for a petty reason like disgust. We weren't, in other words, destitute and scrabbling for survival. Like everyone else here.

I tried to play along. "Squirrel Girl asks the stranger what he wants," Squirrel Gi… I mean, *I* said.

"Hadrian told the alien not to talk in the third person," Hadrian said. "He wondered if she was an egotist or simply had a poor grasp of her own language."

I narrowed my eyes.

"Tell us what you want," I said through clenched teeth.

"'To help newcomers adapt to life on the station, and nothing more,' the hero lied."

"Did anyone else just hear him say that?" Koi Boi asked, but I didn't have the time to answer.

"He did not enjoy explaining his life story, so he disposed with the exposition as quickly as he could," Hadrian said. "He kept most to himself, naturally." In a furtive, conspiratorial voice, he added, "They could not be allowed to know his dark and tragic past."

Something in my head shifted, like several minutes had passed and I'd just become aware of them. They hadn't, really – at least, I didn't think they had. But I knew more about him than I had before he'd said that.

Hadrian had no more wanted to be here than most of these other aliens. At first. He had come here because the passenger starliner he'd been traveling on had been forced off the space lanes by the impending war. He had been too proud to live like the others here, and had taken one of the only escapes available, one that even the most desperate shunned: he had volunteered to serve in the Eradu navy. That was what his uniform signified. The emblem on his chest was an Eradu naval rank. Not even the poetnappers dared stand against the Eradu navy. Hadrian was only waiting for an Eradu picket to arrive and pick him up.

Serving in the coming war was certainly a death sentence. It was both brave and noble for Hadrian to throw himself into it, seeking glory. Look, I'm sure I didn't think that last part, but it shoved its way into my head regardless.

"Okay, I'll bite," Chipmunk Hunk said. "Why do you keep referring to yourself as the 'hero?'"

"The hero frowned. He'd done no such thing. He struggled to think of what the alien might have been implying."

I opened my mouth to object, but was struck with a sudden conviction that Hadrian was right, and that he *hadn't* ever referred to himself as a hero. In retrospect, this was nuts, but at the time it seemed perfectly reasonable. I gave Chipmunk Hunk a strange look.

"The hero told the misbegotten group that he could show

them how to live on the station. Although his motives were selfish… they were not altogether un-altruistic, either. The strangers *did* have a lot to learn about this place. And if the hero was owed a favor for his services – well, that would only be fair."

"We don't need help," Nancy told him.

"The hero smiled thinly," Hadrian said. His flat expression did not shift at all.

Nancy sighed and massaged the bridge of her nose.

"Maybe help wouldn't be unwelcome," I suggested.

"Not from him," Nancy said.

"The hero shifted uncomfortably," Hadrian said – again absolutely unmoving. "He had been humbled many times since arriving at the station. Another blow would have been devastating. It was possible that his social skills were not up to the task to which he kept putting them."

"Simply put," Nancy said, "this isn't your story."

"You can't just waltz right into it," Koi Boi said.

Tippy-Toe's claws tightened ever so slightly on my shoulder. She didn't have to bring up our argument from a few moments ago to tell me what she was thinking.

"What kinds of things could you show us?" I asked him.

"The hero brightened. He outlined some of the things he'd learned."

Hadrian had memorized a rough map of the station, and could tell us which groups had claimed what territories, where to find safe places to sleep, where to get the necessities of life like water for drinking and laundry, and other boring but necessary non-super hero things not ordinarily covered in stories of derring-do. More importantly, he could tell us something of the society and culture that had sprung up here, and how these aliens would interpret (or misinterpret) what we were doing.

Some part of me was aware of what was happening and could talk about it – so long as I didn't contradict Hadrian directly. The experience was too weird to describe – like having two different minds, each aware of different things, that were unable to directly communicate. Listening to Hadrian's narration was like reading a book, or watching a movie. Most of me was immersed in the fiction, and though there was always a part of me that was aware of the split, it couldn't do anything.

"What do you want in return?" Koi Boi asked.

"Though material reward would not be unwelcome, the hero explained that he was primarily seeking friends. Particularly friends capable of repaying favors."

"Oh, I'm good at friendship," I said. "It's one of my superpowers!" On that note: I was starting to feel bad for leaving the Mad Thinker to his shame. I had to do better by him.

"At times like this, I wish it weren't," Nancy groused.

"The hero smiled." For the first time, Hadrian's expression shifted… into a frown. His voice remained level. "His poor luck with friends gnawed at him."

He directed us toward one of the empty corridors that we'd shied away from before. As he explained, er, that he was explaining things, I fell toward the back of the group, toward Mary and Chipmunk Hunk.

"So," Chipmunk Hunk said, "this is a new kind of telepathy."

"I thought I preferred prose over poetry," Mary said. "Until now."

"What is it with this place and English class stuff?" I asked. The universe was a wild place. Full of danger and surprises and things you'd never imagined would be possible. Every time I left Earth, I learned something that changed my view of things entirely.

"So many nerds out here," Mary said. "Infinite nerds in infinite diversity."

"I don't think he's just playing a game," Chipmunk Hunk said.

"He doesn't look like he's having fun," Mary said. "Either he's not having any, or he's having way too much."

"*I'm* having fun," I said. I wasn't even being sarcastic! I liked meeting new people and trying to make new friends. Albeit this one was a little trying.

Neither of them dignified me with an answer.

The Unbeatable Squirrel Girl Vs Diabolus Ex Machina

Our new friend marched down corridors that, while not entirely deserted, were far quieter than the market. There were fewer strange smells here – just a single, overwhelming odor of burning rubber and plastic. Maybe half of the lights in these corridors were working. The ones that were left didn't seem quite attuned to human visual preferences anyway. They shone red-orange in a way that seemed to rob everything of other colors.

I could finally hear the smaller sounds. Ventilation hissed. Voices murmured just around the corner. Strange, oily liquids dripped from the walls.

Hadrian did not tell us anything, strictly speaking. He *told* us about telling us things, and then we knew them. He taught us how to read marks scratched on the walls that signified directions. How to tap into the water pipes. Who had set up water purifiers, and how many stanzas they charged per liter. Whatever misgivings I had earlier, this all seemed like genuinely useful information. If it was true.

Nancy hugged her arms to her side as the air chilled. "I really hope we're not staying long enough to take advantage of all this," she said.

"Knowledge is power," I said, miming a sparkly rainbow over our heads[37].

"I just really wish he wouldn't call himself a 'hero,'" she muttered.

"It could be that he understands 'hero' to mean something different than we understand it," Brain Drain said. I winced at the volume. "Not all heroes are admirable. In the literary canon, heroes could be miserable, unlikable characters, like Achilles sulking in his tent, or Oedipus killing his fa—"

"Okay, okay!" I said, mostly to get him to hush up.

Hadrian was still talking. "…pointedly ignored the babbling of callow youth he was leading, wondering whether it would be worth his time allying with them, or if his loneliness was overriding his better judgment."

That was interesting. I picked up my pace until I was beside Hadrian again. The next time he paused between his lines, I asked, "You've been feeling lonely?"

"The hero startled, shocked," Hadrian said. "Had he been so obvious? With a quick twitch of his head, he denied it."

"Huh," I said. "Just a hunch."

"But it was too late. The floodgates of memory had opened. The faces of old friends, lost friends, flickered through his mind's eye. All of them ripped away by unhappy fortune, until in his desperation he turned to the dregs of this alien space station."

---

[37] It involved lots of finger waggling. – SG

"Um," Nancy said.

"The hero swallowed his hurt, and reminded himself that it was not the aliens' fault they had stepped into an emotional tripwire, especially after he had so carelessly laid one down so clearly in front of them."

"How long is it going to be until you get shipped off to the front?" Nancy asked, making a valiant attempt to change the subject.

"The hero avoided the question with a quick, tossed-off lie–" (At that instant, the words 'two weeks' appeared in my mind) "– and, lest he accidentally give away anything else of his dark and ill-starred history, turned the next corner and began searching for sleeping quarters for the group." Hadrian's boots squeaked on the deck as he turned on cue.

I stuck close to his heels. "Is there something you want to tell us?" I asked.

"The hero answered that he would like to keep showing them around the station. He waved at each door they passed, pointing out which of them had markings indicating claimed territory, and which had char marks indicating recent fighting."

For someone summarizing exposition that would have taken a lot longer to actually say aloud, Hadrian could sure go on and on. When I looked back, Mary was twirling her finger in midair. A perpetual loading icon.

He stopped by a door that had been left open. All its neighbors were closed. Shadows blossomed inside. "'Here,' the hero said, pointing out to the others the lack of door markings, or of scuffing on the floor indicating recent traffic. This room seemed as good a place as any to serve as their shelter."

I wasn't sold. The red-orange light didn't penetrate very far into the next room. The air hanging around the entrance smelled musty.

"Little did the hero and his new companions know," Hadrian intoned darkly, "that they had walked into a trap."

It took my mind a second to catch up with what my ears had heard. Shadows shifted across the open entrance. An instant later, the doors directly behind us opened. Two doors farther down the corridor popped open too.

I got my game on just in time. I ducked, and a sizzling, electrified club swung through the air above me. It crashed into the wall. Sparks exploded from the impact, showering my shoulder. Tippy-Toe squeaked and ducked under my sweater collar.

I was already ticked, but hearing Tippy-Toe made me mad. I grabbed the what-I-thought-was-an-arm holding the club (turned out to be a tentacle), and yanked a squid-faced alien out from the shadows and into the corridor. Another attacker had stepped in front of me, holding another electrified club. With what I dare say was balletic grace, I whirled the squid-faced alien into this new one, and sent them both crashing back through the doorway.

Brain Drain reacted with the grace of a professional, stepping in front of Mary and Nancy to shield them with his giant body. A club whanged off his side, sending sparks everywhere. Chipmunk Hunk and Koi Boi each faced off against their own attackers. Koi Boi held his ground, but Chipmunk Hunk was falling carefully back to cover Mary's other side.

Nancy darted out from behind Brain Drain, charging Hadrian. She must have figured he was responsible for this. But if he was, he'd been betrayed. Two alien attackers were going after him. Since he'd been at the front of the group, he had too many sides left undefended. He sidestepped one club, but would have stumbled right into the sweep of another if I hadn't kicked the second club away.

When my boot brushed the club, lightning arced across my ankle, over my leg, into the floor. Good thing I was still wearing Light-Horizon's spacesuit. My tail frizzed up, but more from adrenaline than shock as the suit kept my body insulated. I'd placed myself between Nancy and Hadrian. Nancy stopped just short of crashing into me.

We had to get out of the mess first, ask questions later. The good news was: we were doing great.

Koi Boi tripped his bulbous, frog-like assailant, knocking the alien to the ground. Chipmunk Hunk dodged his attacker, and then Mary planted her boot in its backside, sending it sprawling. It landed atop its own shock-baton, and convulsed. And Brain Drain was still absorbing blows left and right.

"OUCH," he said, and then added: "IS PROBABLY WHAT I WOULD HAVE SAID IF I COULD HAVE FELT THAT."

We had this. We could fight loose, escape, and stay safe.

Then I heard Hadrian speaking.

"... it was clear from the start that the attackers had the advantage on the hero and his companions, and they did not hesitate to cruelly press it ..."

I didn't know where the new attackers came from. I didn't even know if there *were* new attackers. All I knew was that, faster than I would have believed, my friends and I were encircled, and being pressed back into each other.

A shock baton landed in Chipmunk Hunk's stomach. Like the rest of us, he was still in his spacesuit and that gave him some protection, but the impact doubled him over. Mary yelled, grabbed the club by its insulated handle, wrenched it out of the alien's grasp, and jabbed it into the *alien's* stomach.

"Light-Horizon, was there any way you could have warned us we were about to get mugged?" Koi Boi asked.

"I was watching!" Light-Horizon's telepathic voice protested. "They came out of nowhere. I mean… like, literally, nowhere."

"The hero was caught completely by surprise, could not defend himself against the strange assailants, and fell," Hadrian said, distantly, and I suddenly realized he was on the ground. He shook as though he'd been shocked, which surprised the heck out of me, both because his voice was level, and I hadn't seen the elephantine, tusked alien standing over him until just now.

The mugger pulled his baton back, sparks still settling on the deck beneath Hadrian. Sure enough, there was a burn mark on the front of Hadrian's uniform.

"Fear pounded through the hero's heart. He tried to speak, but the brush of the baton had paralyzed him, robbing him of his voice as the universe once again realized his nightmares–"

"Oh, *crap*," I said, when I realized what was happening. My stomach fell through the deck.

Hadrian wasn't a telepath. His narration wasn't just putting information in our heads, or compelling us to act certain ways. No – when he spoke, he was *causing* things to happen. He was narrating reality. It made my head spin, but I couldn't think of many other ways to explain this.

"Going along with this may have been a bad idea," I said.

Nancy glared at me.

"… condemned to be alone, forever, lest those around him be dragged into his suffering–"

"Ouch," Brain Drain said again, this time with no follow-up.

More and more sparks flew from his chassis as harder blows landed. He took what sure looked like an involuntary step back.

"... hero could not help but watch as the prospect of companionship, dangled in front of him, was snatched away yet again, in the cruelest manner possible. When properly struck, the batons' shocks were lethal. His friends fell one by one–"

"Everybody!" I shouted. "Do what I do!"

When I was sure I had at least a fraction of their attention, I dropped to the ground. Just folded up like a collapsible chair. Like I said earlier, squirrels don't need dignity.

I hadn't been struck by a baton, or caught off guard by anything. I fell because I made myself. The important thing, though, was that I had done it. Exactly as described.

Nancy boggled at me between dodging batons. "*What?*"

The tusked alien I'd been fighting stepped over me, unconcerned. It must have known that it hadn't hit me with anything, and that I shouldn't have fallen. But it was suddenly heedless of me.

Brain Drain's assessment of heroism had been onto something. Hadrian saw himself as a hero, all right.

The hero of a tragedy.

Nancy and I had been through more in the past year and a half than most people have in three lifetimes. We'd fought frost giants from Jotunheim, tag-teamed giant robot dinosaurs, and, most stressful of all, studied C++, Fortran, and Haskell together. Our friendship was tighter than any other I'd experienced with another human. We had a couple of emergency buttons – things to say only when we really, truly meant it. I slammed my hand on one of those now.

"*Trust me,*" I said.

A fraction of a second later, Nancy dropped, albeit a little more gently than I had. Her attacker didn't even shift his gaze to follow her on the way down. It was as though she had stopped being its concern as soon her butt hit the deck.

"I mean everyone!" I yelled. I grabbed Koi Boi's ankle, but didn't have to yank. He got the message and dropped. Mary went next, although not without a roll of her eyes as she realized what I was trying to do.

Hadrian's words were narrating things into reality. It seemed like, one way or another, the things he said were going to happen. The force of his narration was going to bowl us over unless we played along.

One by one – just as Hadrian had described – we fell. Brain Drain was the last to drop. He hit the deck like a bag of bowling balls.

"Oof," Brain Drain announced.

"Watch my tail!" Chipmunk Hunk hissed.

Just like that, the fighting was over. The aliens stood over us, unmoving. For verisimilitude, I closed my eyes.

Hadrian said, "When the chaos of battle cleared, the hero found himself alone amidst the carnage. His assailants had swiftly and mercilessly dispatched his companions, and, with practiced efficiency, checked their bodies for paper, data media, or anything else that might hold precious literature."

I only just managed to resist the urge to object as one of the muggers patted me down. Just across from me, I could *feel* Nancy biting her tongue to do the same.

If any of the aliens were concerned that we were faking dead, they showed no sign of it. If my friends and I had sprung back into action, I was confident that, in ordinary circumstances, we could have taken them down in seconds. But we weren't fighting *them*. If we tried to fight again, we'd be beaten back just as suddenly.

Nancy had told Hadrian *This isn't your story*. To him, though, it was, and we were minor characters.

"The bandits did the same to Hadrian, ripping open his uniform and pilfering the folded papers the hero had secreted there," Hadrian said, as exactly this happened. "It was a mixed blessing that they had mistook him for dead rather than paralyzed, for at that moment the hero would welcome an end to his struggles. The muggers did not kill him, but, having found their booty, merely left him for dead. They disappeared into the shadows whence they came with not even a glance at the misery and tragedy they had left behind."

On the other side of group, Mary made a noise halfway between a snort and an annoyed grunt. I kicked her shin, and she stopped.

A long minute passed before Hadrian haltingly got to his feet. He moved shakily, as though just recovering after a bad shock. He fell to his knees beside me.

"The hero wept, disconsolately," he said, deadpan.

I cracked an eye open. His expression was the same as it ever was.

"Trouble and misfortune followed him as a pestilence," he said. "The hero had realized this before, but never had the courage to admit it to himself. The evidence was irrefutable. He was cursed. He should not have tried to seek companionship, for he had known, deep in the recesses of his nightmares, that this would be the outcome. As it had for all of the times before."

Part of me wanted to say, "Aww, buddy," and let him know that he was going to be all right, too. I very nearly did. What stopped

me was his tone. Dispassionate. Clinical. Most of his attention
was going into sentence construction[38] rather than feeling what
he professed to feel.

There might have even been a little glee in it. The same kind
of excitement authors felt when putting their characters through
awful things.

We were not dealing with Hadrian. I was not sure "Hadrian"
was real. We were dealing with Hadrian's narrator, and Hadrian's
narrator was a jerk.

At length, Hadrian stood. "He accepted now his lot in life,
though that was different than coming to peace with it. He was
doomed. Everyone around him would share his fate, either from
happenstance or his *dark past* catching up with him – and so it
would be best if he marched off to meet it alone."

He turned, and trudged down the corridor. I listened to his
footsteps recede.

Once he was gone, I propped myself up by my elbows. Nancy
let out a long-suffering sigh just as dramatic as anything Hadrian
had said.

(She puts up with things so well. I love her.)

"Life outside the molecular cloud sure is exciting, huh?"
Light-Horizon asked telepathically.

"I would like," Koi Boi said, "to speak with the editor."

---

[38] FREELANCE EDITOR HULK AVAILABLE FOR HIRE. NO JOB TOO
PUNY. RATES REASONABLE. (P.S. ARGUE WITH RATES TO MAKE
HULK SMASH.) – ED

The Unbeatable Squirrel Girl Vs The Space Station Blues

Three days later, we had settled into a routine that was almost comforting in its domesticity.

I didn't know where Nancy had gotten the needle and thread. She sat in our quarters, at a desk we'd built from scavenged junk at the market, stitching up a hole an alien had torn in it yesterday. (They'd thought the material looked delicious. And, apparently, it was). Nancy held the sleeve under the lamp that Koi Boi assembled from a (once-broken, now repaired) flashlight and a table clamp.

Even the Mad Thinker camped out in our quarters. After he'd had his quiet little breakdown, he'd come along with us. He didn't have anywhere else to go, or anyone to watch his back while he slept. He said little to us, except when he wanted to provoke us for petty reasons of his own.

One of the many complaints we had about our quarters was about the poor lighting. It hadn't taken us long to realize, though, that it was a hidden blessing. The lights elsewhere on this level couldn't be turned off. Though that red-orange light was softer than daylight, it was alien, somehow piercing. It got underneath your eyelids and painted your imagination in that overwhelming, monolithic color. I didn't want to think about what it would have done to my dreams.

I set today's share of nutribricks on Nancy's desk. The bricks – exactly as appetizing as they sounded – were the most acceptable food source we'd found so far on the station. Nobody needed to carve off chunks of ourselves. The bricks didn't have all the nutrients a human (or squirrel) needed. No proteins, no vitamins. But they had enough simple sugars and other carbohydrates common to life throughout the galaxy to keep us going for a while.

She didn't look up. "I would thank you, if I were looking forward to those."

"That's fair."

Our quest for answers continued. Yesterday, Brain Drain had written a particularly incisive Spenserian stanza about deontological versus teleological ethics. He'd traded it for a beaten-up scanning device. Out in the market, he'd discreetly aimed it at the robots.

"If I am reading this correctly – a fact of which I am even less certain than I am of most things – then these machines are constantly sending bursts of radio signals."

"Chatting with their bosses," Nancy murmured. No, I wasn't sure why she was keeping her voice down. Brain Drain's speakers were blasting as loud as they ever did. "Can you tell who's getting those signals, or where they're going?"

"Not even slightly. The signals are omni
directional. If the robots themselves are receiving
orders, either I cannot distinguish it from
background noise, or the orders have been sent via a
narrow-beam signal I have an infinitesimal chance of
intercepting."

"Keep on them, buddy," I'd told him.

We'd traded more poems for mattress pads. I reclined into
mine. Tippy-Toe scrabbled from my shoulder into my neck. I
tossed my tail over both of us to keep us warm, and block what
light there was.

All our clothes were in pretty poor shape, to be honest.
The super heroics business isn't always glamorous, especially
when you're stuck in space trillions of miles from the nearest
costume shop.[39] A water pipe with a cobbled-together tap
spigot provided our water. It was enough to do laundry, but
you would not believe the opportunities this place gave you
to stain your clothes. I'll spare you the details about those
other than to say that some of the gelatinous aliens aren't
familiar with human norms of personal space. You have not
experienced adrenaline until an alien tries to budge ahead in a
line by engulfing you[40].

Our spacesuits were propped up against the wall. They were
too clunky to wear around casually, and you do *not* want to know
what the inside of those suits could smell like after days spent
inside.

---

[39] An astoundingly useful resource for the up-and-coming or frugal super hero!
Especially during post-Halloween sales. My squirrel-ears headband came from
one. – SG
[40] IF HULK ENGULFED BY RUDE ALIEN, HULK SIMPLY PUNCH WAY
OUT. – ED

We took turns managing our daily tasks. Today was my turn to discreetly trade our poetry crop for nutriblocks and information. Koi Boi lay on a mat, his arm over his head, plainly trying to sleep. From his long, drawn-out sigh when I entered, though, he didn't seem to be having much success.

Chipmunk Hunk and Mary were huddled in the corner. It was their turn to write poetry, which explained why Mary looked extra-miserable.

"Programming language ought to count as poetry," she was saying. "At least you can actually *do* something with it."

"My body runs on a programming language," Brain Drain said. He was also writing poetry, a tiny pen clasped in his enormous claw. It wasn't his shift, but he just liked doing that kind of thing. "My mind runs on philosophy. But my heart on poetry."

"Brain Drain," Koi Boi said. "Maybe that's not the counterargument you think it is."

"I have a heart," Brain Drain, who ran on microfusion power cells, said. "Poetically speaking."

"I would cringe at that if I weren't cringing already," Mary said.

Trying to get a bunch of STEM students to write poems was exactly as fun as it sounded, which made it as much of a delight as everything else on the station. I actually enjoyed writing poetry! Really! I try to enjoy everything, and there are a whole lot of words that rhyme with "butt".

Everything loses some of its joy when you have to do it for a living, though. This was business poetry, not pleasure poetry. Dangerous poetry, too. Having too much poetry, and being too good at it, would get you abducted by the station's overseers. None of the aliens we spoke to knew what happened after that.

You wanted just enough to pay the overseers' tolls to move from place to place.

Chipmunk Hunk made a valiant attempt to change the subject. "Any sign of Mr Tragic Hero?"

Hadrian was still out there, somewhere. I'd asked around, and a few aliens had seen a person matching his description, haunting the far corridors like a lost specter. You don't even have to be in the super hero business to recognize a superpower when you see one. Just open eyes and an open mind. Whatever Hadrian had, it was definitely a super... something. The more I thought about it, the more powerful it seemed.

For now, it seemed wisest to stay out of his way. I wasn't sure we could find him if we wanted. After the ambush, he seemed to be staying away from public areas like the market. Afraid of his "bad luck" harming people around him.

That seemed to mean *some* level of conscience. Although whether it was genuine conscience, or a narrator trying to evince conscience, was a real question.

"I'd much rather never see him again," Nancy said.

I shrugged. "Maybe." I still wasn't sure how much of the person who'd been narrated to us was real. It seemed worth finding out.

Our space whale friend, now going by Rolling-Pulsar, confirmed that Hadrian was still somewhere in the station. "He's got a very peculiar mind-feel," they said. "Bitter on the outside. Bitterer on the inside. With a soupçon of depression."

"But you can't tell us where he is," Koi Boi said.

"Not *can't*. *Won't*." When the rest of us expressed our indignation, they said, "Look, when *you're* a powerful telepath, *you'll* figure out real quick to keep your probing to a minimum. I read emotional impressions and language centers only. If I wanted to find out more, I'd have to do mind-reading. And I don't do mind-reading without consent."

"Wish the X-Men were here," Chipmunk Hunk groused. "Charles Xavier wouldn't hesitate."

"Yeah? Maybe Charles Xavier is a bad person," Rolling-Pulsar said.

We'd been over all this before. The only exception to Rolling-Pulsar's principles had been about locating the poetnappers in charge of the station. After a long discussion with Brain Drain about consequentialist theories of ethics and the unintentionally harmful effects of absolute codes of conduct, Brain Drain had come out on Rolling-Pulsar's side.

It was up to us to locate the poetnappers. So far, no luck. We'd made some connections here, but no one claimed to know them. The robots standing guard at the airlocks were their only representatives.

"One thing I *can* tell you, though," Rolling-Pulsar said. "No ships have left this region since I got here. Not even the pirates. Unless the poetnappers have got some kind of portal or wormhole thingy, the beings they've abducted are probably still aboard the station."

"No sense in letting your merchandise out of sight until you're ready to transport it in bulk," the Mad Thinker said.

The Mad Thinker sat in the corner with his back to us, like a kid in time out. He stayed out of most of our conversations but plainly eavesdropped on all of them. He'd said airily, "Our chances of returning home are such that they seem to require one of those interminable hero-villain team-ups."

He didn't rotate work shifts with all the others. All he did was work on poetry. He'd scrounged up a bigger notepad than the rest of us. He wouldn't say where he'd gotten it or how he'd paid for it[41]. He'd already used up half its pages.

"You can't calculate your way to maximally efficient poetry?" Nancy had asked him, the first time he'd started scribbling.

"I'm trying," he said, apparently missing the barb in her question. "It seems like I have a perfect plan when I start, but it never comes out as I imagined."

"Sounds about right," I said.

"I don't understand it," the Mad Thinker snarled, tearing out a scrap of paper and balling it up. "I love the ideas when I have them. But not when they're on the page!"

"Sounds about right," I repeated.

The Mad Thinker wasn't all poetry pratfalls and hijinks, though. Every once in a while, he roused himself to prod and irritate us.

"Have you told the others that you wouldn't go home if you were offered the chance?" he asked me. "Or, in spite of their laggard wits, have they figured it out for themselves?"

Nancy looked up from her needlework. The others stared at the Mad Thinker, and then at me. Brain Drain's eyes rotated particularly ponderously.

"Oh," the Mad Thinker said, sounding disappointed. "Neither of the above."

"Doreen," Nancy said. "Is that true?"

"Well…" Actually, the Mad Thinker had undersold things. I hadn't even admitted it to myself, not until he'd mentioned it. "There's a lot going on out here right now. Poetnappers, interstellar wars… I think we can make a difference."

---

[41] Paper, or paper-like materials, was in not-so-astonishingly short supply on a space station without trees and whose economy revolved around creating literature. – SG

"*Doreen Green*. We have finals."

"I can multitask!"

"I enjoy lying to myself too," Mary said cheerfully from her seat beside Nancy. "Sometimes."

"Okay, fine. Maybe I can't multitask things trillions of miles apart." My tail lashed back and forth. "But all this stuff is important, isn't it?"

"So is looking out for *our* world," Nancy said. "Not to mention ourselves."

"Yes, that's important, and I wouldn't stop any of you from going back. But I also know that there are people out here *now* who need help, and we can get it to them."

"We're going to be undergraduates until we're forty," Nancy said as she massaged her temples.

"Look at it this way," I said. "None of this matters because, to get home in the first place, we're going to have to do *something* to get out of here. That means making things better here."

"Exactly," Koi Boi said. "We want to get home, we help."

He looked at Chipmunk Hunk who, after a glance at Mary, nodded.

The Mad Thinker had provoked this argument deliberately. I glared at him. He didn't even give me the satisfaction of seeming pleased with himself. He only looked bored.

"You don't *have* to be a jerk," I told him.

"Freedom of choice is an illusion," he said, looking to Brain Drain for confirmation. Brain Drain, for once, did not take the philosophical bait.

"If I've learned anything about spacetime, it's that nothing is set in stone," I said. "And, frig – even if this *is* a completely deterministic universe in which everything is already set in stone, from our perspectives, that doesn't make a darn bit of difference! We still have the experience of making choices regardless."

"WHAT SHE SAID," Brain Drain said.

"You only have the 'experience' of making choices because you can't see far enough ahead."

I furrowed my brow. The Mad Thinker steadfastly refused to meet my gaze. The more I learned about him, the more horrifying his worldview seemed.

It wasn't just others that he saw as easy-to-predict automatons. To some extent, he saw himself the same way too.

"Leap before you look," I told him. To the others, it must have sounded like an insult of the short-walk-off-a-long-pier genre, but I knew otherwise, and I was willing to bet he did too. He looked at me, eyebrow raised. "You might find a new perspective on experience."

"WHAT SHE SAID," Brain Drain repeated.

I should have been tired. A few minutes ago, I'd been ready to doze off with Tippy-Toe on my neck. But now I was agitated.

Being a super hero gave you some good excuses to take walks to clear your head. Back home, we called them patrols. There was always some crime to fight, some good to do, and that was a hundred times as true on this station as in New York. Once Nancy finished with my sweater, I donned it and my squirrel-ears headband and headed out.

There were always crimes to stop, things to investigate. Yesterday, Tippy-Toe had been jitterier than usual the entire afternoon (or what passed for afternoon here). She constantly crawled from shoulder to shoulder, nose twitching. "I swear I'm smelling squirrel."

"There's a lot of strange smells here," I told her. Once I thought I'd caught the scent of falafel, but it turned out to be some alien's skin sheddings.

"Don't patronize my nose," Tippy-Toe said.

"Sorry," I said.

"You're forgiven," Tippy-Toe said magnanimously. "Keep your eyes peeled for squirrels."

You might have thought Tippy-Toe would have been happy to see another squirrel, but she's no fool. Squirrels don't like to leave Earth. A squirrel here either would have meant some kind of alien squirrel[42] ... or someone trying to trick or entice her. Or us.

Today, the market was as much of a hubbub of bustle as usual – so far as I could tell, there was no such thing as a commonly agreed upon day-night cycle here – but a murmur spread through my little section of it when I stepped in.

My friends and I were already getting a reputation. Some aliens bowed, nodded, or tried to give me free slips of poetry (that I felt obligated to turn away). Others spat or dripped or gooped on the deck when they saw us. Since I didn't know the nuances of alien expressions, I chose to interpret that as being friendly.

Folks knew there were crime-fighters on the prowl. Very few of the aliens we aided turned away from us anymore, like the first alien I'd helped. We'd been here long enough, and behaved consistently enough, that even the jerks among them trusted us not to hold them up or charge for our services. I'd started to get to know some of the regulars.

---

[42] Of course, Tippy-Toe believes her nose is honed enough to detect that. – SG

A handful of alien teens[43] were there almost every day. They'd become stranded here with their parents and didn't have anything better to do than lounge around and do teen things. That made them a good source of gossip. Sarcastic and not necessarily accurate gossip, but better than nothing.

There were too many aliens around here to get to know them all, but I had started to recognize some of the larger groups. Every day, a cluster of leathery-skinned, rhino-horned aliens in monk-like robes gathered at the center of the market, silently and devoutly writing poetry. They didn't seem to know what was going on here. They presented their poetry to the robot guards even when they didn't have to go anywhere, and always with an air of holy dread.

On the rare occasions when the guards would take one of their members away, the rest would raise their arms to the ceiling as if in celebration.

There'd been eight of them when we'd first arrived. Now there were five. If anything, the monks were writing even *more* fervently than before.

"They think translators are *sacrilegious*," one of the teens explained to me later. The sarcasm layered in her voice was so heavy it might as well have had its own gravity. "People've tried to help them before. They won't even talk to anyone but the robot guards. Probably think they're being tested by their gods, or something."

There was so much to patrol. This market wasn't the only space like it aboard the station. There were dozens of others. The station

---

[43] Seven-foot-tall teens with indigo skin and eyes on the back of their bifurcated skulls, but, still, teens. Awkward and full of hormones and making bad jokes and ogling each other with the eyes in the backs of their heads when they thought they wouldn't be seen. – SG

not only snaked its windowless way all over the asteroid's surface, it burrowed underneath. There must have been tens of thousands of aliens aboard. We found more aliens who could confirm that this *was* the Milky Way galaxy, but, other than our space whale friend out there, hadn't found any species we recognized. No Sh'iar, no Kree, or the likes. Some aliens had heard of *them*, but not of Earth. It turned out the Milky Way galaxy contained hundreds of billions of stars, and that even empires that seemed impossibly huge from Earth's perspective could still be small in the grand scheme of the cosmos. Who knew?

I wasn't looking for Hadrian, exactly. I wasn't *not* looking for him either. I didn't know what I *was* looking for. Whatever it was, Tippy-Toe found it first.

"Squirrel," she said.

She was right.

There was a *squirrel*. Sitting atop one of the market stalls, scanning the crowd. Not an alien squirrel, either. (I've seen alien squirrels.) No purple or pink fur, no pointed ears, no flying around in an adorable squirrel-sized spaceship. Just a typical, healthy, adult eastern gray squirrel.

This was all kinds of wrong. Not only was there a squirrel *from Earth* on the other side of the galaxy, but it was exactly the kind of squirrel you'd find in Central Park. There could not have been a more obvious "I demand your attention, Doreen Green of Earth!" sign if those words had been written on a placard being smacked into my forehead.

The squirrel was watching the crowd. A half second after I spotted it, it spotted Tippy-Toe and me out of the side of its eyes[44].

---

[44] Squirrels, like most prey animals with eyes on the sides of their head, don't spot you by looking right at you. They have great peripheral awareness. – SG

It froze. I froze. Tippy-Toe froze, probably. I wasn't watching her.

The instant after the other squirrel got its wits back, it leapt off the top of the market stall and took off into the crowd. It ran from me as fast as it could.

"Oh, man," I said. "I'm feeling so many things right now."

"*Don't just quip!*" Tippy-Toe said, which was how you knew she was serious. She's usually all about the quipping. She climbed onto my head. "After her!"

The squirrel had been far enough away that even I couldn't read the squirrel's gender presentation, but I trusted Tippy-Toe's instincts. I bolted into a denser part of the crowd, barreling past elbows and tentacles and other, stranger appendages.

"Sorry!" I said as I rushed through. "Sorry!" And then, again, "Sorry!"

Anybody but a lifelong friend of squirrels would have lost our quarry in the crowd. But I've lived with and among squirrels everywhere from Ontario to the American Midwest to Central Park. I'd long ago learned how to trace the chaos and startled gasps that follow an unexpected squirrel leaping from shoulder to head to shoulder. Even among aliens, some things are universal.

Under different circumstances, I would have been suspicious that this squirrel was leading me into a trap. But she was doing too good a job of evading me. I had to strain every single one of my instincts to keep on her trail.

Eventually, even those weren't enough. The squirrel made it to a less-populated part of the market. There weren't enough annoyed and startled aliens for me to pick up a trail.

I stopped in between aisles of stalls, tail flicking back and forth because I wasn't sure of my balance and where I'd need to leap next. An eight-eyed octopoid in front of the next stall snapped its beak at me. The other aliens around didn't pay any attention to us.

All I could do was pick a direction and walk. "Beg pardon," Tippy-Toe said to every alien we stepped past, "but have you seen another one of me around?" Heroic reputation or not, the number of aliens willing to humor us could be counted on her foreclaws[45].

If this was some kind of trap, someone had set up the blind so well that they'd forgotten to hide behind it. I finally had to face the fact that I wasn't going to find the other squirrel like this.

But I was far from giving up.

---

[45] More squirrel facts! Squirrels have four claws on each of their front feet, but five on their hind feet. This is why squirrelese uses both base 8 and base 10 digits, and *that* is why squirrels are a lot sharper at math than they seem! – SG

The Unbeatable Squirrel Girl Vs Wholly Justified Paranoia

I made a show of looking confused and dejected, pretending to be looking for the other squirrel, and then left the market. After we'd taken a few twists and turns down one of the emptier corridors, I doubled back around.

Two nights ago, while exploring, Tippy-Toe and I had found a crawlspace in a corridor ceiling that led straight back to the market. It was only a twenty-foot jump off the ground. No problem for someone with both the powers of squirrel and the powers of girl.

"*Hup*," I said, bouncing from wall to ductwork to a ventilation duct with a loose grille. I tugged the grille off, slipped inside, and carefully replaced it behind me.

After two seconds of crawling along the duct, I was covered

headband-to-boots in grime, snagging my clothes on loose bolts. Nancy was going to be ticked. She'd just stitched up this sweater, and here I was, crawling around all sorts of things with sharp edges.

The duct emptied out into the market, in a shadowed gap in the dome ceiling high above the ground. The space up here was cavernous, a poorly lit dome full of old, half-functioning ventilation equipment. Aliens streamed heedlessly past below. I'd seen flying aliens, but even most flying aliens stuck to a dozen or so feet off the ground. There were too many obstacles up here.

It's a common feature of humanoids that they don't look up. Not unless they, like squirrels, evolved as prey animals in forests as labyrinthine and three-dimensional as Earth's.

So it was a mark in favor of our quarry being an *actual* squirrel when she spotted us.

The thing was, we'd spotted her just two seconds earlier. She'd been hugging the roofs of some of the market stalls, staying low, and peeking out only when getting ready to survey the aliens below before making a jump. Then she tilted her head in just the wrong way, and caught sight of us looming above her. Her tail went frizzy. Another point in favor of her being a real squirrel: she had the reflexes of one. She bolted.

Unfortunately for her, Tippy-Toe and I had the reflexes to match, and we had a two-second head start. Being able to take controlled leaps and land gracefully was just another trick in my bag of squirrel-powers. I landed atop the stall running.

She juked, evading my grab. Tippy-Toe nimbly leapt off my shoulder and crashed into the other squirrel. I caught both of them. The three of us fell off the stall's roof and rolled, bowling-ball-style, through a (mostly) empty aisle.

By the time we came to a stop, I had a grasp of the squirrel's scruff in my left hand. And Tippy-Toe's in my right.

I kept my grip tight enough to keep the new squirrel from getting away, but she had stopped trying to escape. She crossed her forelimbs and glared at me. Side-eyed glare like a squirrel, naturally, but a glare.

"A-ha!" I said, for want of anything else to say.

"Are you proud of yourself?" she asked.

"Yes!" I answered. "Also, after going through all that, I think we deserve to know: *what the heck?*"

"Yes, yes, you're doing a really good job of impersonating Doreen," the squirrel said. "I'm *so* impressed."

I have an extremely good memory for squirrel faces and names, but it's not infallible. A moment ago, I didn't think I'd ever seen this particular squirrel before. Now something in that expression tickled a memory. It took me an awkward moment to place it.

I *had* seen this squirrel before. But she hadn't usually appeared to me *as* a squirrel. I'd filed her name in my memory under a different face.

"G'illian?" I asked. "G'illian Blax'zthor?"[46]

"As though you didn't know!"

I blinked. "I mean, I do. You can show me your real self now."

That just made her glare sharper.

"Come on!" she said. "You're still expecting me to believe this? What are the odds of me running into Doreen Green all the way out here? It's like you're not even trying!"

"Hey, I'm trying really hard!" I said, because it was true.

---

[46] GESUNDHEIT. OR EXCUSE YOU. WHATEVER SITUATION CALL FOR. – ED

Okay, story time. G'illian *was* an alien – a Skrull, specifically –
but the last time I'd seen her had been on Earth. Those of you
really out of the loop, the Skrull are shapeshifting aliens from
the Andromeda galaxy. The Skrull Empire has tried to invade
Earth, successfully and otherwise, way too many times for
comfort.

G'illian wasn't any old Skrull, though. She was special. [47] And
I thought she'd been my friend. I was almost happy to see her,
but, if she was all the way out here, she was in big trouble. And,
frankly, that meant I was too.

Because she was right. It *was* too much of a coincidence to
believe that I'd find her all the way out here. If she hadn't planned
for it, and *I* hadn't planned for it, then someone else definitely
had.

Keeping a firm grip on G'illian's scruff, I glanced to our left
and right. Nothing leapt out to ambush us in our moment of
distraction. A few disinterested aliens sifted or slithered or rolled
through the aisle, ignoring us.

I've been accused of being a little *too* trusting and optimistic
about human – and alien – nature. This was a level of paranoia
I wasn't quite ready for. One of the first rules of fighting evil is
to understand it. That was what made Deadpool's heroes and
villains flashcards so useful. And one of the reasons why I felt
so adrift on here, far from anything even Deadpool knew about.

The same rules still applied. Know thine enemy, etc.
G'illian wasn't my enemy. Paranoia was. To beat it, I needed to
understand it.

"How do I know you're the real G'illian shapeshifted into a

[47] HULK HAS NOW BEEN INFORMED THAT G'ILLIAN BLAX'ZTHOR
FIRST APPEARED IN Unbeatable Squirrel Girl #37. – ED

squirrel?" I asked. "And not another Skrull shapeshifted into G'illian shapeshifted into a squirrel?"

She waved a claw across her fuzzy body. "No other Skrull could shapeshift into this."

"Oh. Right." G'illian wasn't just a shapeshifter like the other Skrull. She was a mutant. Yes, as in "X-Men" mutant. They have those in space, too! Her mutant power was that she could not only change her shape, like most Skrull, but her mass as well. She could shrink to the size and weight of a quarter, and then up to the weight of a hulking Hulk and back again.[48]

The Skrull Empire did not tolerate mutants. G'illian had kept her power hidden as long as she could. Even more anathema to the Skrull Empire, though, she didn't want to join any of their thousands of ongoing war efforts. As soon as the opportunity arose, she used her power to duck conscription and escape to a world that had faced down the Skrull countless times before: Earth. She'd spent months living as a squirrel in Central Park until we found each other.[49]

"All right, then," I said. I was starting to get the hang of this paranoia thing, though. "But this wouldn't be the first time someone's plucked something out of my mind on this trip. Then how do I know you're not a robot or a telepath or hallucination pretending to be someone I'd recognize?"

G'illian opened her mouth, offended, but then closed it

---

[48] Does this violate laws of conservation of mass? You betcha. Does it happen anyway? Also you betcha. Sometimes superpowers are better experienced than explained. You might as well ask Cyclops about where the energy for his always-on eye-beams comes from. Actually, don't. He doesn't like it. – SG

[49] HULK ALSO INFORMED REAL STORY MORE COMPLICATED, INVOLVING FAKED DEATHS AND ALSO IRON MAN, BUT THIS FAIR SUMMARY. – ED

again. She blinked. After a moment, she said, "Okay, that's a fair question. That is something Skrull Imperial Command would do."

"Tell me something only G'illian would know."

"No! That's something Skrull Imperial Command would do too! They'd *impersonate you* to get close *to me* so that they could learn something that would help *them* impersonate *me* to get close to *you!*"

"You're definitely more paranoid than G'illian was," I said, with a frown. "And that was already quite a lot." Back on Earth, she'd stayed away from me for months despite having learned enough about me to know I was as awesome and friendly as I was.

"I have very good reason to be," she said, putting her little squirrel-claws on her little squirrel-hips. "I'm being hunted by intergalactic shapeshifters."

"For heck's sake, Doreen," Tippy-Toe said, "she's the real G'illian. This all tracks. Remember when she impersonated Tony Stark just to avoid telling you the truth about the mess she was in?"

"I have trust issues," G'illian said, crossly.

I supposed that if anyone had license to have trust issues, it was G'illian. "All right, you're you. But... but, dang it, I thought we left you safe on Earth! With a job and friends and everything."

"I *was* safe on Earth, with a job and friends and everything," G'illian said. "Things were going all right until your Skrull assassination team arrived."

Hearing that drove a spike through my heart. "Assassination team?!" Tippy-Toe and I said, together.

"Acting tip: pretending to be surprised doesn't mean just being an echo."

"I'm not acting. It was an interrogative statement repeating the most surprising element of the previous sentence in the hopes of elaboration."

"Can you just assume I'm not going to cooperate and get to the next stage of the interrogation? The one where you pull your mask off?"

"Whoa, whoa, whoa," I said. "Let's step back and game theory this out."

G'illian looked appropriately skeptical, as you should whenever anybody uses a line like 'game theory this out', but I had a point to make. "There are a few possibilities we need to consider here. First, I'm a Skrull agent, trying to get information out of you. Second, *you're* a Skrull agent or a robot, trying to get information out of *me*. Which–"

"I know that's not true," she interrupted.

"… and I know I'm not a Skrull, but we can't prove that to each other, can we? But the third possibility is that we're both telling the truth."

"Right…" G'illian said, hesitantly.

"Right! So the key here is to make choices that maximize value and minimize risk in all the plausible scenarios. Look at it like a puzzle… or programming for machine learning. What choices will do the most good and minimize harm in all of these scenarios?"

"That video game AI course last semester was not a good influence on you," Tippy-Toe muttered in my ear.

"Hush," I told Tippy-Toe. But she was right about where I was pulling this from. That course had taught me a lot about how a program should attempt to understand human behavior that had multiple possible interpretations – like different opening strategies in a chess game. It *was* a helpful way of looking at things sometimes. So long as you didn't get carried away and remembered that people were people, not game pieces.

I slid to a seat against one of the stalls, and, trying to prove my good intentions, set G'illian the Squirrel on my knee and let go. She didn't bolt immediately. "As I see it," I said, "there's not much harm treating each other like who we say we are. I think it's safe to say that, at this point, we've recognized enough of each other that if someone really *was* impersonating you or me, then they already know so much that we couldn't give much else away, right?"

She was silent, considering this. She glanced to each side, checking her escape routes, but she didn't bolt.

"I'm going to hazard a guess that you're as trapped here as Tippy-Toe and I are," I said. "If neither of us trusts each other, then we lose what's *maybe* our best chance to help each other and get out of here?" In a softer voice, I added, "Not to mention a friend."

G'illian's head tilted sideways as the last of these equations clicked into place.

"I'm risking quite a bit of emotional harm if I let myself hope that you really are Doreen Green," she said.

"Same, friend," I said. "That's part of the super hero business."

With that, she hugged my knee and clambered up to my neck to hug it, too. And then also Tippy-Toe. She remained hesitant, and moved guardedly, but I think I illustrated the cost-benefit analysis clearly enough.

Tippy-Toe awkwardly patted her back. "Um. There, there."

"What the heck is going on?" I asked. "I have a thousand questions. Why didn't you change shape to get away from me when you could?"

"If you really were a Skrull assassin, you probably would have figured out that I can't change shape now," G'illian said. "So it's safe to tell you that I'm stuck."

"What? Why?"

Her tail flicked in agitation before she answered. She really didn't want to be talking about this. "Because the Skrull assassins zapped me with something to stop me. It got in my head, damaged my brain or something, because I can't shapeshift like I used to. When I realized they were coming for me, I changed into the first shape I thought of that would help me get away, a shape I knew, and this was it. Now I'm stuck like this *and* I'm not safe on Earth anymore."

The way her already-squeaky squirrel voice became even more broken made me not want to press further. There was some bad trauma under all that. Come to think of it, that almost certainly explained how she'd been acting.

No matter what Tippy-Toe had said, G'illian hadn't used to be like this. Something had messed her up good.

G'illian went on: "So I got in touch with someone we both knew, whose powers the Skrull couldn't convincingly replicate. Someone who I'm not going to identify if you aren't who you say—"

"It was Loki, wasn't it?"

She stuttered in just the right way to tell me that, yes, it had been Loki. "*Whoever* it was, they didn't trust themselves—"

"You don't need to worry about endangering Loki. He can protect himself."

"Fine, *Loki* didn't trust himself to do brain surgery with his powers, but he said that he was also a bit of an oracle, and that I'd find help out on this station. So I hitched a ride on the next alien tourist starliner out of the system, hopped ship a few more times, and got caught in this mess–"

Weird... I knew Loki pretty well, and I was fairly sure he couldn't see the future. He'd have gotten into *so* much more trouble with that than I (or he) could possibly have imagined. But I had to file that thought away for later. I couldn't get into any of this right now because of the adrenaline rush of hope.

Having taken that brief dive into grappling with paranoia, I understood what G'illian had meant by being afraid of hope. Hope felt incredibly dangerous. *"Does that mean you know how to get back to Earth from here?"*

"Kinda? I mean, I have a good nose for which ships are heading to which quadrant. And it turns out squirrel-sized bodies are good for hiding and stowing away on humanoid-sized things."

"Heck yeah, they are," Tippy-Toe, who always traveled New York subways fare-free, said. A conspiracy of squirrels, my favorite kind.

Most of me had stopped listening after G'illian had said *Kinda.*[50] "Look, if I'm a Skrull agent, I already know where Earth is, right? So it won't hurt if you lead my friends back there. That's the help we most need right now."

She tilted her little squirrel head as she considered. "O... okay, that's fair."

"I rate it more than fair. I rate it *excellent.*"

---

[50] Though not all of me, obviously. This letter is a complete and only-a-little-biased recounting of events as they happened. If you can't trust a Squirrel Girl for that, who *can* you trust? – SG

"First, we've gotta get off this station," G'illian said.

I shook my head. "We've got to stop all this." I waved vaguely at… everything.

"Good luck with that," G'illian said. "Just about everybody on this station has been trying to figure out who's keeping them prisoner. And the ones who look too hard disappear."

"Wait, what?" I asked. This was the first time I'd heard of that. Come to think of it, though, none of the aliens I'd tried to ask about our captors had seemed especially curious. Well, more like hostile, really. Or they'd hustled away from me like I was about to become the site of a meteor strike.

"Oh yeah. You wouldn't be the first trapped alien to look too closely into who's keeping us all here. Even the really villainous aliens would break out if they could."

"The cause of countless hero-villain team-ups through time immemorial," I said. "Someone else being jerks to both of them. I should've been wondering why that hasn't already happened."

"The obvious answer is that it *has* already happened," G'illian said. "And our poetnapping overlords put a stop to it before it threatened them."

"I wonder how they find out who's conspiring against them," I said. The robots guarding the airlocks, our captors' only visible presence, weren't everywhere. Maybe our captors had more complex surveillance than I'd guessed. Mind-reading, maybe. Or spies among their prisoners. Or maybe our captors were *among* their prisoners, pretending to be like them while keeping an eye out for conspiracies and brewing revolts.

It was suddenly far too easy to see everything around me as a potential threat, a traitor waiting to be unmasked. Man, thinking about everything through the lens of game theory is extremely annoying, and I don't recommend it. Going down that mental road with G'illian had been a mistake. I tried to clear my head.

"I'm still not convinced you're not a Skrull agent trapped on this station along with me," she said. "Using me to escape right before you arrest or kill me."

"I know you've got reasons to feel like you do," I said. "But I'm a friend. One problem at a time."

"No," G'illian said. "*Many* problems at a time. Nobody's going to be enthusiastic about getting free from here if that's just going to toss them into a war zone instead."

I snapped my fingers. "You're right." Usually, trying to break a big problem down into solvable chunks is the right way to go, especially in computer science. I'd gotten too bogged down in the details of everyday survival here. Unlike most CompSci problems, this crisis wasn't a combination of discrete steps that could be tackled one at a time. This was... more like a tree. The smaller problems were branches. Even if they went away, they could regrow from the root.

The root in this case being interstellar war. "The other thing holding people back is the fact that there's nowhere *to* go," I said. "There's a war about to happen out there. It's gonna set fire to all of the space traffic lanes, and kill anyone caught up in them. Most beings here are convinced that the pirate ships keeping them trapped here will at least keep them safe from the war."

All of our problems, from the local aliens' unwillingness to take on their captors to my friends and me being trapped here, stemmed from that root. Tear out the root, and the rest of the tree would topple. The poetnappers wouldn't have a hopeless, captive populace. My friends could safely get back to Earth.

We could get G'illian help for whatever the Skrull assassins had done to her.

"How long have you been here?" I asked G'illian.

G'illian gave me a little squirrel shrug. "I left my watch at home because it's about half my size now. Not really any clocks around here. Two, three weeks, maybe?"

"All of that can't be common knowledge. You didn't find all this out by talking with the locals." The locals had been terrified into keeping all their rebellious thoughts to themselves.

"No, but I'm great at hiding and have good ears."

I rubbed my chin, and then smiled. "You know, I haven't seen many tiny aliens around here. You and Tippy-Toe are probably the smallest sentient beings on this station."

"Oh, no," Tippy-Toe, who knew what I was thinking, said.

"We may not have the thousands of squirrels of New York here to be our intelligence network," I said, scritching Tippy-Toe's head. "But two's a good start."

The Unbeatable Squirrel Girl Vs The Poem Factory

The next morning, I made sure everyone was in our quarters – even the Mad Thinker – and, after checking to verify that nothing and nobody was out in the corridor, shut the doors.

"You guys are not gonna believe what we just discovered," I told the others. As soon as Tippy-Toe, G'illian, and I had figured it out, I'd come right here.

"I don't think I'm capable of disbelieving a single thing right now," Chipmunk Hunk said.

"Please, no dramatics," Mary said. Her migraine had kept returning. "That is, unless it's for something really cool."

"All right, all right," I said, because we were sure to get into plenty of arguments over the next few minutes and we didn't need to start now. Between our awful food supply, general exhaustion, and stress, we were running some serious risk of tempers fraying.

"You know the robots guarding the airlocks? The ones just lifelessly standing there day in, day out, collecting tolls and hauling the good writers away?"

"How could we *not* know them?" Mary asked.

"*They're* the poetnappers."

"I don't believe that," Chipmunk Hunk said.

I clapped my hands in triumph. "I *told* you you wouldn't!" It was nice to be right. In tough times, I took my victories where I could get them.

"The lifeless automatons that stand there looking straight ahead all day," Chipmunk Hunk said. "The faceless cops who don't care about anything except collecting tolls and kidnapping aliens. The ones we've verified are in constant radio contact with someone or something else. They're the ones obsessed with poetry."

"No," I said. "That's the point! They don't appreciate poetry, or probably even understand it, and that's why they're farming aliens for it."

They may not have had a sense for art, but they certainly had a cruel sense of humor. I should have paid more attention to them the moment they'd played that joke on me about the translator back when we came aboard. They were more malicious than they let on.

But just because they were cruel, that didn't mean they could be creative. They were the worst thing – something that even STEM and English majors could look down upon together: *business majors*. MBAs. *Managers*.

Unlike living beings who felt fear, interstellar war didn't strike any terror into their hearts. No fear, horror, or empathy clouded what they must have thought of as rational business judgment. They'd found an opportunity for profit: wartime poetry. They knew that poetry composed in the middle of wars, preferably from the trenches, commanded a premium price and long-lasting attention. They couldn't compose poetry themselves, they'd made themselves a poetry mine. A literature sweatshop.[51]

In AI theory, there's a problem – more of a doomsday scenario, actually – called the Paperclip Maker. Take a hypothetical super-intelligent AI. Task it with figuring out how to manufacture paperclips as quickly and efficiently as possible. It starts by designing better machines to make paperclips. Then it designs and runs factories for making paperclips. Realizing that it could make paperclips more efficiently with more brainpower, it designs better computers for itself to run on. It never stops thinking about the problem. Then it starts coming up with unorthodox solutions that never would have occurred to the people who made them. For instance, there's a whole bunch of things, like streets and cars and trees, that could be broken down to parts to serve the cause of making more paperclips. All those pesky complaining people around, too, had useful molecules that could be rearranged into more paperclips. And before you knew it, the AI had converted all of Earth into paperclips and was spreading out into the rest of the galaxy to convert all of it into paperclips, too. Not good, especially since natural selection suggests the only survivors will be talking paperclips, forever waiting to help someone write a letter.[52]

Someone, somewhere – maybe the leadership of an interstellar publishing house, maybe something even more inhuman and alienating – had instructed these robots to talent-scout poets and acquire their most valuable poems. They'd figured out an unconventional way to fulfill their orders. They held aliens

---

[51] DULCE ET DECORUM EST POSTHUMOUSLY PUBLISHING DEAD SOLDIERS' WARTIME POETRY. YES, HULK KNOW POETRY. ANGRY POETRY HULK'S FAVORITE. HASHTAG HIDDEN DEPTHS. – ED

[52] MAKES HULK SMASH! – ED

hostage in a poetry-based economy and abducted the most promising poets to pack off to war: the greatest source of tragic-ironic poetry and literary movements on Earth and elsewhere.

Nancy looked to the Mad Thinker. "I suppose you had this predicted from the start."

"You wouldn't have trusted me if I'd told you," the Mad Thinker said mildly. "That, in fact, if the idea had come from me rather than your friend, you would have viewed it with enough suspicion as to actually reduce your chances of making use of it."

Nancy raised her hand, ready to angrily object. Then she halted and reconsidered. "Nah, I'll give you that one."

"But you *can* help us now," I told the Mad Thinker.

He slid the hand on his chin back and forth. Since he would have predicted this turn of the conversation from the beginning, I figured his hesitation didn't come from surprise, but from genuine indecision. Several different futures had unraveled before him, and he was struggling to choose between them.

"Leap before you look," I said.

He didn't seem to hear me. When he spoke, his voice and his expression were opaque. "I can help you."

I met that flat stare, trying to divine from little hints and wrinkles which decision he had made. But I couldn't read anything.

He said, "You'll want me to calculate which groups would be most likely to help revolt against the poetnapper-robots. "I already have."

"Good," I said, hiding my unease. "There are well-meaning aliens trapped here along with the criminals. If we can put together a coalition to challenge the poetnappers, we might be able to break out of here."

"And then what?" Koi Boi asked.

"Tell me we get to go home," Chipmunk Hunk said.

"Then we stop this war before it happens and bring about interstellar peace," I corrected.

Across the room, eyebrows lifted.[53] Chipmunk Hunk and Koi Boi looked at each other. Mary blinked, frowned, and briefly stared off into space, as if this was the first time the thought of having anything to do with interstellar politics had occurred to her.

"I like that," Mary said. "Especially if we can enforce peace on the combatants by getting bigger guns."

"You'd probably need something the size of a sun," Chipmunk Hunk said.

"Don't be silly," Mary said. "That'd be impractical. We'd need something that would destroy a sun."

"Okay, first rule: *no destroying suns*," I said.

"If they come from binary or trinary systems, they'll have spares," Mary said.

Such a kidder, that Mary! Just in case, I changed the subject. "The aliens here have just hunkered down and accepted the war as inevitable. They don't believe there's any hope. You and I and everybody here knows how fast things can change when enough people have hope."

Chipmunk Hunk and Koi Boi both nodded. Brain Drain, to the extent that he had an expression, was unreadable – but I would have sworn I saw his brain dome tilt sideways.

"*Meddling*," Tippy-Toe whispered from my shoulder, tail flicking in agitation.

I'd taken my history Gen Eds. When victorious Roman

---

[53] Excepting Brain Drain, of course. And the Mad Thinker, though not because he didn't have eyebrows. He just wasn't surprised. – SG

generals marched through the city upon their return from triumphant battles or conquests, they supposedly hired people just to whisper into their ears a reminder that they were mortal. Big shades of that from Tippy-Toe. I resisted the impulse to glare, or even glance, at her.

This was what the super hero business was all about. Finding problems. Fixing them. Helping people. All of us knew that. I didn't understand this reluctance I was picking up from some of them. I rubbed my hands together, thinking about where and how to start.

"Doreen," Nancy said, "do you even know who's fighting, or what they're fighting about?"

"I do," the Mad Thinker said.

"Yeah. Right. Did you calculate that?" Chipmunk Hunk asked.

"No. I asked around."

I had too, but I hadn't found many more people willing to talk to me about the Itrayans and the Eradu, the combatants in the war everyone was bracing for. However lacking the Mad Thinker was in social graces, though, with his incisor wit mapping out conversations before he experienced them, I trusted that he could at least get more information out of the locals than the rest of us.

"We're going to need a lot more information before we dive in," Chipmunk Hunk said.

"We'll get it," I said, with a glance to the Mad Thinker.

"So," the Mad Thinker said, already sounding exhausted by the prospect of explaining this to us, "the Itrayans and the Eradu could have been galactic superpowers on a par with the Skrull, the Sh'iar, or the Kree ... if they had wanted to be. They have the technological capacity, the nanotechnology-based automated factories, to take millions of star systems by storm. But they've never shown interest in that. They stick to their own tiny little home planets. And so the grand sweep of galactic politics passes them by, and they have thus far sat around and done nothing."

"Until now," Koi Boi supplied.

"I said *rarely*, not never. The Itrayans and the Eradu have gone to war before. Three hundred thousand years ago, they went to war over a cause lost to history. It took tens of thousands of years for the quadrant to recover.

"Even by alien standards, the Itrayans and Eradu are... for as many times as I have planned out this conversation in my head, I still want for a better word than *alien*. Very few claim to understand them. I don't believe anybody even knows what they are fighting over. Their peculiar forms of speech resist translation. Whatever the causes, the last time they went to war, millions of beings perished because of them."

The reminder of the stakes chilled the others' skepticism. Even Tippy-Toe's tail stopped flicking. Brain Drain's brain dome straightened.

Time to press the point home. "We've stopped wars before," I said. "I don't need to tell you how many billions of lives are going to be affected by this. How many people could die and how widespread the suffering is going to be."

Koi Boi's jaw set. Chipmunk Hunk pressed his hands together and raised them to his lips.

"Are you with me?" I asked. I didn't want to go this alone.

But I would have if I'd needed to.

"Definitely," Chipmunk Hunk said. Koi Boi nodded firmly.

"The universe is replete with suffering," Brain Drain announced. "I cannot overemphasize the slimness of our odds of success. Many varieties of decision theory prize advise taking choices with an extremely low

PROBABILITY OF SUCCESS IF THE PAYOFF IS PROPORTIONATELY LARGE. I WOULD BE REMISS TO IGNORE THE CHANCE, HOWEVER SLIGHT OR IMPOSSIBLE, TO ALLEVIATE SO LARGE A SHARE OF THAT SUFFERING."

I looked to Nancy and Mary. Mary had pulled out her pad of paper and was busily scribbling. The muse of poetry could speak even to her when the subject of war and weapons came up. Nancy glanced at Mary, her lips set in a line.

"You don't have to go along," I told Nancy.

"I'd never leave you to face something like this without me," she said.

I hoped I had explained my perspective on this to her well enough. There was still something about hers that I wasn't quite grasping.

This was the kind of moment on which friendships hinged. Some kind of disconnect had split the air between us, and I didn't know why it had happened. The fissure had opened wide enough that none of us wanted to talk about it.

Whatever her reasons, the sources of her hesitation… I was glad she was with us. I wouldn't want to save the galaxy without her.

One more being I needed to check in with. I glanced at my shoulder. "Tippy-Toe?"

"You are going to owe me so many belly scratches," she said.

I grinned. Tippy-Toe would have seen the tremor in it, but I was starting to feel more like myself again. "Just say when," I told her.

"*When*," she said.

The Unbeatable Squirrel Girl Vs Genre and Tropes

G'illian had already found a few things that the rest of us hadn't managed yet. Like the commanders and crew of some of the pirate ships keeping everybody penned in.

They kept their identities to themselves. They would have gotten mobbed if anyone here had known who they were. But they didn't get everything they needed in orbit. They came through here to trade with each other, in person. Even goons needed to socialize.

They came in discreet groups, each no larger than three aliens. None were the same species. G'illian had been watching them for a while. She'd stalked them from the shadows, from vents and behind leaking pipes, and saw everything they did. They found quiet chambers, disused cabins, and talked quietly about trading water and fuel and plasma weapons cartridges.

They were the only ones that the robots didn't collect poetry tolls from at the airlocks. They mimed giving the robots tablets and slips of paper – and the robots mimed reading them – but, from her perch, G'illian saw that they were blank. It was just an act.

She pointed out a group of three in the market: a furry little guy with toothy white ridges all up and down his back, a humanoid with eyes where her ears should have been, and a dramatically cloaked alien with features hidden underneath something like a biker's helmet. They gave their papers to the robot guards, just like everyone else, but it was plain that these guys were special. The biggest thing that set them apart was that they moved with confidence.

The first time she'd noticed them, G'illian had thought that these aliens were in charge. It was only natural to wonder if the crews of the ships holding everybody hostage were the monsters behind the curtain. "Hey, yeah," I said. "Why *are* we assuming they're not the bosses?"

"Just keep watching," G'illian said.

This bunch was on its way out, but the airlock door was already grinding open. Another three aliens stepped through with just as much swagger as the last bunch.

That swagger disappeared when each group saw each other. In a very dangerous, very low-key kind of way, things became tense fast. Each group spread out quickly, visibly struggling to keep things seeming casual. The alien with the biker's helmet kept a hand near the pistol poorly concealed underneath its cape.

They nodded at each other as they passed by. Exchanged a few friendly-sounding words, but without quite ever turning their backs on each other.

"They don't trust each other at all," G'illian said. "Someone's playing them against each other."

That night, I filled in the others – all except the Mad Thinker, who'd taken one look at me and rolled into his sleeping mat – on all this. "Interesting fact about those pirate ships, my dudes," our space whale friend, today going by Malevolent-Logic, piped in. "They've got plenty of cannons and missile ports and other weapons all over their hulls, but some sides have more than others. They have their best firing arcs facing each other more often than anyone else."

"It'd be a shame if all those pirates found a good reason to turn all those weapons on each other," Mary remarked.

"It *would* be a shame," Nancy said. "There are a lot of civilians and innocents around, and I doubt those pirates are the discriminating type."

"I'm not sure there's anybody innocent here," Mary said, but, from the fact that she didn't raise the issue again, she seemed to have conceded the point.

"Worth knowing there's a fault line we could exploit," I said. "*Carefully.*"

There was someone else here who might be able to help us with that. And he seemed like he needed our help just as much as we needed his. When I started to describe Hadrian to G'illian, she shook her head. She knew exactly who I was talking about.

"The soap opera guy," she said. "Mr Dramatic."

"Officer Sad Sack," Tippy-Toe offered.

"Lieutenant Casting Call Reject," G'illian said.

"That's the one," I said. "Also, don't be mean."

"You know, everybody else around here figured out how dangerous he was darn quick," G'illian said. "Are you sure you want to mess around with him?"

"He needs help," I said.

"You've got that right," G'illian said.

"What did I say about being mean?"

Tippy-Toe found him first. She came scampering back from searching, bouncing from overhead vent to my hair to my shoulder.

"Sergeant Drama Club is hanging around in an atmospherics plant," she said. "Some of the pirates almost ran into him, and were about to gank him for eavesdropping on them. He told them that he'd hidden just in time and that they walked by without noticing him. And then they did."

"Are you starting to see what I mean about calling that talent a superpower?" I asked.

Tippy-Toe had been skeptical on that score, but she didn't argue now.

The air in the station had to come from somewhere. It turned out to have come from a production plant the size of Galactus's socks but with none of the charm or cute embroidery. It was like walking around in the universe's biggest, emptiest chemical factory.

Someone had built it with the aim of it being staffed by a crew. There was no sign of that crew now, but whether by dint of being maintained by someone we hadn't met yet or just by being built well, those machines still functioned.

From what I could figure by walking through the metal-and-rock labyrinth, the station's atmospherics plant drew raw material – oxygen, nitrogen, water, the stuff of life – from vast, pressurized reservoirs deep in the asteroid's crust. It churned through pipes larger than the space whale we'd ridden in on, and whirred around in tanks that sounded like the universe's most haunted cotton candy maker.

It made me hungry for cotton candy, because even haunted cotton candy is still cotton candy. But that could have just been days of nutribricks taking their toll on my imagination.

Shadows abounded. The unpredictable clinking, clanking, groaning noises seemed calculated to make any being jumpy. It was no wonder that the place was even emptier than some of the station's least-used back corridors. Coming here was just asking to be jumped.

Two kinds of people came to places like this: those like Hadrian, who really wanted to hide, or those who had business they absolutely could not conduct anywhere else. The kind of business that, if anybody overheard them conducting it, they'd draw weapons first and ask questions later. It was no wonder the pirate crews came here. It was the only place they could talk business without anyone else on the station finding out who they actually were.

Tippy-Toe and G'illian scampered ahead of me, jumping from pipe to pipe, scouting a clear path to Hadrian. They found him in the deep shadows, seated and hunched against a rusting gas tank. I took several deep breaths, in and out, and closed my eyes while I got myself into the mindset for this.

I didn't need to understand what I was about to do. I just needed to believe it.

I'd spent days going over my first melodramatic encounter with Hadrian in my head. Hadrian's world, and his powers, had rules. I *think* I had them figured out. If I hadn't, though, this was about to get incredibly dangerous. Heck, it was going to be incredibly dangerous even if I *had* figured them out. Just to be safe, I told Tippy-Toe and G'illian to keep back out of sight.

Then I stepped out from the shadows and sauntered toward Hadrian as casually as I could.

However much he'd kept his emotions bottled under his narration the last time we'd met, this time it was plain just from his expression that he was not doing well. His uniform was filthy and his eyes had shadows that hadn't been there before. He stared into space, dry lips moving as he narrated something angsty to himself. But that only lasted until he saw me.

His eyes locked onto me. He did something I'd never heard him do before, and cut himself off with a choke. His eyes went wide.

"Somehow, Doreen Green returned," he said in a hushed voice.

The last time he'd seen me, my friends and I had play-acted our deaths. I'd thought it obvious that we were faking – but that had been on our level of reality, not his.

"Hi there!" I said.

"The dead speak!" Hadrian yelped.

"Pretty lame, buddy," I said. Then I reconsidered that tack. Nobody likes a critic. "But it's an interesting start. Let's workshop that a bit, all right? I've been looking for you."

"Was she a hallucination, or a revenant? Doreen Green must have known that Hadrian had caused her death. Though it had not been intentional, intentions perhaps did not matter to the dead. Death and misery followed the hero like pestilence, and on the other side of the veil, the ghost might have recognized that – regardless of intentions – justice would best be served by dragging the hero back into death with her, bringing his ill-augured influence on the world of the living to its end–"

I swished my tail and bapped his nose. He started, staring wide-eyed at me.

Stick a squirrel-tail-bapping in your dramatic story and try to keep the mood.

"I'm not a ghost or a victim or anything that gosh awful dramatic," I told him. "I'm not even the comic relief." Being the comic relief buddy was just asking to be bumped off at the end of act two. I sat next to him, bunching my knees to my chest just like he was. Hadrian tilted his head. It was plain that he didn't understand. I wondered if his narrator did. "That's not the kind of story we're telling here."

For a moment, there was a curious owlishness in Hadrian's eyes. A hint of something on the other side of the tragic hero archetype. It was gone just as quickly.

I'd broken through the fourth wall. (It's one of the many things I'm good at.) I have to admit, it was satisfying seeing actual emotion in him. It was either a sign that I was doing something right or something very, very wrong, and was about to find out shortly.

"I'm your inspiration," I said. "I'm the character the big turn in your story hinges on."

"The hero listened, his heartrate slowing," Hadrian said. "Maybe there was sense to be drawn from her words… if only he could tease the meaning out."

"You want drama?" I asked him. "All right – here's the drama, because this is the scene when you tell me the truth. Confess *everything.* Tell me what your backstory really is."

Hadrian said, "It had been ages since the hero had told anyone the truth. He had gotten so twisted in his lies that he nearly believed them himself."

I raised my eyebrow. Rested my chin in my hand. Waited.

"Doreen Green was a hard interrogator," Hadrian said. "Looking at her, the hero did not see any alternative but to tell the truth."

And into my head it popped, fully formed.

Hadrian *was* a soldier. Like he'd said, he'd come to fight in the war between the Itrayans and the Eradu. But the uniform wasn't real. It was just a mockup. He was a mercenary. He hadn't been conscripted by any of the combatants, as much as he'd wanted to be.

He'd come from a planet of dramatists, storytellers, and artists. Reading between the lines, it was plain this meant people with powers like his own. Aliens who didn't quite fit onto the stage of our reality. Not all that different, really, than oddball heroes like Deadpool and (sometimes) like me. People who saw the shape of the stories they lived.

The others kicked him out. Hadrian might have said (in that other layer of narrative reality, *did* say) that it was because "ill luck followed him everywhere". Accidents and calamities struck him, and anyone near him, at the worst possible time. Like everyone else here, he was trapped on this station.

He'd marched off to war because he was seeking an ending to his story. The only end that might have fit the rest of it. It was like a… a meta-death-wish.

He thought he knew what genre he was in. I shook my head.

"This is an underdog story," I said. "It's about tiny, flawed, heroic people working against cosmic injustices. And it's not a tragedy. In an underdog story, the underdog never loses." That just wasn't what audiences wanted. In writing this, one of the things I've started to understand about storytelling is that writers are a part of their own audience, too.

"The hero continued to stare, nonplussed, as he tried to comprehend," Hadrian said. "But this time, he thought he could pluck a few strands of meaning from her tangled web."

"I'm on the team of the underdogs. That's how I came back from the dead. The heroes of *this* story just can't be put down. Especially not when things are at their worst. That just wouldn't be satisfying."

Maybe the smart thing to do would have been to leave Hadrian out of this. But I believed in him. I'd started to see something in him that I'm not sure anyone back at his home would have. He desperately wanted to be part of any kind of story other than the one he was telling for himself.

"The hero had been focused on the tragedies that surround him." After a moment's thought, he added, "But… he is not inured to the other injustices around him, least of all on this station."

He was in. For now. I smiled.

Some of the exhaustion that had marred his features earlier seemed to have vanished. "During the weighty pause, the hero measured his next words. In spite of himself, he was curious, and asked her what her plan was."

I opened my mouth to answer. Then stopped.

That wasn't a real question, at least not on this level of narrative reality.

In TV or comics, whenever a character tells you about a plan, if you, as a viewer, actually witness the discussion, that means the plan's going to fail when the characters execute it. If they whisper it to each other and don't let the audience in on it, though, then it's going to work in every detail. It's a basic law of tension and storytelling economy. After all, it'd be boring to hear about a plan in full detail and then just see it happen as advertised. [54]

Hadrian's superpower took his words and made them a reality. I wondered if that was the extent of it. Or if reality could push back into his narrative layer.

I pondered a moment. I'd tried speaking like he had before, but now I understood more about it. And only one answer seemed appropriate:

"In a hushed tone, the Squirrel Girl told him exactly what they would be doing next."

Hadrian listened to the line with an air of complete concentration.

He nodded slowly. "In spite of himself, the hero was impressed. This was, at the very least, going to be interesting."

---

[54] HULK NEVER SPOT THIS TROPE BEFORE AND NOW HULK MAD. SPOILS MANY THINGS FOR HULK. – ED

The Unbeatable
Squirrel Girl
Vs
Fire, Explosions, and
Other Big Budget Effects

All we had to do now was lead a revolution, build a fractious alliance of mostly criminals and pirates, stop an interstellar war between powerful megacivilizations, and cross trillions of miles of space to make our way back home.

And I'd promised Nancy we could do it all before finals week. With time to study.

Easy peasy.

Maybe.

Okay, not really, but confidence was half the battle.

As Nancy and I weaved through alien traffic in the market, I told her, "You can always start studying now."

"My textbooks are at home," Nancy groused.

"Between you, me, Chipmunk Hunk, Koi Boi, and Mary, I bet we could put together a pretty good study guide!" I said.

"We could do flashcards or something. I highly recommend flashcards."

Nancy paused before answering while we ducked under a many-tentacled floating orb. "I don't just need the material, I need the time," she said. "I'm going to have a heart attack if I can't focus on class soon."

"We all need emotional support before finals," I said. "Brain Drain is good at helping me keep things in perspective."

She could not give me the stink eye without losing her place in the crowd. "You know how many of my scholarships are GPA-dependent," she said. "This is serious business. Also, we're coming up on the robots. To the left."

"I see them." We were approaching the airlock we'd first entered. The same two robot guards stood watch.

Speaking of serious business – it was serious super heroing time. The key to taking out oppressors like the poetnappers was not to identify and disrupt their power base. That came second. More often than not, the first step was to show other people that they *could* resist.

The poetnapper-robots hadn't gone public with their identities. They were perfectly happy to let everyone captive here jump to the conclusion that they were servants, tax-collectors and toll-takers. Deception suited their purposes.

So, taking that deception away from them would… well, if it didn't harm them, it would at least *un*suit their purposes. So that would be something. Probably.

Brain Drain had kept up monitoring the poetnappers' radio signals. He still hadn't found any centralized source. There *could* have been one, with signals so well encrypted that they looked like background noise, but I doubted it. More likely there was no centralized command. Our captors operated in a distributed system, a neural network. The downside was that they had no obvious target to attack. The *upside* was that an attack on them anywhere was an attack on them everywhere.

Empire State's IT security courses had drilled into us, over and over, that the most reliable way to take down a distributed system was through an equally distributed denial-of-service attack.[55]

Tippy-Toe scrambled down my arm, into my hand. "Ready," she said.

"I love it when we have a chance for a fastball special," I said.[56]

In all the chaos and din of the crowd, the robots didn't seem to see the blur of oak fur and a pink bow until she was halfway to them.

The fastball special, the most famous team move in super heroics, traditionally worked by knocking the recipient off balance with the momentum of the flying super hero, and committing further violence from there. But the laws of physics didn't have our backs on that one. Tippy-Toe didn't have the mass.

Like justice-loving attack rodents everywhere, she'd learned to go right for their eyes – or, in this case, a black sensor strip along their heads that we figured functioned as the eyes. So what

---

[55] Basically, this is spamming a system with so many junk requests that it can't process them all, or determine fake requests from real ones. It's not the *best* way to take down a system (distributed or not). That's always going to be through "social engineering" attacks. Basically, manipulating people into letting an attacker in, through phishing emails or texts or some other similar scam. Be extremely careful about what emails you click on! Lacking that option, though, we went with this plan instead. – SG

[56] I wasn't sure I was allowed to commit a fastball special without calling it out first. Even out here, there were Laws. – SG

she did, as she flew by and bounced herself off the robot's head, was rake its strip of sensors with her claws. Never underestimate the strength or sharpness of squirrel claws.

Tippy-Toe glanced off the robot with balletic grace, and landed on an overhead vent.

Squirrel reflexes are no joke. Tippy-Toe was already bounding into cover before the robots raised their wrist cannons.

The robot with damaged sensors wheeled its wrist about, blocking its companion's shot at Tippy-Toe. The second robot didn't bother tracking Tippy-Toe anyway. It leveled its wrist cannon at me instead.

Nancy had slipped through the crowd. Its attention focusing on me gave Nancy the opening she needed to slip past the stumbling robot and *whang* the back of its head with her homemade club.

We'd gone over this beforehand. Neither of us seriously expected a club, no matter how strong, to take out one of these robots with a single blow. Its memory and processors were almost certainly hardwired to deal with shocks. *Sensors* were a different kind of hardware altogether, though. By necessity, they had to be, uh, sensitive. Much more difficult to shield against shocks.

The robot stumbled ahead, knocked off balance and disoriented. I broke into a run. By the time it managed to straighten itself out and get its wrist cannon aimed at Nancy, I was on its back, wrenching its arms behind it.

Without having tangled with these robots before, I had been afraid that my squirrel strength wouldn't be a clean match for whatever these were made of. I was relieved to find that wasn't the case. (And also relieved that these were robots, and so I didn't have to hold back from family-unfriendly violence.) I slashed through that robot, and then its wildly-gesticulating partner, so efficiently that even the Mad Thinker wouldn't have found much to criticize.[57]

They fell onto the ground in pieces. Gauging the emotions of alien beings (heck, even assuming they *have* understandable emotions) is problematic at the best of times. But it was easy to read the sudden stillness around us as shock. Nancy, Tippy-Toe, and I had taken down the airlock guards in under ten seconds.

After another moment of this stillness, chaos erupted.

I was ready to dart aside to avoid a stampede, but none of the aliens were taking advantage of the guards' absence to dart through the airlock toll-free. They were all bolting away. From us.

Of course, we weren't the first to have attempted to take on our captors. We'd heard what had happened to those who'd tried. So had the aliens. That was why they were running.

"And another thing," Nancy said, dusting off her hands and picking up our last conversation, "if I don't see my cat soon, and if she doesn't see me, both of us are going to lose our friggin' minds."

"Mew is a strong, dignified creature," I said. "She can handle herself."

---

[57] Fun and occasionally useful Squirrel Girl fact! I have claws! (Really, check all the fan wikis! They're canon! I'm not making them up! My claws are not always-on, but I can bring them out when I need them. They *snikt* out from my knuckles like a certain X-Man's. I don't like to use them, because I'm not *that* kind of super hero, but they're there. This was a perfect opportunity to use them. Like Saturday morning cartoon writers around the world have discovered, violence against robots doesn't seem as awful as violence against biological beings. Whether or not this is fair is an exercise left to the reader. – SG

"Mew," she said, "got stuck in a wastepaper basket the other day."

"She would have gotten out eventually!"

Nancy and I weren't doing this alone. Our other friends had broken into teams to attack the robots in the other places we'd seen them. Mary and Chipmunk Hunk were going after another pair, and so were Koi Boi and Brain Drain. We couldn't follow their progress from here, but I had no doubt they were acquitting themselves well.

According to aliens who'd witnessed it, the last several times the robots had been attacked they'd had reinforcements roll out of concealed cubbies in the corridors, wrist cannons already hot and ready to fire. They'd annihilated the wannabe rebels, anyone standing nearby them, and anyone who'd tried to use the confusion to slip through the airlock toll-free. Mary and Nancy had discreetly investigated them. They'd found all different kinds of fluid feedlines, pumps, and storage vessels. Nancy said it reminded her of things at Empire State University's 3D printing lab. That was her best guess as to what those niches were: 3D printers that could flash-manufacture any number of those robots.

The overhead lights flickered. The deck *thumped* underneath our boots.

Mary had made some gifts for the newly manufactured guards. She'd scavenged some empty antimatter storage vessels from the market. To her immense disappointment (and my equally immense relief), the vessels hadn't had any antimatter left in them. They had, though, powerful magnetic containment systems. Magnetic containment systems that, with Mary's expert tweaking, could be converted into EMP grenades. She'd rigged them to go off just as the cubbies were opening.

I was under no illusion that we'd located all of the robot printers. But I was willing to bet that we'd found enough to make a difference.

"And last week, we had to rescue Mew from the top of the refrigerator," Nancy said.

"And we shouldn't hold that against her if she learned–"

"Twice."

"There was a second time?" That was genuinely news to me.[58] The things I miss while I'm out on patrol. "Dang. But our neighbors are still going to check up on her."

We lingered in front of the market's airlock, arguing long enough to demonstrate, to those aliens still watching, that retribution hadn't come crashing down on us.

Mary hadn't been able to make enough EMP grenades to cover all of the robot-printers. We certainly hadn't found all of them, either. But this was a start.

"Let's see what else they've got!" I said. When it was time to eat nuts and kick butts, I was a bottomless well of energy.

And I would need it.

Deep-throated, low-to-the-point-of-being-subsonic alarm klaxons reverberated through the station. I'd wondered if there would be any. It didn't seem likely that the robots that ran the station would have needed them. Then again, they wouldn't have needed all the life support machinery, either. If they had hermit-crabbed into a station that someone else had built… it

---

[58] Mew is honestly extremely smart but, as the Mad Thinker demonstrates, extremely smart people can extremely, smartly talk themselves into doing awfully unwise things. – SG

only made sense that security wouldn't have been set up for their needs. This whole system was exactly as much of a hodge-podge as it felt.

With the robots and robot-printers incapacitated, at least temporarily, we had to worry about their other means of exerting power. At the top of that list: their pirate lackeys. The alarms would get their attention, at least.

We had a man on the inside for that.

Last night, I'd followed Brain Drain to the same life support factory where I'd found Hadrian. G'illian and Tippy-Toe had scouted out the pirate crews' gathering spots. I clambered along pipes and vents overhead, lingering in the shadows to make sure that our spy's insertion went as planned. Ahead, three alien pirates shared drinks in the dark.

"GREETINGS, FELLOW PIRATES," Brain Drain boomed.

He strolled straight toward the pirates. Their hands twitched toward their concealed weapons, but they didn't draw. I've mentioned before that the secret of Brain Drain's "Brain Drayne" disguise was that it was so obvious that everyone immediately believed that it couldn't be a disguise.

The same trick worked here. After all, if Brain Drain knew who they were, then he knew how dangerous they were, and he wouldn't possibly have been ridiculous enough to approach them like this. The only being brave enough to act like that would be another pirate.

Brain Drain knew this as much as anyone. And he loved it more than the rest of us. He wore a strip of black fabric around his brain dome. His left eye bobbed in and out, but mostly stayed hidden behind it.

The nearest alien rolled its eyestalks. "Keep your bleeping voice down, friend."

Honestly, that was what I heard. Our machine translator must have had some modesty.

"I CANNOT CONTROL THE VOLUME OF MY VOICE," Brain Drain said. "IT IS A SIDE EFFECT OF MY PROSTHETIC TORSO, LUNGS, HEAD, AND OTHER ORGANS."

The pirates were no strangers to workplace injuries or prosthetics. After a moment's thought, they nodded in solidarity.

"Bleep," the same alien said grudgingly. "'Suppose that's fair."

"IT IS ACTUALLY EXTREMELY UNFAIR," Brain Drain said, "AND YET I MAKE THE BEST OF IT. IT IS THE SUBJECT OF FAIRNESS THAT BRINGS ME TO YOU."

He had their attention and professional respect, which meant they treated him like they treated each other: with suspicion. Pirates from different crews didn't mingle. An alien with a beak the size of my forearm asked, "What are you doing here? Your captain send you?"

"THE MASTERS OF THIS STATION PROMISED OUR CREW OWNERSHIP OF A PLANET IN EXCHANGE FOR OUR SERVICES." Brain Drain raised a claw. "YOU MAY THUSLY ANTICIPATE OUR SURPRISE WHEN WE DISCOVERED THAT THE SAME PLANET HAS BEEN PROMISED TO THE CREW OF ANOTHER VESSEL."

The aliens, to the extent that they had readable moods, seemed suddenly uneasy. They either looked at or rotated their eyestalks to face each other a moment.

"You were promised a planet?" a frog-faced alien croaked.

"We can't discuss compensation," the beaked pirate said.

The others ignored the beaked alien. "We're just being paid in bleeping mining rights and stock certificates," the alien with the eyestalks said.

"THAT DOES NOT SEEM LIKE SUFFICIENT COMPENSATION FOR THE GROSSLY MORALLY OBJECTIONABLE ACTIONS OF EXTORTION, KIDNAPPING, AND THEFT OF INTELLECTUAL PROPERTY," Brain Drain told the eyestalked-alien. "IT WOULD BEHOOVE YOU TO MAKE SURE THAT YOUR PAYMENT HAS NOT BEEN PROMISED TO ANOTHER PARTY. WE BELIEVE THAT OUR EMPLOYER INTENDS THAT NOT ALL OF US SHOULD SURVIVE TO RECEIVE OUR JUST REWARD."

They looked at each other, and back at him. They were on the edge of believing him, but the "just reward" wordplay might have gone too far. From high up in the shadows, hoping that one of Brain Drain's drifting eyes saw me, I waved my hands forward to push him on. He needed more to convince them he was one of them.

Brain Drain's drifting left eye passed over me. I think he understood.

"ARRRRRR," Brain Drain told them.

Brain Drain had kept working overnight. He insisted he would do better without sleep.

"I REITERATE THAT SLEEP IS A WAKING NIGHTMARE FOR ME," he said. "I WOULD MUCH PREFER THE SISYPHEAN WORK OF HEROISM TO THE PRISON OF MY OWN IMAGINATION."

"Always looking on the bright side," I said. "Don't burn yourself out."

"I HAVE A VERY LONG FUSE," he said. "ATTACHED TO A SIZEABLE EXPLOSIVE."

He was still working at it this morning. As the alarms

continued to blare, I spotted him entering the market with a new trio of pirates.

"IT IS A COMMON TACTIC OF MANAGEMENT TO PREVENT EMPLOYEES FROM DISCUSSING THEIR PAY RATE WITH THEIR COWORKERS," he was saying. His voice stood out clearly above the klaxons. "IT PREVENTS THEM FROM RECOGNIZING INEQUALITIES, FAVORITISM, OR OUTRIGHT FRAUD."

At that same instant, more pirates ran in from a neighboring corridor. I recognized them instantly: eyestalks, beak, and frog-face from yesterday. They recognized Brain Drain just as instantly. Their hands twitched toward their weapons.

If Brain Drain was caught off guard, he reacted quickly. "AVAST, FRIENDS," he said to his current companions. "IT IS ONE OF THE CREWS THAT HAVE BEEN PROMISED YOUR PAYM–"

He didn't have the chance to finish that sentence before his current companions drew their weapons, too. He ducked out of the way of a blistering, crackling barrage of laser rays and plasma bolts as the pirates opened fire on each other. Nancy and I ducked for cover.

The abandoned stalls gave even Brain Drain the shelter he needed to crawl over toward us.

"I HAVE AN INCREASING NUMBER OF MORAL QUALMS ABOUT THIS," he informed me. "HOWEVER, IT ALSO SEEMS INEVITABLE THAT THESE SPACE PIRATES WOULD BRING THEMSELVES TO VIOLENCE AND THIS AT LEAST ALLOWS US TO CHANNEL ITS EXPRESSION."

The market's denizens had already either fled or taken cover in advance of this firefight. Still, any risk of anyone getting caught in the crossfire was too big. Not to mention, I had no idea what circumstances had led these aliens into their lives of piracy. Even the ones who'd made poor choices deserved long lives to reconsider them.

They were already divided. All we had to do now was conquer. "We'll take care of it," I said.

Time management is the underrated key to success as a super hero. It took us a few extra minutes to sew up the market, but we did it efficiently and professionally. If the pirates had been working together against us, they might have been a problem. Separated, and more focused on fighting each other than watching out for us, they were easy marks. Tippy-Toe leapt on an alien pirate's shoulder, and when they spun around to try to get her off, I yanked the gun out of their tentacle and clobbered them with it. Nancy tripped another alien, yanked its gun out of its tentacle, and clobbered them with it. Another pirate ran around a corner and directly into Brain Drain, knocking themselves out. I even got to kick a butt or two, or at least what I hoped were butts. We had all of the aliens tied up and seated against the wall in two minutes.

Some of the other aliens were starting to poke their heads up, or back into the market. They were starting to get the idea that it was more than just another doomed rebellion.

Of course, now we had to protect our captured pirates from *them* too.

"I WILL ENSURE THE SAFETY OF MY MATEYS," Brain Drain told Nancy and me. "I WILL ALSO SPEAK TO THEM ABOUT THE ADVISABILITY OF THEIR ACTIONS AND THE MISTAKES THAT MAY HAVE LED THEM TO THIS LOW POINT IN THEIR CAREERS."

"Love ya, bud," I told him. The sounds of fighting echoed down the nearest corridor. Nancy and I had to get moving.

"Things are getting pretty wild out here," our space whale

friend, naming themselves Delayed-Choice for now, told us as we ran. "Dicey, one might say. Higgledy-piggledy perhaps? Pirate ships taking shots at pirate ships. All kinds of electronic warfare, sensor jamming… my eyes weren't made to keep up with this. Some of the ships the pirates are supposed to be watching are making a run for it, and the pirates don't seem to care."

"That's great!" I said, and then, "Probably."

"I hope they know where they're going," Nancy said.

"I think most everybody out here knows that order's breaking down, and that they could leave if they wanted to," Delayed-Choice said. "Problem is, there's, y'know, gonna be a war happening."

"Not if we have anything to say about it," I said.

"We *don't*," Nancy pointed out.

Chaos had broken out across the station. There was too much of it to be my friends. Aliens all over the station were waking up to the fact that this wasn't just a riot. It was maybe their only chance to get out of here.

My friends and I had started this, but we couldn't control it. This could get out of hand extremely quickly. We'd known for hours that this moment was coming, and it had felt like I'd been holding my breath all that time, and now it was burning a hole in my chest. Super heroism is as terrifying as it is exhilarating. Imagine how it would feel to be a tiny squirrel riding on the back of a goose. Once the goose is loose, you can never let go.[59]

A crackling cacophony of weapons fire drew us down a corridor branch. One of the 3D printers Mary had missed was

---

[59] And the *honking*. The honking never stops. Or so Tippy-Toe has told me. -SG

spitting out replacement robots. A group of five small, furry aliens had stacked themselves up atop of each other like kids sneaking into a movie theater – but instead of a trenchcoat they were hiding behind a shield made of bulkhead plating. Energy weapon fire splashed all over it.

Nancy and I started to run to help. The furry aliens' improvised shield got them close enough to the robots where, in a sudden flurry of whirling claws and gnashing teeth, they descended upon the robots and tore them to shreds. Their teeth, which must have been diamond-hard, ripped right through metal. Their little noses and button whiskers were disconcertingly adorable.

I gave them a thumbs-up, but Nancy and I steered well clear of them. Just in case. Nancy had fashioned a weapon for herself, a short club like a baton made from a segment of a metal post.

We reached another cavernous gathering hall, the size of the market we'd left. The locals had taken over. Downed robots lay near an airlock hatch, barely visible underneath a riotous throng. Aliens ran and slithered and rolled here and there. I recognized the place.

This was where Koi Boi and G'illian were supposed to have attacked the poetnappers. I didn't see them now but, if they'd moved as quickly as Nancy and I had, they were probably already on their way to their next targets.

Two enormous, elephant-trunked aliens had taken station where the robots had been standing, and had apparently taken it upon themselves to manage the airlock. They were helpfully double-checking the spacesuit seals of aliens making their way through, and held up traffic when the airlock chamber filled to its brim, and kept the remainder from stampeding while the airlock cycled.

It warmed my heart. "Volunteerism is heroism!" I hollered, tail swishing excitedly. Not that anyone paid attention.

Nancy pulled me onward, almost but not quite in time to keep me from seeing pickpockets at work in the crowd. There's only so much crime that even I can fight at once, but you'd better believe I was taking down faces. Darn it. Always more work to do.

We had no destination in mind other than following the sound of chaos, but soon enough the chaos was all around us. We burst into a domed cavity twice the size of the market, full of dead and disused mining equipment. Treaded vehicles with big conical drills, enormous laser emitters, and even shovels. I'd never seen this part of the station before. The floor was bare, pebble-strewn rock. It was the first time we'd seen any actual piece of the asteroid since we'd entered the station.

Chipmunk Hunk, Mary, and a dozen other aliens were hunkered beside the heaviest of the mining equipment. I realized, almost an instant too late, that they had taken cover from something. I knocked Nancy to the ground and fell beside her.

The wall just behind us erupted, blasting squid-like tendrils of smoke and debris all around us. I hadn't seen where the gunfire had come from. My eyes burned from the afterimages. Nancy and I crawled over to Mary and Chipmunk Hunk.

"Hiya," Chipmunk Hunk said.

"Things going well?" I asked.

He shook his head. Mary nodded over behind the next-closest mining vehicle. The dancing purple spots behind my retinas cleared just in time for me to see the Mad Thinker hunkered there.

"He led us here," Mary said.

"The movements of our captors suggested, to a high degree of certainty, that they were moving to protect this part of the station," the Mad Thinker said mildly. "It turns out I was right."

"You could have told us they'd have turrets set up here," Chipmunk Hunk said.

"Why?" the Mad Thinker asked, and I couldn't tell if he was making fun of Chipmunk Hunk or genuinely confused. Or both. He nodded to two fist-sized canisters dangling from Mary's belt. Her homemade EMPs. "You still have those, don't you?" he asked.

"My last ones," she said.

The backside of the mining car Mary and Chipmunk Hunk hid behind burst into flames. The new afterimages burned into my retinas gave me a rough idea of the direction it was coming from.

Make that "directions". A bulkhead behind Nancy and me shrieked and split apart in a shower of white-hot metal. I hastily moved to shield Nancy, and gave what I admit was a somewhat undignified yelp as sparks bounced off my skin. Nancy helpfully patted out an ember on my tail before it could catch fire.

That blast had come from somewhere new. The angle would have been impossible for the first one. We were under fire by multiple turrets.

Without peeking over his cover, the Mad Thinker hiked his thumbs in two different directions. "Lob them these ways." Funny enough, both directions looked clear.

Mary and Chipmunk Hunk were still safely behind cover for now, but it wouldn't be long before the rising heat forced them out into the open. Mary shook her head, opened her mouth to object, but I spoke first.

"Do what he says," I told her.

Mary glowered at me, but the metal behind her back must have already been starting to heat up. She hit the EMPs' arming triggers and casually tossed the grenades over her shoulder in the directions the Mad Thinker had indicated.

I had to admit, she looked pretty cool doing it. Big walking-away-from-the-explosion-while-not-looking-at-it energy.

Weapons fire spat overhead as the turrets tried to intercept the new moving targets. They must have scored a hit, because one of the *whumph*s sounded sooner than the other. But at that point, it didn't matter. The magnetic containment coils were fully charged, and shooting one just released its energy earlier than the other.

My skin tingled with the second *whump*. The fur on my tail stood on end. The turrets fell silent.

Of course, they could have been trying to bait us into coming out. The only way to find out would be–

The Mad Thinker made a *harrumphing* middle-aged-man noise, pushed himself to his feet, and strolled out into the open.

I wish I'd had his predictive talent, because if I'd anticipated what he'd been about to do, I would have tackled him ten seconds ago. I was already up and running toward him before I realized that he hadn't been disintegrated. Up ahead – and not at all in either of the directions the Mad Thinker had indicated – two of the white-plated robots sat between massive, wall-mounted turrets overlooking the whole chamber. One was aimed at the Mad Thinker, and the other at me. Neither turret seemed to be working. The robots fussed with dead controls.

For the first time, I noticed the Mad Thinker was holding a barbed-handled, alien-looking sidearm.

He fired. A plasma bolt pierced one of the robot gunners through the head. The Mad Thinker may not have had the best reflexes or the steadiest nerve, but, as the second robot jumped from its seat, he knew exactly where it would be. His second shot found its mark, too, cleaving the robot into two burning halves.

The Mad Thinker lowered his weapon. I just managed to halt my momentum right before I crashed into him.

"Where did you get that?" Chipmunk Hunk asked.

"If you're thinking that I'm going to shoot you, bear in mind that I could have already done it," he said. He pointed to where Mary's EMPs had landed, and explained, "There are power conduits for those turrets behind the walls there. That's what your devices hit. You wouldn't have thrown far enough to reach the turrets."

"Are you saying I have a weak throw?" Mary asked.

"No," he said. "I'm saying that, in the fog of war, you would not have known how far away those turrets were, and I didn't have the time to explain their ideal trajectories. So I chose another solution."

The Mad Thinker flipped the pistol around in his hand, and then offered it to me, butt-first.

"You'll be wanting to take this from me," he said. Not a question. Just a fact. He sounded exquisitely tired.

He could have been manipulating me. Giving me a push down a path of conversation he'd foreseen. Time to leap without looking. I had to hope he was genuinely surprised when I pushed it back into his hand and said, "Maybe once we're out of here."

His eyebrows lifted. For a moment, he got that glazed look he had when he was recalculating one of those rare, unexpected curves in a conversation. Then his eyebrows lowered, making a V-shape.

The turrets had folded out of the bulkheads surrounding a large, unmarked cargo door. That had to be what the turrets were protecting. More reinforcements, robots or pirates or pirate-robots, were probably on their way. We didn't have the time to chat through this.

I *always* have time for character development. But sometimes it's got to happen on the go. I was already moving.

The Unbeatable Squirrel Girl Vs Main Character Syndrome

The cargo door was sealed tight, and was so heavy that it didn't look like anything short of a dynamite blast would break through. I was beginning to understand, though, why the robots had decided to steal poetry and abduct poets rather than take up a pen themselves. They had no imagination. We were in a room full of mining equipment. Heavy lasers, drills, and more. It didn't take all *that* much imagination to adventure-game-puzzle our way through this. For the robots, the heavy doors and mining equipment had occupied separate columns on a spreadsheet and never come closer together than that.[60]

An unfortunate number of the implements piled around had been slagged by all the weapons fire. By the time we found

---

[60] That's one of the problems with AI development. It's clever in ways that you wouldn't expect, but makes category errors on things that a human never would. A well-programmed, well-resourced neural network might beat any human alive at chess or *Jeopardy!* but still have trouble telling a picture of a zebra from a picture of a crosswalk. – SG

an intact mining car, Koi Boi – with G'illian on his shoulder – had caught up with us. Hadrian accompanied them. He had a strangely glazed-over look in his black eyes. Every few steps, Koi Boi checked over his shoulder, as if to make sure Hadrian was still tagging along.

For once in his life, Hadrian was silent. His mouth worked but no sound came out. He caught sight of the cargo door, stared at it a moment, and then closed his eyes, still muttering.

"Either Hadrian needs to do something to help us, or he needs to get away," Chipmunk Hunk told me quietly. "We can't trust him here."

"Ignore him," I said.

"After what happened last time, I don't see how we can–"

"He's not here," I said, with what I hoped was enough finality.

Starting a vehicle designed by aliens, for aliens, was no easy task. The seat was made for a being with a butt three times as large as mine (and that's including the tail). It was like sitting inside a funhouse mirror. I had to stretch my arms out as far as they would go to hit the switches that apparently started the mining car's motor. But it worked. The instant the car started humming, it leapt forward. I had only a second to dive out of the passenger door.

The car had a drill mounted on its front, but it turned out to not be necessary. I was too busy rolling to a stop to see the crash, but it was deafening. It made the chamber shake from the floor to the bulkheads. By the time I looked up, the car and door both had become a tangle of wreckage. The contrast between everything in the station we'd seen so far, and the space beyond the door, was jarring.

On the other side of the wreckage, a brightly lit corridor led about a hundred feet deeper into the rock before emptying out into an even brighter chamber. They were swept clean (barring the catastrophic mess we'd just made). Well lit. Not a single one of the light strips had gone out. This was a part of the station, in other words, that its unruly populace had never had access to.

The wreckage and the angle didn't let me see far into the next chamber. What I *could* see, though, were rows upon rows of coffin-sized, clear-topped enclosures protruding from the floor. Coffins, or surgical beds… or stasis and sleep cells. They came in different shapes and sizes, from three times human-sized to smaller than my tail.

All of the aliens that the poetnappers had abducted had to have gone somewhere. Most likely, they were being stored there.

My ears were still ringing from the crash. I didn't hear the clomp of heavy bootsteps until an instant after it was too late.

Nancy was looking out for me. She knocked me to the side just as more robots entered from the same passage we'd come from, their wrist-guns leveled and blazing. My friends and I scrambled to take cover, again, this time facing the opposite direction.

Some of the weapons fire had come from the Mad Thinker. He scowled, frozen in concentration as though surprised again, but his trigger finger kept working. His shots felled two robots, but there were too many arriving for him to keep up with. I lost sight of him as he dove for cover.

"Thanks," I told Nancy. Sometimes squirrel hearing can be *too* sensitive, and leave me dazed after loud noises.

"Hey," Nancy said. "I'm a super hero." That was so true! But that was the first time I'd heard her call herself that. I slapped her on the back. If it weren't for our dire circumstances, I would have dwelled on that moment even more.

If there were more robots in the stasis chamber behind us, and I wouldn't have bet against that, we were pinched. Heck, just the robots we faced now were going to be a serious, possibly terminal, problem. I risked a split-second peek over the drill I was sheltering behind, and caught sight of ten robots. We'd missed a robot printer somewhere, probably more than one. Now all the fresh security was converging on us.

"It's times like this that make me wish we used more weapons," Chipmunk Hunk shouted over the gunfire.

"I know, right?" Mary asked. "How long have I been saying that?"

"None of us are *that* kind of super hero!" I said. It would have been nice, though, to have a little extra carnage at our finger tips.

Destruction rained on the other side of my drill. I was starting to feel each blast as it struck our cover. The air overhead was filling with acrid smoke. The robots were getting closer, keeping us pinned under an avalanche of fire.

I didn't want to use a weapon. Principles are principles, but when your friends' lives are at stake there is something to be said for a little creative flexibility. I eyed the turrets the other robots had crewed before. If they had power back... if one of us could crawl up there without getting disintegrated... well, it would make Mary happy, at least...

Then a burst of weapons fire from *behind* our cover ran the risk of seriously ruining my day.

I reflexively crouched, not that that would have done much, but the bolts sizzled over our heads. The relentless blasting from the other side ceased.

I looked behind me. Most of the coffin-sized pods had popped open, and a disheveled swarm of aliens – most unarmed except the ones in front, who bore pistols or rifles – were barreling down the corridor. And Hadrian ran in at the head of their charge. He was at least a hundred feet away from where I'd last seen him. I couldn't have gotten all the way down that corridor without being shot, let alone setting the captive poets free and arming them. It was like he had teleported.

Some answering fire met the charging poets. The bolts struck the bulkheads or ceilings in dramatic bursts of sparks and smoke. The lead poets kept up a surprisingly accurate barrage of their own, especially considering that they were all running. Hadrian held his own rifle and once in a while raised it to snap off a shot, but without seeming to look first. He shouted as he ran.

"–lost in the fog of war as the ambush was sprung. For hours, he and his newfound companions had lain in wait, and now all their coiled energy loosed like a snake's strike–"

I'd told the others to ignore Hadrian, and had gotten so good at doing it myself that I'd let him slip from my mind. Great work, me! I was starting to think like a storyteller. I'd foreshadowed his appearance, and then kept my focus off him until it was time for his dramatic rescue.

The freed poets had great aim, but, just in case, I took advantage of the covering fire to scramble to a more out-of-the-way position. I pulled Chipmunk Hunk and Mary with me. Nancy's instincts had caught up with her a little faster than Koi Boi's, and she did the same, tugging him out of the line of fire.

"Where'd Hadrian come from?" Chipmunk Hunk asked. "He was just over there. He couldn't have–"

"*Don't say that too loud,*" I hissed. Chipmunk Hunk and Mary boggled at me. "Here's what happened," I told them. "Hadrian got into the chamber hours ago. He's been waking the captives and sneaking arms into the chamber ever since."

"But Hadrian was just with—"

I mimed zipping my lips. On my shoulder, Tippy-Toe mimicked me.

It was true that Hadrian had followed us here. And he hadn't known where the captives were being held until a few minutes ago, when we'd found them. But that was just real time.

Narrative time was more fluid. It could be edited. "Did you just retcon reality?" Mary asked.

"*I* didn't. He did."

I hadn't even seen Hadrian leave us. Storytelling operates under something like the Heisenberg Uncertainty Principle[61]; observing him might have messed up the plan. Half of narrative logic was letting things slip around the periphery of the audience's attention, and then letting them imagine what had happened when they weren't looking. If Hadrian's superpower was half as potent as I suspected, he really *had rearranged* the cosmic narrative of reality.

If there was one non-STEM thing my friends and I understood, it was serialized science fiction. And sci-fi shows pulled this kind of stuff all the time.

That was enough for us to go along with it as Hadrian charged through the entranceway, firing shot after shot without looking where he was aiming, enemy fire dramatically lighting the corridor around him.

The robots' return fire had picked up again, but little enough of it struck my cover. All at once, the fire ceased, although the

---

[61] NOT BEING ABLE TO OBSERVE POSITION AND SPEED OF PARTICLE AT THE SAME TIME MAKES HULK SMASH! – ED

sound of it continued. I risked a peek. More aliens had taken station at the far end of the chamber, just as irregularly armed as Hadrian's crew. The uprising in the rest of the station was continuing apace. The rebels and poets had pinned the robots between them.

Hadrian's poets were sharp enough to seek cover. Hadrian himself was the only one of them who strode boldly forward, scintillating rays searing the air around him. His eyes were glassy as he stared somewhere far beyond the words on his page, but, for once, they burned.

"He gloried in his rage. He *luxuriated* in it. This was the one thing that had made the hero's life worthwhile, and all his losses and tragedies slipped away from him—"

I did not like the way Hadrian's narration was turning. A pit opened in my stomach.

I craned my neck, instinctively judging the distance between myself and him. I knew his power was capable of handling this, but I also knew what *he* was like. My throat was so dry it had started to hurt.

"The hero howled at the universe," Hadrian said, and though he was definitely not howling, in that moment I was sure I remembered a cry of rage. "Rage had breached his horizon, a bold new light shading everything in new contrast. For the first time in his life, catharsis felt only a few steps away. Every face he had ever known, every name he had ever lost, flashed before him as if bracing to be separated from him forever."

Panic surged through me. I didn't stop to think. I pushed myself to my feet. I darted out from behind cover, though I did not have Hadrian's plot armor. Koi Boi tried to grab my ankle the instant he realized what I was doing, but I was too fast.

"He had saved the impossible hero who called herself his inspiration. He offered his chest to the enemy's fire. His life's misfortunes and ill-fated adventures and deeply personal character flaws had robbed him of all other causes to live—"

Hadrian still thought he was in a tragedy. And he'd seen an appropriately dramatic ending for himself.

"—and so, for her, he would die—"

I slammed into his chest and knocked him to the ground hard enough to knock the air out of him. He couldn't finish his sentence. His eyes went wide, and for the first time they snapped into focus on me.

I had no idea if finishing his sentences would do anything constructive or magic or what, but it was worth a try. "—inside if he did anything to embarrass himself in front of her or any of his other new friends!"

Whether my words had done anything or not, he didn't finish the sentence he'd been about to speak, even when he got his last breath back

At least my last "death" had convinced him I was immortal. Or that I would have risen from the dead again if I were killed. He probably would have narrated that I would have been killed in appropriately dramatic fashion in front of him. Another figure stuffed into a refrigerator in the wake of the only thing that mattered to him: his story.

I took back all of the kind things I'd started to think about English majors and poets. STEM students at ESU have to take ethics-in-computing-and-engineering courses to graduate. Ethics and narrative superpowers had plainly never crossed Hadrian's mind.

Footsteps pounded the rock around us, but none of them

were the robots' heavy boots. The blistering firefight petered out. The rebels and the rescued poets had won the day. Wherever they were all going, they paid very little attention to my friends and me.

"The hero had struck his head in his fall," Hadrian said, weakly. He chose that moment to dramatically faint rather than dramatically die, so that was an improvement.

I was fairly certain I'd kept his head from smacking the ground, but his narration must have made it true, so I didn't argue. I let him loll to the rock.

"Things are getting a stitch hot out here," Delayed-Choice's telepathic voice informed us. "Multiple ships escaping into hyperspace, or warp, or portals, or whatever their flavor of faster-than-light travel is. The pirates are shooting at each other, at escaping ships, or running themselves. And, ah, one of them is after me. I think they figured out that I brought you bunch here."

Koi Boi said a very heartfelt "*Heck*" and then, "Can you get away?"

"I know some tricks," Delayed-Choice said mysteriously. "Not that they'll work forever."

"Where's the Mad Thinker?" Nancy asked.

I looked about. There was, of course, no sign of him. He'd melted into one crowd or another. He could have fled us at any time. It was only now, when we'd opened up a way to leave this station, that he'd chosen to escape.

With his talents to predict what we were going to do, the only way any of us were going to find him was if he wanted us to.

I scowled in several directions just to make sure the scowl hit him, but that wasn't going to accomplish anything. We still had Hadrian to worry about too.

I couldn't just leave Hadrian here. He was obviously a danger to himself and everyone else on the station.

We couldn't stay here to hunt the Mad Thinker. We had a war to stop. And our space whale friend was under attack.

There was so much work left to do here. But there was even more to do out in the rest of the universe. Knowing that, and knowing what decision I had to take, was tearing me up inside.

I scooped Hadrian up, hoisted him over my non-Tippy-Toe-holding shoulder, and stood.

"Let's get out of here," I told my friends.

It was a good thing that Brain Drain was easy to spot even among the crowds of panicked, jubilant aliens. I'd recognize that brain case anywhere.

"I AM RELIEVED TO FIND YOU ALL MORE-OR-LESS INTACT," he said, "THOUGH WHETHER WE REMAIN PSYCHOLOGICALLY INTACT REMAINS, AS ALWAYS, DIFFICULT TO SEE."

"Happy to see you, too, buddy," I said, meaning it.

"I HAVE REMANDED THE PIRATES TO THE CUSTODY OF A PARTY I BELIEVE TO BE LEAST INTERESTED IN HARMING THEM," he said. "THE MONKS WHO WRITE POETRY WILL NEED AN AUDIENCE TO WORKSHOP THEIR LITERARY OUTPUT NOW THAT THEIR CAPTORS ARE GONE."

The robed aliens, the ones who'd *tried* to get themselves abducted by the poetnappers, had encircled the pirates, reciting new poetry. The pirates were wriggling in distress.

"They'll learn a lesson," I said. "Some kind of lesson."

"I AM CONVINCED SOME OF THEM HAVE THE SOULS OF ARTISTS," Brain Drain agreed, sounding as happy as he ever did.

Nancy kept me on track, dragging me toward the room we'd

taken over as our living quarters. Our spacesuits remained safe and intact. It had taken some time to get Hadrian fitted inside the Mad Thinker's suit, but, honestly, my mind was in so many places that it still seemed like a blur. I couldn't remember much about our dash to the airlock chamber. Only the fog of flash-cooling air billowing around us as the outer door opened, and the pit opening in my stomach as the artificial gravity released us.

Mary had had to drop her new toys to help the rest of us carry Brain Drain – whose body once again locked up the moment he was back in the asteroid's natural microgravity.

"I AM SURE THERE IS A METAPHOR FOR THE AGING PROCESS, THE LIMITS OF SELF-RELIANCE, AND OUR EVOLVING INTERDEPENDENCE WITH SOCIETY," he said, "BUT EVEN I, A SEEKER OF UNPLEASANT TRUTHS, FIND THAT DIFFICULT TO DWELL UPON AT THIS MOMENT."

"I'm not going to mourn," Mary muttered. "Not going to mourn..." She could not help but look back at the toys she'd abandoned.

Tippy-Toe was content hiding under the shoulder of my spacesuit, but G'illian crammed her way up into Chipmunk Hunk's helmet, smooshing his face to one side. He was too nice to complain.

In spite of the ongoing battle, Delayed-Choice managed to set down on the asteroid long enough for us to labor over to them in our heavy spacesuits. "Left 'em chasing a psychic projection of me on the other side of this rock," they said with a telepathic chortle. "That'll take them a minute to figure out."

G'illian was close enough to Chipmunk Hunk's helmet radio that I heard a squeak when she saw Delayed-Choice. I realized what she must have been thinking. The acanti were fairly scarce in this galaxy, and for good reason. Free acanti were usually in hiding, like Delayed-Choice had been. The rest had been abducted and hollowed out. Turned into mounts, to serve the Skrull Empire.

"We're still not Skrulls," I radioed.

She stared at me. Her squirrel-sharp claws were *very* close to Chipmunk Hunk's face, if she wanted to do some real damage.

She didn't. Or at least she held off.

Delayed-Choice's tail twitched while we climbed into the fleshy chamber that served as their airlock. "Let's go, let's go," they said, antsy, until we were sealed inside. It occurred to me later that Delayed-Choice was talking to itself more than us.

"Has anyone mentioned how gross this is?" G'illian asked.

"No," Chipmunk Hunk said. "Never occurred to us until now."

"Just don't think too much about it," Tippy-Toe advised.

The pirates must have figured out Delayed-Choice's trick, because they were extremely ticked off. Seconds after we stepped into the "lounge" chamber, acceleration shoved us against the fleshy walls before we'd managed to secure ourselves in our seats. The oval-shaped monitor showed the asteroid falling away from us. Seconds after we left, a crackling light show seared across the asteroid's surface, right where we'd been, silently turning a broad swath of it into molten rock and slag.

We should have taken the moment after the acceleration cut to get to our seats. We were all too busy staring at the screen, jaws slack[62].

The destruction, spectacular as it was, covered only a fraction

---

[62] In freefall, your jaw doesn't so much "drop" as "flop loosely", but let's not dwell on that! Not as dramatic. – SG

of the asteroid's surface. It wouldn't reach the station. But it was plain that the pirates no longer cared about preserving it, if they ever had. The revolution was on. The rules were out the airlock. For the sake of everyone left aboard the station and everywhere nearby, we had to go.

Two pirate ships bore toward us. Winking lights played across their hulls. Weapons fire. Missiles or torpedoes or plasma fire or One-Above-All knew what else.

Chipmunk Hunk and I pulled Hadrian's insensate body into a seat and tugged his safety harnesses into place. Everyone else was safely in place by the time he and I found our own seats. Tippy-Toe nestled tightly underneath my spacesuit's neck. Chipmunk Hunk's wince told me that G'illian's claws were digging into him as she held on.

All over the rest of the starfield, the drifting specks of other starships raced off into the void, or opened wormholes and plunged through, or just plain vanished in flashes of light and exotic mathematics. There were as many different mechanisms of faster-than-light travel out here as there were ships.

There were so many incredible things to discover. We weren't going to be able to stay around to find any of them.

All of those ships and the beings aboard them were likely not going to be any safer out there than they were back here. A war was going to start out there, soon. We were going to plunge into it too. And now we had a responsibility, impossible as it was, to stop it.

"Harnesses secure?" Delayed-Choice asked. "I can't feel all that much in there. It's just like a bunch of tickling, you know?"

"*Go.*" I couldn't track how many of us spoke at once, but my voice was one of them. The fleshy walls quivered and distended

Marvel Heroines

as our ride twisted and contorted their body into a new shape. I squeezed my hands together and said, "Find where the center of the war's going to be. Let's go there."

A sound like a telepathic *hmmph* (but less, you know, throaty, and more… mind-y) echoed in my mind. But our friend did not argue. Not yet, anyway. A missile streaked by close enough for the backwash of its exhaust plume to rattle the screen, or at least wherever its camera feed came from.

"New name, dudes," they said. "I'm Abrupt-Destiny now."

The screen blurred as Abrupt-Destiny twisted through impossible space. And then we were elsewhere.

The Unbeatable Squirrel Girl Vs Causality

"Okay," G'illian told us, "I'm starting to believe that you all *aren't* Skrull assassins after all."

After a long moment, Koi Boi looked "up" at her as she drifted past his head. "Excuse me?"

"I'm beginning to believe that you're not all Skrull assassins sent to interrogate me and kill me," G'illian reiterated, as though it were the simplest thing in the world.

"Thank you?" Koi Boi said.

"You're welcome," G'illian said. She flicked her tail back and forth to gyroscopically control her spin, and landed on my seat. "I did come close to clawing Chipmunk Hunk's face off."

"I could have gone without knowing that," Chipmunk Hunk said.

"But I didn't," G'illian said, scrambling to my armrest, and then onto my wrist. "When I saw an acanti waiting for us, I thought for sure that the jig was up. But the real Skrull would never leave an acanti with enough of its mind to communicate telepathically. The Skrull wouldn't put the effort into faking that, not once I'd already boarded. And you wouldn't have kept up with the disguises once you had me aboard."

"Thank you for not clawing Chipmunk Hunk's eyes out," I said sincerely.

"I already said 'you're welcome.'"

This was our second day aboard, and already we'd run out of things to do. Nancy had had to leave her sewing equipment behind during the hasty evacuation from the asteroid station. Mary had spent the last few days mourning the alien weaponry she'd had to abandon. She had the grace, though, not to do so in front of Brain Drain, for whom she had sacrificed them to carry. We had latched him onto one of the chairs. His eyes floated placidly at perpendicular angles. I couldn't tell if he was watching us or sleeping.

We burned through space faster than, frankly, it was healthy to comprehend. A single star shone on the monitor. Like last time. The universe ahead of us had collapsed into a bright blue star, a pinprick of compressed light.

While I watched, the star began to fuzz. It blossomed into a blur, and then a fog. I straightened in my seat.

"We're coming up on the only place I know to go, guys," our space whale friend said. Their name was Variant-Interpretation today.

Most of us were already in the lounge. Nancy and Hadrian arrived moments after Variant-Interpretation's warning. Nancy stayed carefully behind Hadrian. He'd woken hours after we'd fled the asteroid, but he'd kept mostly silent since. He stared bleakly around Variant-Interpretation's innards, occasionally muttering something about aimlessness and the inherent meaninglessness of life. We'd tried to shush him to no avail. With his powers, for all we knew, he *could* make our lives meaningless.

As dangerous as he'd proven to be, we still needed someone to watch him. It had been Nancy's turn. So far, though, Hadrian had done little to provoke us. He did not seem to know what to do with himself. His story hadn't come to the ending he'd outlined. His narrative power had probably never been stymied before.

"Safety first," I reminded everyone, snapping my seat harness into place. Always buckle up, reader! Tippy-Toe slipped underneath my sweater's shoulder while G'illian, after a moment's hesitation, did the same thing with my sleeve.

The universe ahead burst into a dazzling starscape. A swirling blue-green-white marble, half-bright and half-shadowed, spun out of the cosmos. In half a blink, this new world consumed most of the screen.

According to what Variant-Interpretation had told us yesterday, this gorgeous-looking world had no name in any language they'd ever known, but it was important regardless. The Itrayans and the Eradu had kept themselves, and the location of their homeworlds, quite secret. But they still needed to interact with the outside universe. This uninhabited world had once been designated as an Itrayan political outpost. Diplomats, merchants, and scholars who wanted to make contact with the Itrayans could come here to petition them. Most of the time, the Itrayans answered those petitions with firm 'no's. They never explained their reasoning.

Variant-Interpretation hadn't been out this way for a long

time, but they said they would wager that the Itrayans were coordinating their war effort with their allies from here.

Immediately, an orange glow on the continent below caught my attention. It shone with its own searing light. To be visible from this far away, it must've been an enormous firestorm. Smoke blackened the air around it, like a distended char mark. Lightning flickered throughout the volcanic cloud. But the center of the firestorm was so hot that even the smoke had blasted outward.

"Ah, darn," Variant-Interpretation said. "That's where the Itrayan outpost *was*, anyway."

"All those poor animals down there," Tippy-Toes said.

"Don't feel bad!" Variant-Interpretation said. "The life forms there are tough. Big, roly-poly tardigrades,[63] really."

"Does that mean the Itrayans and Eradu are already at war?" Koi Boi asked. My stomach had plummeted thinking about the same thing, as much as anything could plummet in freefall.

"Nah. If those dudes had started fighting, everyone in this quadrant and several dimensions over would be feeling the aftershocks. This was more of a diplomatic tap on the shoulder by their standards." For the first time, I got a sense of the scope of the forces at play. There must have been hundreds of square kilometers of destruction down there. The crater would be carved into that world's geological history forever. A tap on the

---

[63] Tardigrades are the toughest lifeform known to science (I guess barring the Hulk or Wolverine). They're a special kind of life called "extremophiles", and can survive radiation, hard vacuum, fires, and cosmic retcons. If Galactus ever actually *had* eaten Earth, those things would be colonizing his stomach. – SG

HULK HAPPY TO BE COMPARED TO UGLY MANY-LEGGED WORM-THINGS. HULK HAVE HULK-SIZED EMPATHY FOR MISUNDERSTOOD SURVIVORS. – ED

shoulder. Variant-Interpretation added, "But, ah, there's another problem."

"Oh, good," I said. "We were running low."

"You all probably aren't able to believe this," Variant-Interpretation said, "but I would swear that there's another acanti out there."

"*Ouch*," I answered, because G'illian had just dug her claws into my skin.

Not that I could blame her.

"Skrull," G'illian whispered.

I looked to Hadrian to see if his mouth was moving, and if he had somehow caused this. He stared straight ahead, and hardly seemed aware of any of us. It didn't seem like he was narrating this into being.

None of us had gotten out of our seats. It felt like we ought to have been bracing ourselves, strapping in tighter, but we'd already done all we could. One of the big stressors of space travel turns out to be the same thing that wigs me out on airplanes: no direct control over anything. At least I had a friend steering us.

"Something really weird going on here…" Variant-Interpretation said.

"You don't say," Chipmunk Hunk said.

"I did say! With just about any acanti, even ones that have been, uh, altered by the Skrull, I'd feel some shadow of telepathic resonance. Telepathy is superluminal, you know. I should have sensed an acanti light years before we got here."

"But we're seeing one right there," Chipmunk Hunk pointed out.

"Yup, sure are," Variant-Interpretation said.

An indicator light to the side of the screen, a light that had never turned on or done anything at all until now, started blinking a dull red. "What's that?" I asked.

"What's what?" Variant-Interpretation asked.

I actually had to describe the light to Variant-Interpretation. "Oh *that*," they said. "Probably a radio signal. I don't know, really. Not much of the equipment in there has a direct line to my nervous system. It wasn't made for my use."

Unlatching my safety harness was a risk, but the other acanti hadn't done anything aggressive so far. And, though Chipmunk Hunk and Koi Boi's superpowers were not to be underestimated, I was the hardiest of all of us. I pushed myself away from my seat, toward the blinking light, and hit the button closest to it.

The screen blinked, and I found myself face-to-face with my mirror image.

It *seemed* like a mirror image at first, anyway. It was a view of the lounge, exactly as it would have appeared if taken from the front of the room. But there were differences.

The Doreen Green in the image was floating in the center of the room, where I was off to the side. The other Nancy had her arms folded, while the one seated near me was gripping her armrest with white knuckles. Brain Drain was in the same place too, except that his eyes were staring forward rather than drifting off in their own separate directions. And there was no sign of Hadrian on the image. On *this* side of the screen, Hadrian was still seated with us.

The other Doreen let out a long, exasperated breath. "There's always more to unpack with you," she said. "Jerk."

"Uh," I said. That's me – always quick on the comeback.

A squirrel tail flashed over the edge of the screen. It was

about where the other crew's radio controls would have been. Either their Tippy-Toe or G'illian was wrestling with the switch.

The image vanished, replaced by the horizon of the planet beneath us. Against the blue-white halo of its atmosphere, space bent and twisted like someone had run a convex lens over it, and then snapped back into shape. I had never seen it from the outside, but I was willing to guess that was what Variant-Interpretation looked like when they bolted at faster-than-light speeds.

"They're gone," Variant-Interpretation said.

A hundred comebacks popped into my head too late to use them. Give Spider-Man some respect (or more respect than you already do). Quipping on the fly is hard.

"I mean, if they were ever here to begin with," Variant-Interpretation added. "I *still* never sensed anything telepathically."

"So," Chipmunk Hunk said. "Time travel?"

I have some experience with time travel, and even meeting past and future versions of my former self (or selves?[64]). But all those other Doreens had at least felt like *me*. I'd had more to say to myself than, well, that.

"Nah," Variant-Interpretation said. "I mean, probably not. There's no reason time travel would block my telepathy."

My tail flicked back and forth irritably. I admit it: I was frustrated, I was antsy, and I was hyper[65]. The adrenaline of our escape from the asteroid station, of losing the Mad Thinker, and then being cooped up inside a space whale's organs for days

---

[64] HULK NEED HAZARD PAY BEFORE PROOFREADING TENSES WITH TIME TRAVEL INVOLVED. – ED

[65] Just don't call me squirrely. – SG

afterward was getting to me in a way things usually didn't get to me. I wasn't used to me treating myself so poorly. I wanted to bounce from the walls and get into about ten different arguments.

I tried to force myself to come up with more ideas. "Okay, what about holograms?" I asked.

"Holograms that know exactly what the inside of this room looks like?" Nancy asked. "That can mimic us all *and* do a perfect impression of your voice?"

"That *wasn't* a perfect impression of me!" I said.

"Yeah, it was," Chipmunk Hunk said. "She sounded *just* like you."

"But it was too high-pitched, and–" I cut myself off. Nobody's voice sounds exactly like it does in their head. "I don't sound like *that*, do I?"

All the others nodded.

"Bull poop!" I said.

"Nobody likes the sound of their own voice, Doreen," Nancy said. "But that was you. I'm pretty sure the rest of us were us. I even fold my arms just like the other Nancy did."

"Yeah, you do," I admitted, and dropped the argument before one of them thought to do an impression. "What would make us all see perfect images of ourselves, doing different things, but not leave a telepathic echo for Variant-Interpretation to sense? Variant-Interpretation, you said you saw them, right? So that means that regular light also reached – wait. *Dang it.*"

"I don't like it when you swear like that, Doreen," Koi Boi muttered.

"*Au contraire*," Mary said, looking pleased. "That's when I know things are about to get good."

I hardly heard them. "Variant-Interpretation," I said. "*How* did you say you traveled faster than light, again?"

"I didn't say," Variant-Interpretation said. Somehow, they lowered their telepathic voice. "I mean, I don't know that well…"

Freefall takes all the weight out of dramatic moments. You can't, for instance, sit heavily when you're given some information that floors you. (There isn't even a floor!) You just kind of… hang awkwardly. I hung awkwardly for a while.

Nancy stared off into space, chewing her lower lip. Then her eyes widened. "Oh, *dang*. That's what happened, isn't it?"

"Exactly!" I said, clapping. Nancy and I had taken the same fall semester physics course. None of the others had spent their electives there, though.

Science lesson time. Does it make it sound more appealing if I call it science lore? Science lore time. Have you ever wanted to know the reason physicists get so itchy about faster-than-light travel, even when it's been shown to be possible by the many alien races that visit Earth to invade it (secretly or otherwise) or bounty hunt or smuggle out bootleg cassettes of old sitcoms?[66]

It's because, in order for faster-than-light travel to be possible, one of two things can't be true. The first is the theory of relativity, which is one of the most thoroughly tested, ironclad theories ever developed. If the theory of relativity turned out to be untrue, there were so many observed phenomena in the universe that would become anywhere between difficult to

---

[66] Astonishingly popular! If you ever find yourself stranded in space, and you happen to be carrying a VHS (or, worse, Betamax) library of tape-recorded *M*A*S*H* episodes, watch out – you've just become a target for every pirate and robber from here to the Sombrero Galaxy. – SG

HULK CHECKED. SOMBRERO GALAXY IS ITS REAL NAME. IT LOOK LIKE YOU EXPECT. – ED

frigging impossible to explain, and so relativity is still thought of as ironclad. Or better… vibranium-clad.

There is, however, *another* way that both relativity can be true and still allow faster-than-light travel to be possible. But physicists are even more loath to discuss it, because it involves sacrificing an even more important principle: causality.

Yes. Causality as in *cause-and-effect*. As in, having causes always precede effects. And being sure that effects cannot happen before their causes.

Without causality, everything we know about our universe – heck, even the parallel ones, too – flips butt-over-head upside-down. Faster-than-light travel (or even just signaling) without causality means that you can do things like receive a text before the sender ever typed it.

Imagine a race car. Imagine that race car crossing a finish line. Now, you look back down the track, and see the driver still warming up that car's engine. You see the *effect* before you see the cause. The present-driver can see her past self, too. They can flash signals back and forth at regular old light speed and have a conversation with each other. Or, if you're a space whale or that space whale's humanoid passengers, you can look ahead and see the light of your future self – just out there violating causality like nobody's business.

You can understand why physicists just hate this kind of thing. You get all the paradox problems of time travel, but it's even more confusing.

What happens if the winning driver tells her past self *not* to go through with the race? And her past self just gets out of the car and goes home?

Nobody knows. It's not a question that doesn't have an

answer. It's a question that *can't* have an answer, and it makes a mess of everything. At least time travel comes with a coherent conceptualization of time. Without causality – with effects coming before causes – what "time" even means breaks down.

Another day out in the cosmos, another day learning the terrible secrets of space. I was learning enough about the universe to know that I *couldn't* understand it.[67] But here we were. I had to deal with what we'd seen.

It occurred to me that, if that other Squirrel Girl's screen had been positioned like ours, she hadn't been looking at me. She'd been staring at what, to my angle, had seemed like up and a little to the right. Right at the seat we strapped Hadrian into.

Something tickled the back of my mind, trying to tell me something was wrong. Frankly, a *million* things were wrong, so I didn't pay close attention to it. It took me a minute too long to realize that my subconscious was trying to tell me about something in my more immediate environment.

I looked around. "Where's Hadrian?" I asked.

After spending the past few days hardly sensate, he'd slipped out of the lounge without anybody noticing.

"Getting some harsh vibes from in there," Variant-Interpretation remarked, as I pushed myself toward the exit to search for Hadrian.

---

[67] If you want to get a little more freaked out about causality, look up the delayed-choice quantum eraser experiment. That's where a choice made randomly, about whether or not to delete or erase certain information to keep it from reaching the experimenters, seems to influence the behavior of a particle in the past. (Well, that's one possible interpretation. A second interpretation of the data is that nothing is real, or ever was!)

Whatever the explanation, it's been verified many times in many laboratories. Science! It's frigging weird! And cool! Just don't eat lunch right before you learn some of it! – SG

I found him near the same hiding hole where I'd found the Mad Thinker a lifetime – I mean, days – ago. He looked like a mess: pale, scruffy, unwashed. That was his new normal, though. It was all of our normals, honestly.

"Do you have any idea what that was about?" I asked him.

His mouth worked soundlessly. I twisted my lip and tried again.

"She asked the 'hero' if he understood what had happened in the lounge, and then he told her what he knew," I said.

He looked at me bleakly. His mouth had stopped moving. No new information magically exposited its way into my imagination.

Okay, so I may not have had Hadrian's superpower to turn narrative into reality – at least not when he wasn't cooperating with it.

"I'm sorry I called you a jerk," I said.

"The hero pointed out that she hadn't called him a jerk," he said. "She *will* call him a jerk."

He had a point. Assuming Nancy and I were right about what we had seen, if I wasn't going to do what my future light echo had, I would risk breaking the universe by *not* doing what my future light echo had done. I know people who've broken universes, and universes are nothing but hassles to put back together. At some point, I was going to call him a jerk, and that was that.

"Why would I do something like that?" I asked.

"To distract her from pursuing her line of questioning, he answered the other question burning a hole in the back of her mind," Hadrian said. "Yes, her voice really did sound like it had on the call."

"Dang it," I muttered. "But that's not going to distract me from questioning. I mean, okay, it distracted me, but not enough. Why would I call you that?"

"Had he been so obvious about his attempt to change that subject that she would call him out directly? Evidently so. The past few days had shattered all of his defenses, and left him so destitute of grounding, that simply nothing else remained between her and the truth about him, not even the obfuscating half-lies he had told her before–"

"'Obfuscating half-lies,'" I repeated, and it was difficult to keep my voice even at that.

"He had been away from home for so long that he had almost locked the memories away from himself," he said. "His failure to find a heroic and honorable ending, to atone for his poor control of himself, had brought all of them flooding back. He felt no different now than when he left. He might as well have not changed at all."

The flatness of his voice was tempting me to think of all this as insincere. All along, I'd had to force myself to remember that Hadrian was an alien being. Though his way of expressing emotions seemed strange to me, that didn't mean they weren't sincere.

The fact was that he *could* show emotions in ways other than narrating them. I'd seen his expression change plenty of times. Usually when something had surprised him... or gone counter to the story he was trying to tell.

I wanted to believe in people. Especially strangers. His intentional-or-otherwise confession that he had lied – again – was shaking that confidence.

"Hold on a minute," I said. That tickling in the back of my

mind had returned. It was the same way I felt during a really difficult programming challenge, when I started to figure out the path toward answering a question that had stymied me for minutes. A handful of things were starting to add up.

We knew only a few things about the two combatants in this war, the Itrayans and the Eradu. I'd never heard of them back on Earth. They were powerful on a scale with the Sh'iar and the Skrull and other enormous, galaxy-spanning empires... but they had a population low enough that apparently just occupied a few star systems. Maybe even just their homeworlds. When they weren't at war, they left everyone else well enough alone. When they were at war, they could rewrite the political map of the galaxy.

For such a small population to outmatch vast interstellar empires, each individual Itrayan and Eradun must have had enormous powers. Close to, or maybe even on the same level as, the Celestials or the like.

I'd recently experienced a power that, properly wielded, could put someone on that level.

"You're one of them," I breathed. "An Itrayan. Or one of the Eradu."

His expression actually shifted. The shadows under his eyes seemed to grow longer. He looked at me, seeing me for the first time since this conversation had started.

"Which one?" I asked. When he didn't answer, I pressed: "Are you still working with them? Spying for them?"

"The hero *had* left the Itrayan navy, though he did not know how to explain that to her in a way that she would believe. He was so tangled in his own lies and self-deceptions that the now truth seemed unreal, even to him."

"All this time, you could have told us more about the war?" I asked.

"She seemed to have figured him to be a political leader, or someone with power and influence over Itrayan affairs," he said. "He wondered if, after all of the lies he'd already spun, she would believe him if he insisted he'd had no influence even before he fled the Itrayan navy."

I shook my head and waved the objection away. Whether he had influence or not was beside the point. "You can lead us to the Itrayans," I said. "You could have days ago, when we told you where we were going, and why." The weight of it all was starting to sink in, which, yes, *was* difficult to do in freefall but still happened. "And you still didn't say anything that might have helped us. You just floated around with the rest of us, moping, thinking about yourself and your own story."

"His self-proclaimed 'inspiration' had become his tormentor. She had robbed him of his honorable ending, of all of his cover stories, and it still wasn't enough for her—"

"This isn't about you," I interrupted.

I try not to shout very often. Or, more accurately, I try to shout *with* people rather than *at* them. I like to be more *enthusiastic* than *angry*. But I could not deal with this. Hadrian stared at me, wide-eyed.

"You know better than anyone how many billions of lives across the galaxy are about to be upended by this war," I said. "But they didn't figure into 'your' story."

"He kicked off the wall and pushed past her, unwilling to continue this conversation."

Though I never saw him move, as soon as he finished the sentence, he was gone, and I was spinning toward the bulkhead.

I lashed out my arms and tail to control my spin, and grabbed a metal handhold. By the time I came to a stop, Hadrian was halfway down the next bronchial passage.

I didn't go after him. Nothing productive would have come of that. But I still wasn't quite in control of myself, and couldn't keep myself from talking to his back.

"You keep telling stories about bad things happening to you, but you don't spare a moment's thought for the people around you – people who keep getting hurt because of you – except as props in that story."

The first time we'd met, my friends and I could have been killed. I wondered how many other people *had* died in those little dramas of his.

Before the next bend in the passage, he halted himself with a hand on the wall. He did not turn around, and did not speak for a long moment.

Then, in his regular tone of voice, as though nothing special had happened, he said, "The hero muttered the vector and distance to his homeworld Itraya, loud enough for the acanti to hear." After a pause just long to be called dramatic, he added, "And in doing so cemented his damnation."

Then he was gone.

By the time I returned to the lounge, Variant-Interpretation was already breaking away from the planet, and was limbering up for another impossible trip past the speed of light. Tippy-Toe had been on my shoulder that whole time, keeping quiet. She leapt off me and landed beside the screen. "Are you all right?" she asked.

Between losing the Mad Thinker, blowing up at Hadrian, trying to think about how to stop a war involving billions of aliens, and keeping my promises to Nancy about Mew and finals, my head was too full of static to figure out how to gently phrase an honest answer.

"Peachy," I lied.

Variant-Interpretation was already traveling at a healthy fraction of the speed of light when the inevitable happened and we spotted ourselves skimming the light speed barrier and braking toward the planet.

I pursed my lips. The other whale wasn't actually out there, I knew. It was all just light echoes, lost in a labyrinth of time, causality, and ridiculous physics. Radio was light too. I could signal them. Unless I wanted to risk breaking the universe, I would have to signal them.

Hadrian wasn't in the lounge right now, but this gave me another chance to speak with him. And I already knew exactly what I was going to call him.

The Unbeatable
Squirrel Girl
Vs
Continuity

"I'm still trying to understand why we haven't heard of the Itrayans or the Eradu before," Chipmunk Hunk said. He and Mary were lounging together in neighboring seats, and this was how they passed the time during our trip to Itraya. "I mean, yeah, Earth can be a little bit of a backwater, but it's not like we also haven't been in the thick of galactic politics before."

"It doesn't seem that strange to me," Mary said. "Space is huge."

"I know that! But the powers Earth has tangled with before are *also* huge. Like, galaxy-spanning."

"There are hundreds of billions of stars in the Milky Way galaxy," Mary said. "There's no reason we should have heard about two of them in particular. You're just upset because science fiction trained you to think the galaxy is neatly divided into 'territories' and 'neutral zones' between the Klingon Time Lords and Romulan Rebel Alliance or whatever."

Chipmunk Hunk's eye twitched, but he admirably did not otherwise take that bait. "No, no, science fiction trained us to think about how things fit together!" Chipmunk Hunk said. "It's important. Everything has to fit together."

"EVERYTHING DOES NOT, IN FACT, HAVE TO FIT TOGETHER," Brain Drain said. "THE UNIVERSE ADVANCES NOT TOWARD ORDER BUT CHAOS AND HEAT DEATH."

This was typically the kind of argument I'd throw my squirrel-ears headband into, but I figured I would be better served by keeping calm, collecting myself, and saving my energy. I'd cooled down since my confrontation with Hadrian.

Calling him a jerk in front of my past self had been cathartic. We'd avoided each other in the hours since. Hadrian avoided everybody, in fact, to the point that, when anyone paid him any attention, he used his storytelling superpower to narrate that they had lost interest in him and left him alone.

"I've got some questions along the same lines," Koi Boi said. "I mean, take the acanti, like our friend here." He gave the fleshy wall a pat. "I thought we'd all heard that the acanti Prophet-Singer had been freed from the Skrull, and the rest of the acanti with her."

"That's right," our whale buddy, Lightning-Apparition for now, said.

"But after that, we saw the acanti again during the Skrull's last invasion of Earth,"[68] Koi Boi said. "There were Skrull riding lobotomized acanti like nothing had changed."

"Hey, that's right," Chipmunk Hunk piped in. "I remember seeing them in news photos."

---

[68] WAS NOT GOOD TIME. HYDRA CONTROLLED UNITED STATES. CAPTAIN AMERICA OUTED AS HYDRA SLEEPER AGENT AND ON RELATED NOTE CANCELED ON TWITTER. – ED

"I wasn't there myself," Lightning-Apparition said. "But I believe you saw it."

"So... what the heck?" Koi Boi asked. "Which of those two is it?"

"Dunno," Lightning-Apparition said. "I've been out of the loop. Why does it have to be either?"

"Because they're mutually exclusive," Chipmunk Hunk said.

"Are they?" Lightning-Apparition asked.

"They can't both be true at the same time!" Chipmunk Hunk said. I understood where he was coming from. It was like the universe had forgotten that one thing had happened before the other.

"What's time?" Lightning-Apparition asked innocently.

Chipmunk Hunk opened his mouth, about to answer, and then stopped.

"EXCELLENT," Brain Drain said. "I WILL NEED A PHILOSOPHICAL CONUNDRUM TO KEEP ME OCCUPIED."

For the sake of my developing headache, I finally entered the fray. "Look, yesterday, we talked to our past and future selves just by moving really fast," I said. "Nothing has to make sense in the way you think it does. Space is weird. Time is weird. Everything's weird! Common sense has been falsified scientifically! We still have to live with it."

Nancy had so far remained quiet, though she'd started massaging her forehead minutes ago. I'd never come closer to understanding her than when I'd started getting this headache. "I would really like to go home now," she said.

"My pod-mother had a saying for days like... well, every day," Lightning-Apparition said wistfully. "'Nothing is true, but everything is real.'"

"I think it's the other way around," Mary said.

"Either way is extremely canon," I agreed. "It's even about canon. Hey, are we slowing down?"

On our screen, the blue dot of faster-than-light-whale speed once again started to blur. It blossomed outward like a dying star[69].

"Uh oh," Lightning-Apparition said.

"Please don't say that," Koi Boi said.

"Sure thing. Anyway I'm kind of frightened and you should be, too." That was even worse. "The thing is, I didn't mean to start slowing."

It had scarcely been a day since we'd left our last world, and the light echoes of ourselves, behind. I'd expected another half-week of living through arguments about continuity. The jolt of adrenaline was almost welcome. *Almost.*

The walls were quivering. "Something's doing this to me," Lightning-Apparition said. "I mean, moving my muscles without my control. Wow! Never felt anything like this! I didn't think this was even possible."

G'illian, Tippy-Toe, and Hadrian weren't in the lounge. "Everybody brace for... for something!" I called back. "Just grab onto whatever's closest to you."

"This is extremely cool," Lightning-Apparition said, "but also profoundly uncomfortable."

---

[69] The events of the last few days got me thinking more about literature, science, and the intersections thereof! Science and astronomy can lead you to things that are as evocative as they are beautiful. As suns burn through the last of their fuel, they expand into red giants, and then eventually their outer layers expand outward into a planetary nebula. It's comparatively more peaceful than a supernova – which only stars ten times or more as massive as our sun do – and kinda sweet in a way, in that the ejected mass can be recycled into new stars and planets. (It still roasts any planets that system had, though. Kinda rough.) – SG

The blue fog ballooned into a bright new starscape. Instantly it was clear something was wrong. Some of the stars were too regularly spaced. They were moving. They must have been a fleet of starships – at least three dozen of them, traveling in formation.

Strange new lights sparkled among them. They were not all that dissimilar from the flashes we'd seen when those pirate ships had fired missiles at us.

In fact, I was pretty sure it was *exactly* like that.

"Trying to move," Lightning-Apparition said, considerably more panicked. "Can't."

"–had had enough of these games," Hadrian announced, coming into earshot as he charged into the lounge. I was not surprised that he hadn't grabbed onto something secure like I'd asked. "The nightmare broke, the anxiety-induced mirage vanished, and the hero and his companions were shaken back into the present to discover what had *actually* happened was–"

<A NOISE FOR WHICH THERE
WAS NO ONOMATOPOEIA>

"Hey, are we slowing down?" I asked.

"We were all having such a good time arguing about time that I didn't want to tell you we were approaching our destination," Lightning-Apparition said. "Well, kind of. I just received a signal that said everyone approaching Itraya at faster-than-light speeds would need to pull over for inspection."

That was a lot faster than I'd expected. I leaned back to call everyone else into the lounge, but Hadrian was already there, muttering. I was astonished I hadn't heard him come in. "–that they were slowing for a routine inspection before being allowed to proceed into Itrayan space," he was saying. "In Itrayan space, even in wartime, outsiders were treated with suspicion but never fired upon without cause."

I frowned. When I'd seen the blue star start to expand, I'd had a sudden flash of anxiety, a micro-dream that we had been shot at. But it had vanished as quickly as it had come.

(I am aware of how disjointed this all seems in retrospect. I promise I am recording this exactly as I remember it happening, loud and indescribable tear in reality included. My memories are much clearer with distance, but the discontinuity was extremely tricky to recognize at the time. It took me another cycle recognize why. All I knew at the time was that my ears hurt.)

I called Tippy-Toe and G'illian into the lounge. By the time they arrived, a starfield had bloomed around us. We weren't alone out here. Some of the stars were too regularly spaced. Five of them moved placidly, in a loose formation. Their distant engine plumes sparkled against the void.

"How exactly are they going to 'inspect' us?" Chipmunk Hunk asked, under his breath.

"What are they even looking for?" Mary asked.

I craned my neck to peer at Hadrian. He was the Itrayan; he ought to know. But my question died in my throat. He wore an expression I'd never seen on him before.

He was visibly strained. He floated peacefully enough, but all his muscles were taut and sweat sheened his brow.

His voice was tight, like he was having an argument with someone. "Nothing aroused the patrol picket's immediate suspicions. Though everyone approaching Itraya was to be thoroughly inspected and analyzed, the unmistakable life sign of a fellow Itrayan meant that the whale would not have to be boarded–"

<A NOISE FOR WHICH THERE
WAS STILL NO ONOMATOPOEIA>

"–but the commander of the picket fleet decided that the unusual circumstances meant an inspection was warranted regardless," said a stern voice I didn't recognize. I whirled.

Three strangers, all of Hadrian's distinctive species and wearing uniforms of a similar style, hovered at the lounge's entrance.

They'd plainly spent a good part of their lives practicing how to move in it. Their leader pushed herself toward Hadrian, and halted easily with a tap of her foot on one of the handholds.

I was starting to recognize that strange sense of discontinuity. The thing was that, in the instant it happened, everything felt completely normal. It was only in looking back on it that I started to realize that things didn't add up. Two different stories of my recent past clashed in my head. I felt like the Itrayan boarding team had materialized instantly behind us, but somehow at the same time knew we'd been waiting for them to approach and board us for half an hour.

Adrenaline still burned in my head, but it was already fading. For a moment, I was left wondering why I'd jumped for no reason.

If I hadn't spent all that time around Hadrian, I wouldn't have recognized reality bending around someone trying to tell a story.

Only it wasn't just Hadrian telling it this time.

"The trap was sprung," the Itrayan commander said, folding her arms. She wasn't as affectless as Hadrian, but her voice was still flat by human standards. "The rest of the fleet, awaiting intruders just like this one, had decloaked and taken formation around the whale." On the screen, the number of moving stars had multiplied. Where there were once five, there were now over a dozen. "No intruders were allowed in Itrayan space, and certainly no–"

"–certainly there were no intruders to be found here," Hadrian interrupted. "Only guests of Hadrian of the Luminous Court."

"Hadrian of the Luminous Court was a wanted man," the commander said. "And he would be taken back home under guard."

"Honor guard," Hadrian hastily corrected. "And 'wanted' only in the sense that he had been summoned to appear at the Court, and so they went–"

<IMAGINE THE SOUND YOU MIGHT PERCEIVE IF YOUR OWN HEAD WERE TURNED INSIDE OUT. THAT WAS WHAT IT WAS LIKE.>

In the space of seconds, and with a false memory of days of faster-than-light flight, we were above a bright blue-orange-yellow planet.

When I say "bright", I don't mean that it was daytime, or that the world was reflecting the light of a sun. It glowed with an ethereal, hazy light of its own. So far as I could tell, the light came from everywhere – the land, the gauzy atmosphere, the pinkish-orange clouds, everything. No shadows underscored the clouds. They pushed over shadowless, crinkling mountains. The oceans sparkled as though reflecting the atmosphere's own light back up through it and at us.

I had just enough of my wits to tear my eyes off the screen and look at Hadrian and the intruder.

Both of them started talking at once.

"–the Luminous Court was not in session–" the commander said.

"–given landing clearance with diplomatic permits–" Hadrian was saying.

"–officers with a list of charges waiting for the fugitive and his companions," she said, speaking over him. Her version of reality was louder. "Their eyes had misled them. This was not the Luminous Court–"

<LOOK, IF YOU REALLY NEED AN ONOMATOPOEIA, I FEEL YOU. I LIKE THEM, TOO, BUT THERE JUST WASN'T ONE FOR THIS.>

"–it was the Prison Sphere."

The glowing world vanished, replaced by a dull gray orb, barely visible against the starscape. It was more of an occlusion of stars, a shadow in the void, than an object. But there were still glints and glimmers of reflected light. They were mirror-reflections of engine exhaust from the starships cruising beside us.

It took effort, but I finally forced my thoughts into order and recognized what was happening to us. Judging by the confusion muddling the others' expressions, they were having the same problem. The two Itrayans were dueling their narratives against each other.

Hadrian was losing.

"Editorial note," Hadrian charged. "The 'Prison Sphere' is a terrible name. Suggest revision."

"Suggestion rejected," the commander said.

Both of them were sweating, although Hadrian looked considerably more strained. Clashing their narratives against each other evidently took some effort. I had shadow-memories of a long span of time between our first meeting with the commander and coming here. Only I was getting better at recognizing the artifice. My friends and I hadn't moved.

It wasn't just the story of what was happening *to* us that was changing. It was the universe around us. The Itrayans were writing new and elaborate backstories into every moment. Their powers were changing the past. The memory of the glowing planet was fading from my mind like an old dream. It took a real effort of will to etch enough of it into my mind to record here.

Either this Itrayan's powers outstripped Hadrian's, or Hadrian had been holding back the whole time he'd been with us.

"Can I ask a question?" I asked.

"The intruder could not ask a question," the commander replied. After a moment's thought, she added, "After that question, anyway."

I opened my mouth to ask anyway, but no sound came out. My vocal cords had frozen up. It was, frankly, as horrifying as it was alienating.

I had to fight on their level. I needed a loophole. "Squirrel Girl *would* have asked if she and her friends could be taken to their leaders to discuss a matter of urgent interstellar diplomacy."

Hadrian, for once, looked directly at me. "The hero did not need to hear the Squirrel Girl's question to know what she would have asked. He told her the truth: that he would be taken to the Luminous Court to be given a fair hearing," he said, emphasizing the word *fair* as if to underline it, and make sure it became part of his reality. "And that she should make her case there."

The commander did not contradict him, but subtly changed his meaning: "The intruders' criminality would be judged along with the deserter's. They would have plenty of opportunity to enter their statements into the record then."

"The hero and his companions were swiftly escorted to the

surface, before their 'escort' could find the opportunity to abuse them further," Hadrian said.

> <GO AHEAD, IMAGINE A 'BZZZZT' OR A
> 'CRONK' OR A 'BRRUUUUUM' IF YOU WANT.
> THE IMPORTANT THING IS THAT
> YOU HAVE FUN DOING IT.>

Now all of us – except of course Lightning-Apparition – were walking down a silvered corridor at a measured pace. The commander strode just ahead of us, and we were flanked by more Itrayans. There were three of them for each of us, and, though none of them walked too near, their purpose for being there was plain.

I had a false memory of Lightning-Apparition settling to the ground on a disc-shaped landing pad, complaining about the gravity all the way. A dome had closed over us and flooded with breathable air. The moment we stepped outside, we had been flanked by uniformed Itrayan security.

Of course that hadn't happened. We'd skipped over long stretches of traveling the same way a movie or a book transitioned between scenes: maybe a few lines of explanation or a fade to imply what had happened.

My stomach was turning somersaults and every muscle in my legs, back and tail was screaming, as if I'd abruptly transitioned to full gravity after days of freefall. The non-superstrong members of the group, Nancy and Mary, paused as if winded. Brain Drain walked with the rest of us, but his hydraulics hissed abruptly, as if they'd started working again only moments ago. Tippy-Toe splayed across my shoulder. G'illian sat atop Chipmunk Hunk's head, as alert as ever, but I think she was powered by paranoia.

The commander didn't know us very well. In my false

memories, my friends and I had gone along with this without complaint, and without even asking any questions. At the very least, we would have put some solid effort into irritating our captors. Focusing on the out-of-character moment helped me draw the final line between truth and fiction.

The others exchanged glances. Chipmunk Hunk whispered to Mary, who nodded. When Nancy finished gasping at the muscle pain, she glared at the commander. The corridor ended in an imposing dark gray door. The commander and the other Itrayans, except Hadrian, halted in front of it.

I'd never heard any of the other Itrayans make a sound or join in the storytelling and wondered if they were even real. Maybe they were just novices, learning from their officer. Maybe Itrayan soldiers kept a strict code of silence during operations because of the chaos that would ensue from putting too many storytellers into the brew. Or maybe they really weren't real at all. Props, setting dressing, or plot devices.

I hoped they weren't real. I didn't want to think about the alternative. The crews of the starships we'd seen earlier must have gone *somewhere* when Hadrian changed them into a smaller picket fleet. The people occupying the vanished blue-orange-yellow world *couldn't* have been real people, written out of reality by a narrative flourish. I hoped.

The doors started to grind apart. A glowing blue fog spilled from between them. I instinctively shielded my eyes. The space on the other side of the doors was brightly lit enough to hurt my whale-interior-adjusted eyes (another break from the narrative). The colors matched those of the world we'd seen before it had been replaced by the Prison Sphere. And, just like that world, the light seemed to be coming from the air itself. From the moment we stepped inside, we stopped casting shadows. Even the wrinkles in our clothes lost their definition.

The chamber had dimly perceptible walls, but the glowing air hid all but a distant impression of them. It made the space appear much bigger than it was. It was the same effect as restaurants and stores that placed mirrors along the walls. This had to be the Luminous Court.

Hadrian had tried to visit the Luminous Court first. The picket commander tried to send him to the Prison Sphere instead. Hadrian had retaliated by rewriting the setting so that the Court had come here in order to hold a trial.

A rotund woman stood in the center of the room. She was of Hadrian's species, but her waist-length hair rippled as if in a breeze that none of the rest of us felt, and glowed the same color as the sun (the sun back home, that was). Her white robes were nearly as bright, but they "only" reflected the mist rather than glowing of their own accord. She stood beside a tall, wispy man, whose scraps of remaining hair looked as though they might fly off in the slightest wind – but even those glowed. More figures stood farther back from them, but they neither moved nor approached.

The shorter woman was one of the rare Itrayans who reacted with an expression. She clasped her hands in front of her. Her eyes twinkled with delight. Her companion stared straight on. Hadrian strode ahead of us. Our guards let him past.

"The hero dropped to one knee in greeting and supplication," he said, and then, as if an afterthought, physically kneeled. "He lowered his face not only out of tradition, but to hide the blizzard of emotions he could not contain. Then, with a raspy voice, he greeted his mother."

"Plot twist!" Lightning-Apparition said telepathically.

"Just what we needed," Nancy groused.

"Maybe," I said. I kept my eyes flickering between Hadrian and his mother, alert for the slightest change. I kept myself tense, ready to spring. Nothing here was what it seemed. Or, at least, everyone could be made to be something other than it seemed at an instant's notice.

Hadrian's mother smiled thinly. The biggest difference between her and the other Itrayans was that she displayed even the slightest of her emotions. My gut feeling was that this made her a more advanced storyteller than Hadrian, but I didn't have anything to support that.

"If she was aware of her child's emotional tumult, she was polite enough not to remark upon it. She told him that she appreciated the effort he was putting into showing, rather than just telling, and instructed him to stand."

I had so many questions. Had she always been here, even before this planet had been rewritten into the Prison Sphere? Had the world reformed around her? Or had she been narrated into existence? These seemed unanswerable, but at the same time more important than anything else. If we understood the rules to this game, we could beat it.

The wispy man beside Hadrian's mother spoke: "The adjutant asked, 'Is the deserter ready to answer for his crimes?'"

Hadrian's jaw shifted. "The hero was prepared to–"

"'Is the deserter ready to answer for his crimes?' he repeated."

Hadrian was silent for a long moment.

"The deserter was prepared to answer for his crimes," he said.

His mother's smile grew thinner.

"That was fortunate," she said, "because his contrition would lessen the blow of discovering that he had already been tried for desertion *in absentia* and determined to be guilty by the jury."

Dang, either this wasn't a very complicated court system or she was using her narrative power to gloss the legal details out of existence.

"All that remained to be determined was punishment, but he had complicated things by bringing along co-conspirators." Her eyes traveled briefly to the rest of us. "Their complicity in his desertion would be determined by the Luminous Council's war tribunal today."

"The hero was not surprised that she would have done this to him," Hadrian said, his voice small.

That choice of words, though understated, was important. Not only in calling himself a hero again, but by pinning the responsibility for this on her, he was denying that a jury had ever existed. He had accused her of writing it into the story.

Brain Drain leaned over toward the rest of us. "I DO NOT BELIEVE THIS IS A REALISTIC PORTRAYAL OF A FUNCTIONAL CRIMINAL JUSTICE SYSTEM," he said as an aside. Of course his voice still boomed across the room.

"The horrifying brain floating in a robot was correct," Hadrian said. "It was not a functional justice system. It was a simple abuse of power, with hardly an effort made to disguise it."

"Ms Hadrian's mother," I said. "Er… your majesty?"

The wispy man standing beside Hadrian's mother directed his gaze at me, and didn't hide his distaste. Hadrian's mother looked at me like I was a toddler who'd knocked over the urn at a funeral.

Okay, rewind that. I had to think like they thought. "Squirrel

Girl greeted the members of the Luminous Council respectfully, in the manner most befitting of their station."

Hadrian's mother smiled again, although in that peculiar thin way that was hard to read.

I was too worked up to keep speaking in the third person. I didn't have the power to inflict my words upon reality, anyway. "Look, I'm going to skip over the injustice of all this for now – especially the part about putting my friends and myself on trial, and *especially* the part about punishing Hadrian for not wanting to fight your war – but put a pin in that, because I want to return to it. But what I really need to talk to you about is the war."

Hadrian's mother said, "The war was not relevant to the war tribunal. The Squirrel Girl stopped sp–"

"Zip it!" I interrupted.

In a functional legal system, it wouldn't have made sense that I was allowed to interrupt. But, as Brain Drain had pointed out, this wasn't a functional system. It operated under rules of dramatic license. I'd held that license since before I knew how to walk.

Hadrian's mother looked at her taller companion. He didn't react. Neither of them interrupted me this time. The figures in the luminous fog didn't move. Like the other guards, I wasn't sure that any of them were real, or if they were props – set pieces, extras – for the much smaller number of important characters up front.

"Billions of lives are going to be affected–" I started.

"There were trillions of lives about to be affected, the hero corrected," Hadrian said.

"Trillions of lives are going to be affected by this war," I said. "It's *already* hurt a lot of people, and I don't think it's even started yet. How can you afford to spend any time standing in judgment of Hadrian when you should be doing everything in your power to stop it?"

"Why does this have to happen?" Nancy added.

"Who even are the Eradu?" Koi Boi asked.

"Neither the council chair nor the judge had the time to explain the war's necessity," Hadrian's mother said. "Nor, if they could have, would they have felt compelled to. They let their silence linger long enough to make the point—"

"—linger long enough that the hero felt compelled to fill it, by explaining the facts of the crisis," Hadrian interrupted, earning a sharp glance from his mother. He continued regardless. "Most especially the fact that the Eradu were not from this galaxy, nor any other nearby, but periodically linked to ours through a wild wormhole. He described the overall strategic situation."

The facts flooded into my head. Every few hundred thousand years, an unstable wormhole opened, bridging this galaxy with another far outside our visible universe. It connected the Itrayans and the Eradu, and catastrophic war always broke out between them. Sometimes the Itrayans found the wormhole first, and sent their forces through to the Eradu's galaxy. This time, it had happened the other way around.

The wormhole had opened months ago. Eradu ships had poured into the region, forcing local star systems into their service, and establishing their beachhead in the Milky Way swiftly. Like the Itrayans, they were numerically small and typically stuck to themselves, but reality bent and warped around them. Nothing stopped them from inflicting their perverse designs upon this galaxy. The long-established empires, from the Skrull to the Kree to the Shi'ar, had learned to stay out of their way. The Itrayans and Eradu usually kept to themselves, except when they met each other. Then their forever war began again.

So far, whichever galaxy had been invaded, the Itrayans or the Eradu had pushed them back to the wormhole before it closed. Both sides still dreamed of permanent conquest. Each was anathema to the other.

I looked to Nancy, who returned my glance with her eyebrows raised. We knew each other well enough that I might as well have read her mind. The Eradu's powers sounded remarkably similar to the Itrayans'.

"So what have Eradu done that's so horrible?" Nancy asked.

Hadrian blinked. "The hero wondered if the Squirrel Girl had been listening. They attempt to force their logic, their ways of thinking, and their narratives upon this galaxy."

I stared at Hadrian. Then at his mother and her companion. The latter two showed no signs of self-awareness.

"Their thoughts are poison to us," Hadrian's mother said. "As they would be to the rest of this galaxy, if they were allowed to take root."

"You mean," I said, "that they take their understanding of the universe – their narratives – and write them into fact."

Hadrian's expression clouded and he looked abruptly to his side, lost in thought.

One of the reasons human beings tell stories to each other is to communicate complex ideas through narrative.[70] Lecture children all you want about diligence and consistency, but the

---

[70] One of the reasons I'm writing this letter right now, in fact. – SG

story of the tortoise and the hare is easier to understand. I might have been thinking about the Itrayans the wrong way. Like they were overpowered English majors. Drama geeks, theater majors, that kind of crowd. Maybe the better way to think of them was as philosophers. Ideologues.

I felt like slapping myself on the head. I'd been looking at things on the surface. The most important things about the narrative Hadrian spun weren't the events he spoke into being. The ideas underneath them were the core of the story.

That story being that Hadrian was sad. He was lonely. And he did not believe that anything good could happen to him, not without something more awful falling upon him afterward.

Hadrian's mother was after something much larger and deadlier than that.

"I get it now," I told Hadrian's mother. "You're the real villains of this story."

Hadrian's mother startled like I'd just slapped her with my tail. Which I wished I could do.

"The final bosses, as it were," I said.

I was wrong about that, by the way. I had one more villain to beat, and it wasn't Itrayan or Eradu.

"The Luminous Court and its war tribunal would not be delayed by the defendants filibustering their way through their statements," the wispy man said, sounding bored.

"The hero had smuggled a stun grenade through the tribunal's lax security," Hadrian said quietly.

As he spoke, he reached underneath his uniform's side pockets. That pocket had a lump I was *confident* hadn't been there a moment ago. He pulled out a fist-sized silver sphere.

"But he had actually mista–" Hadrian's mother started to say.

She didn't get a chance to finish the sentence. Hadrian didn't try to out-narrate her. He didn't say anything at all. He threw – physically threw – the sphere onto the floor.

My squirrel reflexes gave me just enough time to look away. An enormous *bang* slammed against both my ears. The shock rattled my skull. My muscles convulsed and then locked solid. An instant after that, and I couldn't feel anything at all.

When I returned to myself, I was on the floor. Every part of me felt like I was being jabbed with needles. My nerves were somewhere between "tingling" and "on fire". It took a frankly silly amount of effort to push myself to my knees.

Almost everyone else was down. My friends, Hadrian and his mother, the wispy man, our guards, and all the anonymous figures back in the luminous fog – everyone except Brain Drain, who was helping Koi Boi and Mary off the floor. He held each of them under one metal claw. I couldn't tell whether he'd been affected by the stun grenade or had just remained standing.

Tippy-Toe had fallen off my shoulder. I scooped her up and staggered to my feet.

Hadrian's mother twitched. She still wore her smile, but it was about ten times goofier. Goofy to the point where it circled all the way back around to tense and creepy.

She'd be all right, probably.

I knelt next to Hadrian. He was doing a little better. He was shaking like the rest of us, but his eyes, unlike his mother's, focused on me as I approached.

"N-n-n-n-n–" he said.

He hadn't really thought this one through. That was all right. It was the thought that counted. If he could make noises, though, the others would soon enough. I tried to help him up, but he regained enough control of his hand to block my arm as I moved it around his shoulder.

"N-n-need," he said.

"You can do it, buddy!" I whispered. "I believe in you!"

He treated me to a rare expression: an exasperated stare.

He couldn't narrate his way out of me helping him. I bapped his hand away with my tail, and then succeeded in at least getting him to his knees.

"T-the Sq-Squirrel Girl needed to get out of here," Hadrian stammered.

"*We* need to get out of here," I said, looking around. I realized I didn't actually know where to go. The scene transition getting here hadn't left me with a memory of the path back to our space whale friend.

He shook his head. "If she went, the Luminous Tribunal would simply rewrite events until she and her friends were recaptured or killed." Huh. That was the first time he'd referred to his powers directly. Maybe he was starting to see more things from our perspective. He added, "Not unless somebody stayed to fight them word-for-word."

"*No.*" I didn't realize how strongly I'd felt about helping him until just this moment. "First of all, we're not leaving you with these abusive jerks. Second of all, we *still* aren't leaving you with these jerks. And third of all – we're going to need your help to figure out what to do next." We couldn't just plunge back out into space without any idea of where to go. We still had a war to stop, and less and less time to do it.

I didn't think I was *wrong* to get peeved at him earlier. Not exactly. But if we'd gone back to that moment, knowing then what I knew now, it would have taken some of the edge off.

He smiled briefly. "The wormhole was not indestructible. Each side had left it intact because they harbored dreams of conquest and could not tolerate the idea that their opponents remained alive elsewhere in the galaxy. But it could be closed with the right tools. The hero told her where to find the wormhole."

The wispy man was starting to stir. His mouth was moving. I'd be lying if I said I didn't feel a trill of fear. I was the Unbeatable Squirrel Girl, but… I'd never gone up against anybody who could, in a scarily literal sense, scratch that first word off my name.

I was going to win, somehow, but I hadn't figured the *how* part out yet. My legs were still quivery. I fought to get to my feet, dragging Hadrian with me.

When Hadrian looked at me, there was steel in his eyes. He looked at the wispy man, whose mouth was starting to move.

Then Hadrian's gaze went unfocused, and trailed out into the middle distance.

"The Squirrel Girl listened to her friend carefully, respected his judgment, and–"

"No!"

"–got herself and her friends safely off the Prison Sphere, without him."

<A NOISE FOR WHICH THERE
REMAINED NO ONOMATOPOEIA>

The Unbeatable Squirrel Girl Vs The Hugest Metaphor

A naked singularity is not as much fun as the name makes it sound like it's going to be.

I mean, everybody likes the word "naked", so I don't think I need to go into detail about that. But the name "singularity" is evocative and cool. It's kind of like "quantum" in that people slap it into anything they want to give the etymological equivalent of mirror shades from techno-AI fantasy utopias to theories of panconsciousness that only Brain Drain would be able to explain.

And then there are astronomical singularities like the one my friends and I orbited.

It *was* evocative. It *was* cool. It was also highly terrifying.

The physics of black holes are fascinating, but you don't want to meet many of them up close. You'll get flash-fried by radiation, crushed by gravity (or stretched into molecules-long filaments as you fall), and a whole bunch of other things that make the environment downright unfriendly to squirrels, girls, and all other kinds of lifeforms in between.

Hadrian had sent us to what he called a "wild wormhole", but he had neglected to say that it was orbiting one of these gorgeous monstrosities.

Or the space around the black hole was gorgeous, at least. The black hole was, well, a black hole. *That* name was simpler than "singularity", if less cool. Like the "big bang", it accurately described the thing in question while, at the same time, enormously understating its weirdness.

It was a hole in space, and in more than one sense. It was a region where gravity so densely warped space-time that the laws of physics as we understood them broke down.

My friends and I were no strangers to picking up physics, snapping it over our knees, and juggling the pieces... but this felt different. This was the kind of *weird* that, the more I learned, the more I got freaked out. It wasn't just weird; it was mathematically, scientifically weird.

If you try to understand black holes using conventional physics, your equations just plain break down. You end up dividing by zero, or making calculations with infinite energy, or worse: ending up with perfectly consistent and verifiable results that also indicate that the rest of the universe couldn't possibly exist. If you thought about it too much, you risked going eating-your-own-hair nuts.[71]

There are so many weird astronomical phenomena, from superdense neutron stars (which are also exactly what they sound like: stars that are one giant neutron) to gamma ray bursts to Galactus, but black holes are hard to top.

A black hole doesn't look like much from the outside because

---

[71] My hair tastes like chestnuts. Ask me how I know! – SG

it *can't* look like much from the outside. Its gravity is so intense that light can't escape it. So, to the naked eye, it really is just pure black. The deepest, darkest black you can imagine. It traps every single kind of light that falls into it, without exception. No reflections, no nothing.

Of course, if that were the end of the story, it still wouldn't look like much. A blank in space. What made this black hole so wonderful and terrible, though, was the light show all around it.

It had come at a tremendous cost. Hundreds of thousands to millions of years ago, the black hole had passed near another star. The black hole had ripped the star to shreds and then swallowed most of it whole.

Not all of it, though. Some remnants had escaped, tossed out into the wider universe to cool to dust. Others had become trapped in orbit around the black hole, and followed it on its murderous journey through the galaxy.

From the amount of leftover mass, Lonely-Formation guessed that the star had been an ordinary yellow sun, not all that different from Earth's. Because most star systems didn't bear life, the odds were that the star system hadn't had anyone living there. But, if there had been, there wasn't any way to tell. Every trace of them would have been completely annihilated.

As the star had broken down, it had mostly stopped burning. All that was left of the star were shreds of gas, mostly unfused hydrogen. There was no longer enough heat or pressure to support fusion, the engine that made stars shine.

Mostly.

The stellar remnants spun in ever-tighter orbit around the black hole. They formed what was called an accretion disk. It didn't look all that different from the newborn stars Lonely-

Formation had shown us back in their molecular dust cloud. Except, of course, for the hungry void at the center.

The stellar remnants weren't perfectly stable. Due to collisions with other objects, or the gravitational influence of other celestial bodies – or a million things, really – a certain percentage of the remnants fell closer to the black hole every year.

Callback time! Remember when I mentioned conservation of angular momentum earlier?[72] How, as you spin in a chair and stick your legs out or draw them in, you change the speed of your spin? Same thing applies to the accretion disk. As the remnants fell farther in, they spun faster. As they spun faster, they crashed into each other more often. That generated lots of friction and, therefore, friction heat. The farther they fell, the faster they spun, and the more heat they produced.

All that heat and pressure, on so much unburned stellar fuel, restarted stellar fusion. The gas ignited. The remains of the dead star shone one last time as they were drawn into the maw of oblivion.

The black hole had a brilliant, yellow-orange accretion disk. The solar nebula spun outward like filaments of dew on a spider's web, or the petals on a sunflower. It was beautiful but somehow still felt like nails in my stomach. The beauty was the inverse of the planetary nebula we'd seen earlier. Rather than coalescing around a newborn star, a dead star was caught in a whirlpool above oblivion.

Most of the disk was yellow, orange, and red. The pieces that had fallen closer to the black hole, though, spun faster and

---

[72] WAIT, HOLD ON, STOP WRITING. HULK STILL TRYING TO FIND WHAT PAGE THIS WAS ON. – ED

brighter. Their colors changed to blue, violet, and white, and burned much brighter. It made the dark of the event horizon seem sharper. Razor-edged, even.

Lonely-Formation said that the hard radiation outside tickled a little bit. It would have swiftly killed an unprotected human, though. Millions of miles away, the black hole was still lethal.

That wasn't the only way this black hole could kill us. Close to the black hole, the magnetic fields were so intense that they alone could disrupt the human nervous system, and cause brain death.

If you somehow got closer than that, the black hole's gravity was so steep and so intense that there would have been a big difference in gravitational pull between a person's feet and their head. A really steep difference. Close enough in, and a person wouldn't have time to notice their feet and their head departing the rest of their body. The gravitational shear was strong enough to not only tear a person (or a squirrel, or even a Squirrel Girl) to pieces, but it would eventually strain what was left into a noodle-thin stream of matter. It was a process that astronomers had delightfully named "spaghettification".[73]

The others were silent too, as they took this in.

My friends and I were all seated in our usual places, ringing Lonely-Formation's screen. Tippy-Toe was no longer perched on my shoulder, but had nestled in my hair – something she only did when she was exceptionally nervous. G'illian seemed to have adopted Chipmunk Hunk, who, in the absence of his own chipmunky friends, was happy to have a tiny furry friend.

---

[73] HULK NOT KNOW WHY ASTRONAUTS ALWAYS SAY THEY SHOULD HAVE BROUGHT POET. SCIENTISTS PERFECTLY GOOD AT POETIC METAPHOR. – ED

She curled around his shoulder. I couldn't tell who needed the comfort more.

Brain Drain's claws were locked around one of the handholds, and we'd curled up his non-functioning body into a seated position so that he wouldn't swing around. We expected that there might be some turbulence ahead.

"IF IT IS ANY COMFORT," Brain Drain offered, "THIS IS NOT THE METAPHOR FOR FINALITY AND DEATH THAT IT MIGHT FIRST APPEAR. NOT EVEN BLACK HOLES LAST FOREVER. THEY SLOWLY DECAY BECAUSE OF A PHENOMENON CALLED HAWKING RADIATION. EVENTUALLY, GIVEN UNFATHOMABLE TIME, THEY WILL EVAPORATE. THE DARK AND THE COLD AT THE END OF TIME WILL TRIUMPH EVEN OVER THE HUNGER OF THE VOID."

"Thanks, Brain Drain," Nancy said.

"YOU ARE WELCOME." He paused. "ALTHOUGH NOW THAT I HAVE SAID IT ALOUD, IT IS NOT NEARLY SO COMFORTING AS IT SEEMED."

I'd faced down the destruction of Earth before. I'd talked down Galactus. Galactus and I had become friends, even! Those threats had been alive, though. They'd been people, in one sense or another, no matter how advanced or alien. I could talk with them. There was no negotiating with natural phenomena. I could talk to the black hole all I wanted, but for once that wouldn't help anything. Even the super scientists I knew back home didn't understand black holes, not really.[74]

---

[74] Dang, and I'm even out of time to write about how time slows the closer you get to a black hole. Well, it doesn't "slow" for the person that's fallen in, it's everything else that speeds up, because time is relative to the observer and ... well, it's complicated. – SG

I tried to focus on the material facts on hand: 1) the black hole was incredibly dangerous, 2) the accretion disk around the black hole was incredibly dangerous, 3) the dangers out there could kill a person in ways that would make for fascinating diagrams in physics and astronomy textbooks, and 4) I was going to have to go out there.

The thing was that Hadrian's "wild wormhole" was in tight orbit around the black hole. It skimmed the event horizon, almost at the point where gravitational shear would tear a person to pieces. The energies in play were important to the wormhole's functioning. It took a lot of energy to rip open space between two distant galaxies. If you wanted to find lots of energy, this was where you went.

Deadly, deadly energy.

Nancy checked her watch. After all of the spacetime-twisting superluminal travel we'd done, I didn't think she could trust that it was still telling the time on Earth, but it gave her something to focus on. "Assuming that finals are delayed for a week because of the destruction of a building," Nancy said, "we can make it back in time if we get this done in about… six hours."

She remained laser-focused on getting home. She and G'illian had discussed which direction we needed to go to get to Earth. They'd gone over it with Lonely-Formation, who'd made a confident guesstimate about the time it would take to get there.

"Glad to hear," I said.

"You don't *sound* glad to hear it," Nancy said.

I'm the Unbeatable Squirrel Girl. I wasn't feeling beaten, and I didn't believe I ever would. But I was feeling… worn down. Just because I couldn't be beaten, that didn't mean I couldn't suffer losses along a journey. Hadrian and the Mad Thinker were open sores in my psyche. Both of them should have been here.

And then there was this thing that I was about to do. The reason I'm writing this entire letter, and, after my good editor friend gives it a once-over, going to seal it in a time capsule forever.

Mary saved me from having to answer Nancy. "I really don't need to be thinking about finals right now. I hate tests. Just give me a lab assignment."

"Same," Chipmunk Hunk said.

"*I* like tests," Koi Boi said. "Filling in bubble sheets, getting in the zone…"

"'In the zone,'" Mary repeated dryly, letting the words hang.

"I don't care what you say," Koi Boi said, crossing his arms. "I'm cool."

"You *are* cool," I confirmed.

They were trying to distract themselves from the black hole. There wasn't much else to say now. Other than chiming in with a quip or two to remind them I was still there, I kept my lips sealed. If I told them too much, I worried that I would give away what I would have to do next.

There would still be a little time to talk later.

Part of my problem was that I could no longer be sure which of my memories were real. I *thought* the time since we'd left the Prison Sphere had actually passed.

The moment Hadrian had pronounced his final words, my stomach had somersaulted into freefall. Despite that, I hadn't been able to feel shock. Half of me felt like I'd just been tossed out of full gravity and back into freefall, but the other half felt like I'd been here for close to an hour. The physical reality that I had plunged into freefall clashed with false memories of escaping that Hadrian had given me.

The inconsistencies were obvious once I knew how to look for them. I wondered if this was how characters in books and comics felt between scenes but were never allowed to say.

On the screen, a delta formation of stars – Itrayan starships – advanced toward us. Plumes of engine exhaust burned brightly behind them as they drew nearer. Then they vanished underneath another ear-splitting clash of false memories and unsettled realities. The formation was replaced by a smattering of chaotically moving stars and luminous fog, the remnants of a battle fought between them.

Back down on the Prison Sphere, Hadrian seemed to be narrating a revolution into being.

His version of events hadn't held long. The debris disappeared, and so did most of the starships. I had trouble remembering that they'd even been there, but the afterimages of glowing debris lingered in my retinas.

The Prison Sphere had become an even darker gray. The mirror reflections had vanished. Its surface had become featureless, as if enclosed in an opaque shield. Some kind of lockdown. In another roar of false memories, the Prison Sphere vanished entirely. I wasn't sure it had ever been there, or if everything there had been an illusion.

I had the feeling that the narrative was still being written. The story hadn't settled.

"Well," Brain Drain said, but stopped there. For once, even he'd had no words.

"Um," Koi Boi added. "Huh."

"Quite," Mary said dryly.

There had been nothing left to do but run before we, too, were edited away.

The tricky part had come afterward, thinking back on what Hadrian had told me. A new sentence had popped into my mind that I was sure – well, *maybe* sure[75] – he hadn't actually said at the time. Either during the battle or afterward, he must have retconned it into my head.

"The hero told the Squirrel Girl, in exacting detail, what must be done to collapse the wormhole," he'd perhaps said. "She was not going to appreciate it."

He was right. When the knowledge popped into my head, my skin went cold.

Finding the components for the device Hadrian had instructed us to make wasn't difficult. They were things whose purposes eluded me: a tiny rare-metal asteroid from a gas giant's rings, a filament of iron exposed to a flash of radiation from a rapidly spinning pulsar, a glass of heavy water[76]. I supposed the important thing wasn't how they physically worked, but how significant they *felt*. We were still operating under Hadrian's narrative rules here.

The important thing was that we hadn't had trouble finding them. We'd assembled them into a device the size of my palm. It looked like a clockwork rat's nest, was studded with blinking containment devices, and certainly felt like it ought to do *something*. That last part was the important one.

For as deadly as the environment around the black hole was, we *did* have the means to survive it, thanks to alien super science. One of the spacesuits Lonely-Formation traveled with – the largest, least comfortable-looking one – could protect a suitably hardy Squirrel Girl for about an hour. According to Lonely-

---

[75] Call it a fifty percent chance of certainty. Or somewhat absolutely sure. – SG

[76] That is, water molecules where the hydrogen atoms were deuterium isotopes rather than regular hydrogen. – SG

Formation, it didn't so much contain shielding as surround its wearer in an artificial pocket universe with its own laws of physics.

It could have been nonsense, and *sounded* like nonsense, especially given Lonely-Formation's grasp of their own means of travel. But I believed Lonely-Formation wouldn't try to harm me. However the suit actually worked, they weren't mistaken about its capabilities.

Navigating to the black hole had taken some doing. As Hadrian had said, their enemies, the Eradu, had seized territory throughout the region.

Lonely-Formation had ducked vast sensor webs strung across space. Patrol ships sweeping the area for intruders. Fleets mustering in battle formations, testing planet-killing weapons. And a distress call from a ship whose holographic entertainment programs had attained sentience and were subjecting its crew to endless jazz,[77] lounge singing, and charming rustic villages. But that last one didn't seem relevant or urgent, and so we made a note to return there later.

We slipped through without notice this time. Now that Lonely-Formation knew to keep a low profile, they crept through the lines stealthily. They said they could appear to be debris to most sensors – squishy, blubbery debris, but that still didn't seem to arouse any attention.

There was no telling which ships were Eradu and which were locals that had been impressed into their service. We avoided them either way. If the Eradu had universe-editing powers on the scale of the Itrayans, the only way we were going to beat them was by slipping their notice.

---

[77] This is just what the translator told me! I assume it's an alien equivalent of jazz. – SG

My friends passed the time by making plans for getting home. "Earth isn't safe for me anymore," G'illian said, hugging her little squirrel arms around herself. "The Skrull know I tried to live there. Even if they're not around, I'm going to see them behind every tree, in every alley…"

"Are you not going to see them everywhere else?" Chipmunk Hunk asked gently.

"Well," G'illian said. "No…"

"You can admit that part of you still thinks we're Skrull right now," Nancy said.

"Is it that obvious?" G'illian asked, kneading her claws.

"You've survived a lot of trauma," Nancy said. "We get it. You know, we're a pretty happy-go-lucky group, but I think all of us have been in some pretty bleak places before."

"Have I told you what it is like when I try to sleep?" Brain Drain asked.

"Yes," everyone answered.

"The point is," Nancy said, before Brain Drain could delve deeper into that, "is that we're super heroes. There's not a month when one of us isn't facing down some kind of clone, or parallel universe self, or time-traveling future self, or having our bodies stolen, or being hypnotized into fighting one another. I'm not saying this to minimize what you've gone through. Because it's pretty hard, actually! But you do have friends who understand at least a little bit about what you're going through. That helps me keep it together."

G'illian's twitching tail gave away her nervous energy. Squirrels did that when they were measuring their balance, as if getting ready to leap somewhere to escape.

"Look at it this way," Koi Boi said. "Loki sent you in the

right direction, didn't he? He's got an, uh, interesting sense of humor, but he *probably* meant well. Sure, a hundred thousand light years or so off, but he knew you'd find friends." Loki must have divined, using whatever flavor of powers he'd decided he had this month, that I would end up out this way. "And that we really are the best people to help you." He looked to me for support.

Look, Loki was a friend. But he was also the kind of friend whose graduating class would vote him Least Likely To Help You Get Home If You're Stranded Across Space. He'd think that kind of thing was a lark. He would have especially gotten a kick out of sending G'illian a million light-years away just to find me – someone that, in ordinary circumstances, she could have found by hopping on the subway.

Loki was also, notably, *not* an oracle. Maybe he'd counted on G'illian and me not knowing that. But I had Deadpool's deck of flashcards with me and I'd double-checked: no abilities to read the future.

He was up to something here. Playing some kind of game. But I had no idea what and telling G'illian this would have just undermined her new trust in us.[78]

"Friendship and squirrels are kind of our thing," I told G'illian.

When the others were suitably distracted by each other quipping, I quietly slipped away, into one of Lonely-Formation's farther bronchial passages.

The suit resembled a metal-clad dinosaur: ten feet tall, all sharp angles, and with an extruding jaw. There was no visor.

---

[78] HULK DETECT SEQUEL HOOK. -Ed

There was also a strange shimmer around it. Like a heat mirage, though I felt no actual heat involved.

As I approached, the front of the suit split open like a blossoming flower. For all the suit's ugly bulk, it looked easy enough to get into. Inside was a cushioned space, made to be perfectly comfortable for a body shape that was not my own. Whatever species had made this suit, they'd had at least two extra sets of knees and elbows, and had been very tall.

Tippy-Toe was uncommonly quiet. Lonely-Formation had done as I'd asked, and kept my secrets. Other than Tippy-Toe, who would always be with me, none of the others knew I was suiting up now.

"I dunno about this," Lonely-Formation said. "You ever think about how much you have to lose?"

I swallowed back my first answer. "I mean, it *has* been on my mind. A lot. A lot of a lot."

"I have my limits, you know. Once you're far enough out there, I won't be able to pick you up."

"Believe me, I am aware of that."

"I'll go along with what you think the best thing to do is," Lonely-Formation said. "I'm pretty chill about most things. I dunno if I can be about this one."

"War is a crime," I said. "I have never understated something so much in my life and you *know* I'm a serial exaggerator. War is a level of supervillainy beyond what even I'm used to dealing with. And when it doesn't just involve one world, or even one galaxy, I can't let it happen."

They paused for a moment, considering. "Yeah. I see where you're coming from."

"Trust me on this one," I said, and stepped up onto the

spacesuit's platform-sized boots. Then I carefully lowered myself
into the cushioned interior.

Fitting took some adjustment. I'm used to having to squeeze
my tail into tight places, but not my legs or hips. I had to be
extremely careful around the servos around the suit's extra knees
and elbows. Lonely-Formation didn't *think* they would activate,
but couldn't guarantee it. I didn't want to think too much about
what would happen if they tried to bend my arms and legs in
places that couldn't bend. The Unbeatable Squirrel Girl can't be
beaten, but she can get broken bones.

Tippy-Toe skittered from my left shoulder to my right
shoulder and finally wrapped around my neck as I squeezed in.

"Sure you want to do this?" I asked her.

"Where you go, I go," she said.

The suit sealed over us. For a moment, we were in complete
darkness. The sound of my breathing was far too loud.

"Doesn't mean I think it's a good idea," Tippy-Toe muttered.

Then the world sprung back into place around us. The suit had
no visor, but the headpiece held a hundred different holographic
projectors. The rendered world was so complete that I saw the
outside world as fully as if I weren't wearing a helmet at all. The
illusion only broke when I looked down and saw the rest of my
suit. Some of the flexible neckpiece had fuzzed where the suit
sensors weren't quite in a position to find it.

Experimentally, I raised my right arm and flexed my fingers.
The arm moved easily enough, if on a delay. Servos in the suit
responded to my muscle movements. Finger movement was
another matter. Whoever had built these suits had hands with
nine fingers, and whichever of them moved with mine seemed
random.

The heat-mirage shimmer persisted, but it wasn't right in front of me. When I looked to my sides, I caught glimpses of it. Hadrian's clockwork device fit snug into the suit's left hand. With all the device's unnecessary bits and bobs sticking out all over, I'd have no trouble keeping a grip on it.

"So why aren't you trying to talk me out of it?" I asked Tippy-Toe.

"Because I trust you to know what the right thing is," Tippy-Toe said.

At the time, that had felt good to hear.

The Unbeatable Squirrel Girl Vs Main Character Syndrome (Round Two)

Inside the alien spacesuit, my mouth tasted like I'd washed it out with soap.

I tried one more time to talk Tippy-Toe out of coming with me. "You have other friends besides me," I said. "Lots and lots of squirrel friends. You won't be able to see them for a while."

Dead silence from the back of my neck. But I felt Tippy-Toe's claws dig a little deeper.

Text hovered around the fringes of my sight. Whoever had designed this suit had a much wider field of vision than humans. Eyes on the sides of my head was one of the few squirrel traits I *didn't* have. I wouldn't have been able to read the alien words, anyway. Moving in the suit was surprisingly easy, if on a weird time lag before the servos kicked in. I freefall-swam toward Lonely-Formation's "airlock", hoping past hope that none of my friends heard the clomping and squishing noises.

"Oof," Lonely-Formation said, and then, "Ouch. That thing's more massive than I remember."

"You okay?" I asked Lonely-Formation.

"Let you know as soon as you stop banging that thing around," they said. "Good thing I have twelve kidneys. Gonna have to take that one offline for a bit."

"Sorry," I said, sincerely. I guess I'd underestimated the strength of the servos as I swung my arms around.

"No biggie. Probably."

I pushed into the airlock. The inner passage irised closed behind me. Fortunately, Lonely-Formation didn't leave me alone to think for long.

After a fog-burst of freezing escaping air, I got intimately acquainted with the universe.

No spacesuits I'd worn had given me such a clear view outside. Tony's suits might have had more capabilities, but even he would have been jealous of the view.

The escaping atmosphere gave me a little kick out into space. Stars strung the sky over my head. The dead sun burned under my feet.

The suit had its own thrusters, controlled via finger movements in the gloves. Switch the controls on, and, when you crooked a finger one way, the boot thrusters fired. Crook a different finger, and the shoulder thrusters fired. Again, though, these suits had been made for wearers with nine fingers. It took effort, lots of tumbling, and a spin back into Lonely-Formation's flank[79] before I found a semblance of control.

The suit had held up well for however many years Lonely-

---

[79] Oh boy, can you get dizzy in zero gravity. I hadn't eaten for hours before this for a reason. – SG

Formation had it. Everything seemed to be working except my rear shoulder blade thrusters. Their exhaust plume sputtered and coughed in several directions. I made a mental note to avoid using those. Facing backwards, with Hadrian's device gripped in my other suit glove, I dove away from Lonely-Formation.

I caught a glimpse of one of Lonely-Formation's eyes. I hadn't seen either of those since the day we met.

The last time I'd been outside Lonely-Formation had been in the dark around the asteroid station. The light of the accretion disk showed me all of them. Their skin was leathery, and the pits of micrometeorite impacts cast steep shadows across them. Pale, smooth scar tissue sealed their cybernetic components and prosthetics into their body.

Their eye was solid black, and seemed tiny against the rest of them. It had a rheumy film. Lonely-Formation had several transparent eyelids to protect them from vacuum and cosmic radiation.

I'd forgotten how ancient Lonely-Formation looked. When they spoke, their telepathic voice ran a spectrum between bubbly and chill. To my inner ear, they sounded about twenty.

I carefully turned away. Though Lonely-Formation hadn't hidden from me or asked me to look away, I wanted to remember them as they chose to present.

It wasn't long before things got worse.

I fell toward the wormhole as fast as my suit thrusters would take me. Before long, gravity had outmatched the thrusters. I wasn't that close to the black hole, not yet, and already the gravity gradient between my orbit and Lonely-Formation's orbit was enough to send me plunging away.

The dead sun burned so brightly that, whenever I looked down, everything else disappeared. The stars, my suit, and even the outer edges of the accretion disk. The suit's sensors were overloading just trying to block the radiation.

My target was just visible. The wormhole was a speck in the accretion disk, the dark center of its own whirlpool of light. It was a microcosm of a black hole system.

It wasn't long before things got worse.

"So," Lonely-Formation told me. "Some things are happening."

I'd much rather have solved a problem than spent more time alone with my thoughts. "That doesn't sound good," I said, cheerfully.

As soon as I finished speaking, the suit's radio crackled, and Nancy's voice filled my helmet. "Doreen, *what the heck?*"

I swallowed. I *had* counted on my friends finding out what was going on, so that I could talk to them before doing this. "Look," I said, "I've been thinking about some things."

"You can think about them back here, *right now*. Doreen, we've been discovered. There's some kind of unimaginably powerful battle fleet heading this way."

"It's true," Lonely-Formation said. "The Eradu or one of their allies must have double-checked their sensor logs and found that I was too warm and squirmy to be regular space debris. There are about seventy warships heading our way."

"Hurry up. There's probably time to get back here," Nancy said.

"Maybe," Lonely-Formation chimed in.

I was still much closer to Lonely-Formation than I was to the wormhole. In space travel and orbital mechanics, though, distance is a little less meaningful than it is on a flat surface. The gravity of the black hole meant that it would have taken me a lot more time and energy to climb back toward Lonely-Formation than to keep falling. To put it another way – in terms of physical measurements, I wasn't all that far from Lonely-Formation. In a much more real sense, I was already closer to the wormhole and the new universe on the other side.

"Not sure Nancy is right, to be honest," Lonely-Formation said. "Each ship in those fleets is staying in formation, but some of them look smaller than the others, and have bigger engines to boot. Advance ships could peel off at any moment. I bet they could beat you to the wormhole."

"Heck," I swore. "Frig." Deep breath. I had contingency plans. "All right. Nancy, I'm going to need your help figuring something out."

I wasn't just scooting about in a straight line. I'd started this trip not only where Lonely-Formation was, in orbit around the black hole, but traveling at the same speed they were. The way orbital mechanics worked, you couldn't just point a spacecraft (or spacesuit) at something, fly straight, and expect to get there. Though I could see the speck of the wormhole, I had to crane my neck. I'd plotted out my trajectory in advance, using the flight computers in Lonely-Formation's lounge while the others slept.

The black hole's magnetic field had etched fields of radiation around like waves in a pond, and I'd taken care to steer clear of the worst of them. Only now I was going to need to take a chance and plunge through those belts. I had to reach the wormhole faster. And that meant I needed new calculations.

I needed the computers back aboard Lonely-Formation. And I needed Nancy.

"Absolutely not," Nancy said, when I told her she had to give me a faster route to the wormhole. "No. You're out of your mind. Never."

I was starting to get jealous of Hadrian's powers. If *I'd* been writing this moment, I would have turned that into a stock sitcom joke and smash cut to Nancy doing exactly what I'd asked. But I wasn't so fortunate.

As it was, I had already had to lay down the very last card in my hand: *"Trust me."*

There was a long silence on the other end. A lot longer than when I'd used the card last time.

"Working on the calculations," Nancy said, in a quiet, tight voice.

"I think you would've needed to adjust your trajectory anyway," Lonely-Formation said. "You're not where you should be. Might've gotten the suit's mass wrong in the first calculations. Kinda weird."

"There are things going on that I need to explain," I told Nancy.

My friends thought all we had to do was toss the device down the wormhole, and that all Lonely-Formation needed to do was maneuver into position. The truth was a little more complicated.

We weren't fighting a purely physical battle. There was, and please forgive me for writing something like this and I promise I'll never do it again, a metafictional element, too. The Eradu had powers on the scale of the Itrayans. Physically destroying the wormhole wouldn't do much good if they could just narrate it back into existence.

Hadrian had sincerely apologized for this. The only way he could think of to make the loss stick was to make it a good story. A memorable story, with a memorable ending, that still left an opening for a sequel. The Itrayans and the Eradu respected storytelling.

Whoever collapsed the wormhole would need to do it on the other side.

They wouldn't need to die. That wouldn't leave much possibility for a sequel. But they would need to sacrifice their hopes, dreams, and everything else from their lives on their own side of the wormhole.

I couldn't let any of my friends do that.

Earth had a lot of heroes protecting it. That wasn't to say life there was easy, or that we didn't always need more heroism... but Earth was full of heroes I trusted. My friends included.

There were trillions of beings who didn't have that same level of protection. The number of lives at stake out here dwarfed the population of Earth by an absolutely silly order of magnitude. If the war brewing between the Itrayans and the Eradu had made anything clear, it was that the galaxy at large needed more heroism. I doubted it was much different on the other side of the wormhole.

If I could do anything to help those trillions of beings... if I trusted my friends and Earth to stay together in my absence (and I did), I had an obligation to go.

The ethical calculus was not complicated.

I don't like to talk about this because I've got some complicated feelings about it, but my current gaggle of friends wasn't my first super hero team. I used to fight crime with the Great Lakes Avengers. And I'd had to make the hard choice to leave them. There'd been a couple reasons for it. I'd been holding them back, taking too much of their spotlight and not letting them get the experience they needed.

It's the nature of super heroes that we don't stay in one place or one team forever.[80] We rarely get to say goodbye when we expect.

I couldn't tell Nancy all that. It would have hurt the both of us too much. But I did tell her that Hadrian's device needed to be activated from the wormhole's other side. Tippy-Toe's grip on my neck tightened. It was strange that I found comfort in her claws digging into my skin, but there were we.

"When I tell you, fire your thrusters about ten degrees to the left of where you see the wormhole now," Nancy said. She was such a good friend for doing that for me, even when she knew what I'd asked. "You really can't be serious about this. Earth is your home, Doreen. It's where all the squirrels are. And me, and Mew–"

"And all of us!" Koi Boi said. His voice came through distorted. He must have been farther away from the receiver.

"–*Your whole life*," Nancy said.

"I know," I said.

At the start of all this, before we'd discovered we were in the Milky Way galaxy, I was determined that we would cross infinite time and space to get back home. I still believed we could have. Even exiled to the other side of this wormhole, I knew I still could find another way home. The difference between now and then was that now I didn't think it would have been right to.

Panicked chatter filtered through the radio. The others hadn't stopped broadcasting, but they were speaking too far away from the receiver for me to pick up. Plotting how to get me back.

When Chipmunk Hunk spoke to me, he sounded broken up

---

[80] HULK FACT CHECK: TRUTH. – ED

in multiple senses of the phrase. "I don't know how, Doreen, but somehow we've got even more problems."

"He's extremely correct," Lonely-Formation said. "Like I thought, some of those ships are speedier than others. As soon as you started falling toward the wormhole faster, about a dozen of those ships kicked in the afterburners. They're definitely going to reach you before you get to the wormhole."

"How do you know they're warships?" I asked, trying to think of ways to talk through this.

"Most of them look pretty spiky," Lonely-Formation said. Ah. The universal spaceship signifier for "heavily armed". "Also, they're demanding we surrender to the Eradu Empire or they'll turn us into a cloud of carbon vapor, et cetera."

"Oh," I said. "Well, in that case I'm going need a new trajectory."

"Nope, you don't understand. I mean that suit isn't capable of putting out the thrust you'll need to get to the wormhole faster."

Every muscle in my body felt tight. In my ear, Tippy-Toe said, "Doreen…"

"Come back to Lonely-Formation," Nancy said. "We'll talk about things here."

Nancy understood orbital mechanics. It just didn't come to people naturally, and it hadn't clicked with her that it would take me longer to get back than it would to keep going. Or maybe she *did* know, was hoping I didn't, and just wanted me to start back.

When a villain outed my secret identity to the world, back when I thought that would change my life for the worse rather than just change it, the first words I'd thought were *I'm not ready to stop being Doreen Green.*

Ever since I'd left Lonely-Formation, I felt like I'd jumped off a cliff. I mean – I *was* in freefall. But usually I found things to distract me from that. I had plenty to distract me out here, but the feeling wouldn't go away.

The ground was still extremely far away.

I'm not ready to stop being Doreen Green kept repeating in my head now. I tried to stop it. If I'd learned anything from last time, it was that I'd be Doreen Green wherever I went.

My jaw was starting to hurt from clenching. I stayed on course toward the wormhole.

"Doreen, you can't do this to yourself," Nancy said. That one caught me by surprise. I'd expected to hear *you can't do this to us.* Though it would have hurt to hear, I'd emotionally prepared myself for it. "Your home, your human and squirrel friends, your degree, everything you wanted to make in your career, your *mom.*"

"I know that," I said. I had really, really not wanted to think about that right now.

"You're looking out for everyone else," Nancy said. "I know you. I get that. But we have to look out for you. You drop through there, and you'll lose everything."

She was right and that was terrifying. It was selfish to feel that way, though, I kept telling myself. This galaxy, and the one on the other side of the wormhole, needed heroes more than I needed to be happy.

I had to divorce what was good for me from what was good for the universe. I was the Unbeatable Squirrel Girl. With great unbeatability, comes great responsibility.

"You've time traveled!" Nancy said. "You've met yourself from the future. Remember that cool old lady you! She must have stayed on Earth."

"Did she?" Time and space were weird. And, if other super

heroes had proven anything about time travel, it was that the future was never etched in vibranium. "Somebody has to do this. It's best if it's me."

"You alone?" Nancy asked.

"I don't think I'll be alone wherever I go." Tippy-Toe's claws were getting painful, but she was a comforting warm presence regardless.

"Nancy, I've passed the point of no return," I said.

A pause.

"I don't have enough thruster fuel to climb back to a higher orbit," I said. "And Lonely-Formation can't descend to a lower orbit without putting you all in danger."

I thought I heard a choking sound on the other side of the transmission, but I couldn't be sure. It kills me just as much to write this now as it did when I heard it.

"We'll get you back," Nancy said. "Just start a thruster burn and we'll figure the rest out."

When I looked to my side, I saw several stars that weren't there before. There were ten of them: bright blue-white stars strung in formation like beads on a necklace. Not good. Those ships must have been traveling at faster-than-light speeds until very recently. If I could *see* them, then not only must they have decelerated below light speed, but they had to be relatively – on the scale of the black hole system – nearby.

"Get the heck out of here," I told Lonely-Formation and the others. "Whatever they want to do to me, I'll take care of it." I was *going* to get to that wormhole. I didn't know how yet, but I would.

"Hold up," Lonely-Formation said. "I recognize some of those ships."

"Is that good?" Koi Boi asked. "Someone tell me that's good."

"No idea, bud," Lonely-Formation said. "Some of them were at the asteroid station."

As soon as they finished that thought, the sky erupted in dazzling flashes of light.

My helmet reacted instantly: the rest of the universe dimmed to black, just like it had when I looked directly at the accretion disk. The brightness still stung my eyes.

"Aaand they're firing on each other," Lonely-Formation concluded.

"*Is that good?*" Koi Boi demanded.

"We don't know!" Nancy yelled.

Red and violet nebular clouds blasted into being, but the predominant color of the battlefield was a searing white. Lonely-Formation had been right about those ships' weapons. The fleet wasn't just armed, it was *ludicrously* armed.

The fleet had entered the system close to the plane of the accretion disk. The only way I could still see the disk was when I tilted my helmet to look away from the battle. When the brightness limiters reduced, I saw dimples in the accretion disk. They grew rapidly even as I watched. Shockwaves from weapon detonations. The energies being tossed around out there would have boiled a planet.

My helmet radio crackled as someone else joined our transmission.

"Good day, Squirrel Girl," the Mad Thinker broadcasted. "Just so you're all aware, you *are* all using an open, unencrypted channel. I would avoid discussing your dramas on it. Have your acanti friend relay specifics telepathically if you really must."

If my heart had been beating any harder, it would have burst through my ribcage.

"Hi, buddy," I said, trying not to put too large an audible question mark after *buddy*. "What, uh, brings you out to this neck of the galaxy?"

"The word is 'arm', Squirrel Girl." He enjoyed nothing more than being pedantic, but given the circumstances I'd let him have that one. But only that one. "Like you, I'm debating whether or not I want to continue my work back home or not. I still left a great deal of business unfinished on Earth, especially with that Reed Richards. But, as it turns out, you can go quite far as a fleet captain when you have an uncanny genius for calculating trajectories and firing arcs. After you were forced to depart our last station, I steered the remaining mercenaries and pirates away from taking revenge on each other. It was more profitable to sign up for mercenary service with the Eradu. Our ships joined up with other Eradu fleets."

"And then you betrayed them," I said.

"They were planning to betray us, we were planning to betray them," he said. "It's all part of the business." I almost admired his villainous nonchalance about the whole thing. His voice broke up into static as a particularly bright flash drowned out the starscape. "... Apologies. EM noise will make hash of just about every radio frequency shortly, so we should keep this brief."

"Why are you here?" I asked, voice tight. If the Mad Thinker and his new friends had been waiting to betray the Eradu, and blown their surprise right this moment, I figured he'd seen profit in it.

"I thought it was obvious," he said, sounding genuinely surprised. "I'm here to help you."

"I don't believe that," Nancy muttered. She must have been sitting right next to the radio because it still picked up her voice.

"I'm trying something new," he said. "I don't know if it will, ah, take… but I have had a chance to recalculate a few things, based upon what you told me. About an exchange of favors, a give-and-take relationship, mutual aid–"

"You mean friendship," I blurted.

"Don't make me say it," he said. "I don't know if it will take, Squirrel Girl, so don't get your hopes up." Too late. "This is transactional. It's only that, ah, your side of the transaction is to be decided." All the pauses and hesitations said he hadn't mapped this conversation out in advance. He was surprising himself as much as me. "The fact is that the Eradu and the Itrayans cannot be allowed to tear this quadrant of the galaxy apart–"

More static interference buzz-sawed through his voice. When it ended, he was saying, "–I saw the spacesuit falling toward the wormhole, I knew it would be you. So, my gift: my ships can keep the Eradu away long enough for you to reach the wormhole. But that is not all I can do. You no doubt think you've passed your point of no return. I've calculated an alternate trajectory for you. The wormhole has a substantial gravitational pull of its own. You and the wormhole are orbiting the black hole at such different velocities that you'll be able to leech some of its velocity via a slingshot trajectory. That will give you the boost you need to get back to a safe distance."

"What about closing the wormhole?" I asked.

"It will stay open. After that… I don't think I can predict. You know, that still hurts to say." He sighed. "Suffice it to say that you, your friends, and I *will* find another way to seal it."

"Can you say that with certainty?" I asked.

He paused. Then: "I don't know that I can say anything

with certainty anymore," he said. "Quite a thrilling way to live, isn't it?"

"Come back to us, Doreen," Nancy interjected. "We'll be here to catch you."

"I don't…" I started to say, but I didn't have any words to go after that.

"You should return to your friends, Squirrel Girl," the Mad Thinker said. "It will be best for you."

"I can't watch," Tippy-Toe said. She scrambled down my shoulders, into the tight and dark space in the small of my back, where she didn't have to see or hear anything.

They were all worried for *me*. And they were right to be. Leaving home would shred me apart inside.

But that ethical calculus hadn't changed. This wormhole had to close, and I couldn't accept any ambiguity about that. There was so much I could do out there. So many lives hinged on whether this war would be allowed to continue.

At the same time, what Nancy said had torn open a hole in my chest, and it just wouldn't close. All that heat and pain bundled tightly under my ribcage. They were absolutely right. I belonged on Earth, and with them. Anything else would have been like me without my tail. I wouldn't have been whole.

Heroes made sacrifices. The thing about heroism is that heroes rarely had a chance to be whole.

"Get ready for the slingshot course correction," the Mad Thinker said, voice breaking up with more static. "Stay facing exactly that direction. Fire rear thrusters – now."

And now we come to why I'm writing this. The problem I told you about at the very start of this letter, the thing rattling inside my head that I need to talk about but can't ever let my friends know. They had made every argument they could. Given me all the reasons they could think of to stay. I made my decision.

"Okay," I breathed. "I'm ready."

They thought that I meant I was going to come back to them. They will go on thinking that was what I meant.

I pulled my fingers back from the thruster controls, curled them into my glove, and let gravity draw me toward the wormhole.

I had a few seconds to myself to think about how much I was about to lose. Then the shimmering around the suit, at the edges of my vision, coalesced into solid colors. Dark gray metal and a shiny black visor rippled into being.

It was another suit, clinging to the back of my own. Its gloved hands had a solid grip on what I'd thought were my malfunctioning shoulder thrusters. They hadn't been malfunctioning at all. Their exhaust had splashed on the cloaked suit holding onto me. Now that cloak had dropped.

"The hero's timing was exquisite," Hadrian radioed.

Still holding onto me with one hand, he reached forward and grabbed my right glove – the one that controlled my suit thrusters. He clenched the empty fingers, and yanked them all back.

My thrusters fired. I couldn't force my fingers back through the glove. He had squeezed the glove's fingers and pinched them off.

My brain still hadn't caught up with my senses. "Frig!" I said, eloquently.

"The EM static of the battle prevented the Squirrel Girl's friends from hearing that she was not alone," Hadrian said.

I found a few more words: "What the heck? Did you win back home? Did they agree to stop the war–"

"No," Hadrian said. "The Luminous Council had in fact defeated him in humiliating fashion."

"Oh," I said, and paused. "Then how–"

"The hero couldn't change his people, not this time. But he had effected an escape for himself. Given the directions he had given her, it had not been a difficult task to find her whale friend and smuggle himself aboard." I had no idea how much of that was post-hoc retconning. It didn't seem to matter. "But the more important matter was that the hero had discovered what kind of story he wanted to be in."

"What kind of story is that?" I asked because I had to know.

"He had once again abandoned his home and set out into the universe alone. But he was embarking on a journey, not a tragedy. He had given up thinking he knew the ending. He was ready, now, for new adventures on the other side of the universe. He had been given the courage to forge new friendships and to make for himself a new home. He could inspire others as she had inspired him.

"The point of heroism was not to take everything upon herself," he continued. "It was to show others that a better universe was possible, and that they can help make it. Then those she inspired could step in to support her, too. He needed a new home, but she already had one. Friends, family, and a community that could make a difference. *Because* of her heroism, not in spite of it, she did not need to sacrifice the rest of her life on the altar of doing good."

With the hand on my glove still keeping him linked to me, he released his grip on my suit. He reached to the clockwork device

I was still holding, and plucked it out of my palm. I still had all my fingers in that glove. I could have stopped him.

Then he pushed away from me.

His suit's thrusters fired. He fell toward the kaleidoscopic gyre of the accretion disk and the wormhole spinning within it. I didn't see how far he got, because his cloak shimmered back into place.

Without his grip on my glove, I could have pushed my fingers back onto my thruster controls and gone after him. I could have pulled away from the Mad Thinker's slingshot trajectory.

I didn't.

Sometime later, Tippy-Toe scrambled onto my neck. "Are we all right?!" she asked. "Your shoulders went all tense, and I couldn't get back up. I thought I heard–" Then she saw that I no longer held Hadrian's device. "Are we on the other side?"

"In a manner of speaking," I told her. "But we're a lot closer to home."

There was no blame when I got back, but a lot of tears. Happy tears, mostly. They had every right to be angry with me, but I think they understood why I'd almost done that. There would be time for anger later. Right now, we had more to celebrate.

Like stopping an interstellar war.

On my way back to Lonely-Formation, who soon thereafter started going by the name Willful-Chorus, I hadn't looked behind me. Tippy-Toe had been on the back of my head, though. She'd seen everything.

The way she'd described it, the wormhole had turned into a gyre of different colors. Reds and golds and violets. They'd whirled tightly around each other until, abruptly, the dark speck of the wormhole had collapsed into itself and vanished. The colors lost their violent energy, and dispersed into the rest of the accretion disk.

"What did you do?" Nancy asked, when she found her voice, after the third time we'd embraced. "You just told us Hadrian said that his device needed to be activated from the other side."

"I think that was a narrative conceit." I wasn't used to lying, but that seemed the least hurtful way out of this. "I had to try everything I could … so on my way back I let the device go. It fell in, and I guess it still worked."

Getting out of the suit was much more of a hassle than getting in. I had a serious kink in my back from staying tense for so long. My muscles had turned to jelly. Sweaty, stinky jelly. Sweat had glued my skin to the interior cushions. The super hero stories I grew up on didn't delve into the locker room realities of the business.[81] Not that that stopped Nancy, Koi Boi, and Mary from trying to give me a hug. Friendship is a really special thing.

It turned out that hugging in freefall was astonishingly difficult! Mary clonked her head against mine the first time we tried, and I still felt guilty about that.

I'd missed the best part of the lightshow, but it still hadn't ended by the time I got back to the lounge. Tippy-Toe had seen it all, but she still leapt off my shoulder to get a better look. Koi Boi and Mary had come with Nancy to greet me and help me out of my suit. Chipmunk Hunk had stayed in the lounge to keep Brain Drain company. G'illian had mounted herself atop Chipmunk Hunk's head and wouldn't let go. He kept trying not to wince at G'illian's claws in his scalp as he, too, hugged me.

---

[81] Tony had to invent his own brand of industrial-strength deodorant. There are very few problems that man can't solve with a product. – SG

"FORTUNE ONCE AGAIN FAVORS THE FOOLISH," Brain Drain said.

"Foolishness is our heroic edge," Nancy agreed, giving me a meaningful look.

On the screen, shreds of superheated gas – the remnants of the wormhole's own microcosm system – continued to disperse into the rest of the accretion disk. The disk itself was nowhere near as even as it had once been. Pockets of void, whorls, and shockwaves were still spreading across it. The pressure waves amped up both heat and friction near the black hole. The dead sun glowed brighter than it probably had alive.

A cluster of starship exhaust plumes formed an artificial constellation just[82] ahead of us. The Mad Thinker's ships. The Eradu and their loyalists had outnumbered them, but, after the wormhole's destruction, their cohesion had broken down. Most of the other ships here had been mercenaries, like the Mad Thinker's new gang. When they'd seen the wormhole die, they'd scattered.

There *had* been an Eradu ship among the fleet. The Mad Thinker had targeted it first, and blasted it apart before they'd had any warning to deploy their narrative powers. "THE DEATH OF THE AUTHOR," Brain Drain intoned, and started telling us something about literary theory. I loved him, but I wasn't listening. I didn't think the others were either.

This wasn't over yet. Nothing was ever over, not really. There were still more Eradu on this side of the wormhole. They wouldn't go so easily. If the Itrayans stayed true to their history, they'd stick to their own world for the next several hundred

---

[82] "Just" here meaning thousands of miles, give or take some zeroes. – SG

thousand years, until the wild wormhole opened again, and leave the rest of the galaxy to tell their own stories. In the meantime, though, they would still be out looking for Hadrian. And they had a grudge with us.

We couldn't stay here forever. Just as with the asteroid station, we were about to be chased out. The last time anyone had spoken with the Mad Thinker, he'd reported plenty of distant engine signatures lighting the sky. Some of them were coming this way, and fast.

"We still have three hours if we want to make finals," Nancy said.

"Hold that thought," I said, pushing my way out of the lounge.

Willful-Chorus's subspace radio equipment was in a different chamber. Like all of the rest of the technology inside Willful-Chorus, it was mounted in their fleshy walls, but that was no longer as off-putting as it had once been. I only had to fiddle with it a little before I found how to contact the Mad Thinker.

The console's tiny screen showed the Mad Thinker seated in the central chair of an alien bridge. Tentacled creatures slithered from station to station behind him. His lap and broad armrests were piled with tablets, calculators, and even pen and paper.

"What's next for you?" I asked.

He'd been waiting for the call. He didn't even look up from his scribbling. "It's going to be very difficult for us to stay alive as interstellar politics snap back to normal," he said matter-of-factly. "It would be safest for my mercenary 'friends' and me to disperse. I think I'll be heading the same way as you eventually. Back to Earth. I'll try to make some, er, transactional alliances–"

"You mean 'friends'," I said, flicking my tail excitedly.

I have hope for everybody. Funny thing was, for as much as I was still piecing myself back together and hating myself for lying to Nancy, I had more hope for myself than I remembered having for a long time.

"... Friends," he said, as though trying the word for the first time, "along the way. After that, for once, I cannot and will not make promises about what comes next." Finally, he set down his calculations, and looked at me. "But you have a question for me."

"When you sent me that slingshot trajectory," I said, "did you predict what I would do with it?"

The way his eyebrow raised said it all.

"There was a very good chance you wouldn't listen to me," he said. "Close to one hundred percent, actually. But I wanted to try. Somehow, nothing seems certain when it comes to you."

"Ready whenever, my dudes," Willful-Chorus said cheerfully when I returned to the lounge. "Earth sounds neat. Looking forward to meeting the local whales."

They told us a little bit about the journey we'd be taking. According to G'illian, Earth was on the other side of the galaxy from us. We couldn't go in a straight line. Our course was going to skirt the center of the galaxy. The gravitational pull there was going to force an arc in our course.

I'd always wanted to see the center of the galaxy. From a safe distance, that was. There's a supermassive black hole there, grinding away at everything. Almost everything in Earth's night sky, barring other galaxies and give or take a Magellanic Cloud or two, revolved around it. Black holes still terrified me, but now I had some happy memories associated with one of them. I could always make a few more.

It would have been a shame to travel all the way to the center of the galaxy and not do some educational sight-seeing.

"You know," I told Nancy, "I bet we could get an extension on those finals..."

"No," she said instantly.

"Yes," I answered.

"No."

"Yes," I countered.

"No!"

"Yes," I said, enticingly.

Our debate went on for a little while. But, in the end, my thoughtful, cogent arguments carried the day.

NEXT TIME (???) ON SQUIRREL GIRL: UNIVERSE!!

The Unbeatable Squirrel Girl Vs The Planet of the Cat-Boys

"Oh, dang," Nancy gasped as we ran. "Oh, geez. Oh, heck!"

"Frig!" I agreed. I found a second to glance backward as we weaved through the trees.

"Mrrrrow!" one of our dozen pursuers[83] yelled. At least it was not a hiss.

---

[83] *Purr*suers, if you will. -SG

Time for cat facts! Cats only meow at their parents, or humans that they see as parents or authority figures! The cat-boys were still using kittenish language on us, which was either very good, or – I realized just then – very bad.

The jungle canopy overhead was too thick for me to grab Nancy and jump. Nancy and I had to stay on foot. We'd run long enough that we were gasping for air, which just made things worse.

"That smell!" I said for the fifth time.

"It's not their fault!" Nancy said. "There's sand *everywhere*." It was true. The soil here was unusually dry and coarse for a world with so much plant life.

Our trip had started off on the wrong foot, literally, with every step a potential horrible surprise. And that had been before the cat-boys had started running in front of us, trying to trip us to get our attention.

Things had only gone *really* bad until Tippy-Toe had poked her nose out of the collar of my shirt. I'd forgotten she'd even fallen asleep under there.

"This isn't like Cat-Asgard at all!" Nancy said.

"You were the one who wanted to come here!" I pointed out.

"You thought it would be fun too!" Nancy said.

There would be enough time for blame later. The others had had it right when they'd stayed inside August-Omen (our space whale friend's name today).

"We just want to *plaaaaay!*" one of our (admittedly cute and fuzzy-faced) pursuers yelled.

"Maow!" another added. The raptor-sized extended claws made that a lot less cute than it might have been.

The cat-boys were gaining on us. They leapt through the foliage with speed that shouldn't have astonished me, but somehow still did. I could not help but admire their murderous grace. They leapt lightly, avoiding loose soil, fallen branches, and anything else that might have left tracks. Still more were even laying in wait ahead, wriggling their butts as they readied to pounce.

"This was not a good idea," Tippy-Toe informed us.

"The important thing is that we learned a valuable lesson about planets with names like this," I said. "And not thinking through the implications and consequences."

"I admit," Nancy said, "I have my weaknesses." From the moment she'd overheard this world's name in that seedy space convenience store, Nancy had forgotten all about finals.

"Mew is going to hate us when we get home and she smells this on us," I said.

That was about when the pouncing started.

"I still love cats!" Nancy said, and although those would be far from her last words, they would have made fine ones.

Acknowledgments

Squirrel Girl Universe wouldn't exist without more people than I could name, but that's not going to stop me from attempting it.

The two editors who worked with me on this, Charlotte Llewelyn-Wells and Gwendolyn Nix, are indispensable members of the Aconyte Books team. I owe both of them an incredible amount for their stamina in putting up with me and my shenanigans. Extremely gracious thanks also to Sarah Jane Singer of Marvel and copyeditor Claire Rushbrook.

Absolutely none of this book would have been possible without the incredible writers and artists at Marvel, most especially Ryan North, Erica Henderson, and Derek Charm, whose work this novel directly follows. That team's legendary four-year Squirrel Girl series is unmissable and you should absolutely read all of it – and if you've already read it, reread it. Right now! Do it!

The work of more writers and artists than I have the space to name made Squirrel Girl the kick-butt super hero she is today, but I cannot miss mentioning Squirrel Girl's creators Will Murray and Steve Ditko.

The incredible art on the cover of this novel was created by Merilliza Chan. You can find more of her work at her website, *merilliza.com*.

Aconyte publisher Marc Gascoigne's continued faith in me has been astounding. Thank you to him and to everybody on the Aconyte Books team, including Anjuli Smith, Nick Tyler, Jack Doddy, Vanessa Jack, Joe Riley, and Amanda Treseler.

Finally, an incredibly special thank you to my perpetual beta reader (and life partner!), the Unbeatable Dr Teresa Milbrodt.

About the Author

TRISTAN PALMGREN is the author of the critically acclaimed genre-warping blend of historical fiction and space opera novel *Quietus*, and its sequel *Terminus,* and the loosely linked Marvel novels *Domino: Strays, Outlaw: Relentless* and *The Siege of X-41.* They live with their partner in Columbia, Missouri.

tristanpalmgren.com
twitter.com/TristanPalmgren

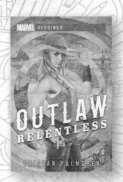